The
Osiris
Ritual

The
Osiris
Ritual

A NEWBURY & HOBBES
INVESTIGATION

GEORGE MANN

 A TOM DOHERTY ASSOCIATES BOOK
TOR® NEW YORK

THE OSIRIS RITUAL: A NEWBURY & HOBBES INVESTIGATION

Copyright © 2010 by George Mann

A Tor Book
Published by Tom Doherty Associates, LLC
175 Fifth Avenue
New York, NY 10010

www.tor-forge.com

Tor® is a registered trademark of Tom Doherty Associates, LLC.

The Library of Congress has cataloged the hardcover edition as follows:

Mann, George.
    The Osiris ritual / George Mann. — 1st ed.
        p. cm.
    "A Tom Doherty Associates book."
    ISBN 978-0-7653-2321-7
    I. Title.
  PR6113.A546O75 2010
  823'.92—dc22

                                                        2010032650

ISBN 978-0-7653-2323-1 (trade paperback)

First Edition: August 2010
First Trade Paperback Edition: June 2011

Printed in the United States of America

10 9 8 7 6 5 4 3 2 1

For Emily May Irene Mann

ACKNOWLEDGMENTS

Thanks, as ever, must be extended to Emma Barnes and Liz Gorinsky for continued support. Also to Gordon Fletcher for superb pedantry, and to Jonas Eyles and Craig Caithness for goading him in the pub (and for making me feel better about losing every round of golf to them both). Mark Hodder kept me busy with inspirational reading matter, and Michael Rowley and Mark Newton debated the meaning of life over a number of excellent curries. Lou Anders shared in all the highs and lows. And Fiona, James, and Emily put up with me spending long hours locked away in the study when I really should have been doing something else.

The
Osiris
Ritual

CHAPTER

1

LONDON, FEBRUARY 1902

George Purefoy was running late.

The young reporter hurtled down the street, his notebook clutched tightly in his hand. He dodged the other pedestrians, who eyed him warily as he raced by like some crazed animal pursued by an invisible pack of hounds. His sand-coloured hair stung his eyes where it whipped across his face in the driving wind. His dinner suit was crumpled, and now, to top things off, it had started to rain. The biggest assignment of his career to date, and things had already started to go terribly wrong.

Purefoy skipped around a red post box, narrowly missed colliding with an elderly gentleman in a top hat, and finally flung himself around a bend in the road. There, in the distance, was

Albion House, the home of Lord Henry Winthrop. The street outside the house was bathed in bright yellow light from the windows, and even from here, a good hundred feet away, the noise of the party spilled out, a cacophony of chatter in the otherwise quiet London evening.

Purefoy, catching his breath, slowed his pace to a steady walk. He tried to regain his composure, smoothing his jacket and straightening his tie. Rain pattered lightly on his face. Other guests were still arriving at the big house, and whilst he was most definitely late, it didn't look to Purefoy like he had missed the main event. At least he hoped not; his career as a reporter depended on it.

Purefoy had made his way here, across town from the office, for *the* society event of the year: to cover the return of the explorer and philanthropist Lord Henry Winthrop from his expedition to Egypt. It would also be the grand unveiling of Lord Winthrop's greatest find: the mummified remains of an ancient Theban king. There had been a great deal of fanfare about the success of the expedition over the last few weeks, accompanied by wild claims from Winthrop that the mummy was a unique specimen. Found still wrapped in its finery, it was said to bear strange markings that were unfamiliar to any of the experts he had consulted at the British Museum. It was the talk of London, and tonight, Winthrop planned to unwrap the bindings of the long-dead king before a select audience.

Much to the chagrin of his fellow reporters, Purefoy had been assigned to cover the event for *The Times*, following the success of his recent piece about the revenant plague— a disease from India that had terrorised the slums since before Christmas—and the government conspiracy to hide the fact that it was still spreading unchecked through the London slums. He'd set off in plenty of time, of course, first picking out his best suit and selecting a brand-new notebook from his pile. But then the ground train he was on had shuddered to a halt a few streets away, and word had spread throughout the carriages that a spooked horse had caused a cart to overturn, spilling its cargo of rags and bones across the tracks up ahead. Knowing that he didn't have much further to go, and sure that waiting for the engineers to clear the tracks would cause him to miss the party, Purefoy had taken matters into his own hands and set out on foot. Now, uncomfortable, damp, and late, he was starting to wonder whether the assignment was more of a curse than the blessing it had at first appeared to be.

Purefoy quickened his step. Grand houses loomed over him from both sides of the wide street. This was a London as unfamiliar to him as the slums he usually found himself writing about. The people who lived in these enormous mansions moved in circles entirely outside of his experience, and he found himself feeling not a little nervous at the prospect of having to hold his own with a crowd of such gentlemen, lords, and ladies. Nevertheless, he was anxious to see what Lord Winthrop had brought back with him from the Middle East, and, most of all, to bear witness to the unrolling of the pharaoh himself.

He stopped at the bottom of the steps to let a lady in a billowing, cream-coloured dress step out of a private carriage and enter the party before him. She smiled graciously as he stepped to one side to allow her to pass. He eyed the butler by the front door as the man checked the lady's invitation and showed her inside. Judging by the standard of the servants, Purefoy was starting to feel a little underdressed. He checked his suit again, conscious that he was a little crumpled and damp. Sighing, he patted his pockets and located the invitation. Then, warily, he mounted the steps and presented the card to the older, balding man, who looked Purefoy up and down and raised an eyebrow before examining the card he'd been handed.

"Ah, yes sir. With *The Times*. Won't you come this way?" It was as if the man's entire demeanour had changed upon seeing the invitation. Purefoy gave him a quizzical look. He couldn't tell whether the butler had altered his previously haughty attitude because of his respect for the newspaper, or because, upon realising that Purefoy was a reporter, he had lowered his expectations. Either way, he supposed it didn't matter all that much. He followed the butler in through the grand porch, which was impressively decorated with a series of stained glass panels and Minton tiles, and stepped through the inner door that the butler held open for him on the other side. A moment later he was standing in the grand hallway, where the party was already in full swing.

Purefoy gazed in amazement. It was like nothing he'd seen in all of his life. An enormous staircase dominated the space, its sweeping banisters curving up to form a large gallery that looked down upon the bustling hall. Glass cabinets had been erected at regular intervals all around the tiled floor and filled with the most wondrous gilded treasures from the tomb of the mummified king. People milled around these cabinets,

drinks in hand, cooing appreciatively and courting one another with sidelong glances and averted gazes. Purefoy almost
laughed out loud. It was like every cliché he could have imagined, and more sumptuous and extravagant than even those.
The women floated around in the most magnificent dresses
of coloured silk, brandishing their drinks like talismans. The
men looked austere in their formal attire and clustered together in little groups, talking in hushed tones. *This*, Purefoy
thought to himself, *is all of London society, here together in
one room*. He didn't know whether to be giddy or appalled at
the thought.

Feeling a little lost, Purefoy cast around for anyone he
recognised. There were faces he'd seen in portraits and photographs, but no one it would be proper for him to approach at
a party, at least without a formal introduction. He looked up
at the gallery and noted that Lord Winthrop himself was
resting against the balustrade, surveying the scene below.
He was sporting a wide grin. When he spotted Purefoy looking at him he gave the reporter a little wave, then pushed
himself away from his perch and began making his way along
the landing towards the stairs.

Purefoy had met Lord Winthrop only once before, when
the lord had visited the offices of *The Times* the prior week
to discuss an exclusive on the finds with his editor. He was a
gregarious sort of chap with a welcoming manner, but Purefoy was not so naïve as to miss the fact that the only reason
Winthrop was making a beeline towards him was because his
inflated ego compelled him to entertain the reporter who
would be providing a write-up of his event for the morning

edition. Purefoy smiled and held out his hand as the lord approached him, the other guests turning to see who their host had decided to grace with his presence.

"Mr. Purefoy! A pleasure. Are you enjoying the party?" Lord Winthrop was a tall, stocky man with broad shoulders, a long, greying beard, and a receding hairline. He carried his weight around his jowls and his waist and his voice was friendly but with an overbearing boom.

Purefoy smiled. "Alas, I've only this moment arrived. An accident in the road meant I had to finish my journey on foot. I trust I haven't missed the main event?"

Winthrop patted Purefoy easily on the shoulder. "Not at all, my good man. Not at all. It's been four thousand years since the Theban was confined to his bandages. I'd say there's no imperative to rush, wouldn't you? Now, let's get you a drink. . . ."

Chuckling, Winthrop gestured towards the row of statues situated along the back wall, to either side of the huge staircase. Purefoy watched, fascinated, as one of the statues stepped down from its perch, collected a tray of drinks from a nearby table, and made its way jerkily towards them. Purefoy had assumed the statues were part of the display, items brought back from the expedition by Winthrop and his team. The one coming towards them looked every bit the part, a flawless, life-size replica of an ancient Egyptian statue, replete with carved headdress and blank, staring eyes.

Winthrop laughed when he saw the young reporter's expression. "Dear boy, haven't you seen one of these new Ottoman automaton devices?"

Purefoy shook his head.

"Why, they're all the rage. Much better than those terrible

British things we had last year. No, these truly are wondrous machines. Look here . . . " He waved at the device as it came closer, and Purefoy stood agape as Winthrop took a flute of champagne from the proffered tray. "It has a brass framework of unsightly cogs and things underneath, but a porcelain veneer over the top, designed to order. I had these made up in the style of the twelfth dynasty. Remarkable, aren't they? Just like living statues."

Purefoy accepted the glass of champagne from Winthrop and took a long sip. "Indeed they are. Very impressive." He watched as the bizarre creation made its way back through the crowd, returned the tray to its place on the table, and climbed back onto its pedestal beside its fellows. He studied it for a moment, unnerved by how easily it had blended once again into the background, becoming nothing but another immobile exhibit. He repressed a shudder then turned to Winthrop, who he realised had been talking at him for some time.

". . . and there are Lord and Lady Buchanan, talking to Sir David and his wife. Oh yes, and there's Sir Maurice New-bury, examining some of the ushabti in that glass cabinet over there. Perfect timing, I should say. You should meet Sir Maurice right away. Come on. I'm sure he'd be delighted to meet a man from *The Times*."

Winthrop led Purefoy through the crowd towards a man who was standing alone at one of the glass cases, examining the items on display inside. The man was wearing a thought-ful expression and the glass of champagne he was clutching in his left hand appeared to be untouched. He looked up dis-tractedly as Winthrop and Purefoy approached, and smiled when he recognised his host. When he came out from behind the cabinet, Purefoy had the opportunity to see him properly. He was dressed in a fitted black suit with a white shirt and bow tie. His hair was jet black and swept back from his forehead, and his emerald eyes glittered above a hawkish nose. Purefoy guessed he was in his midthirties, but he could have been older.

Newbury extended his hand and Winthrop took it firmly. "Lord Winthrop. A pleasure to see you again. I trust you are well, following your return from the Middle East?"

Winthrop nodded vigorously. "Well enough, Sir Maurice, well enough. I see you've been admiring my little collection."

"Indeed. Quite a find you had out there in the desert, Henry. I'm particularly intrigued by the markings on this series of four ushabti." He stopped, suddenly, looking up to see Purefoy standing off to one side, sipping champagne. "Oh. How terribly impolite of me." He stepped over towards Purefoy and extended his hand. "Please forgive me, Mr. . . . ?"

"Purefoy. George Purefoy."

"Please forgive me, Mr. Purefoy. It's just that I get a little carried away when I find myself surrounded by such exquisite objects as these."

Purefoy laughed at the man's obvious embarrassment. Clearly, it was Lord Winthrop's faux pas for not introducing them, but Purefoy took it as a measure of the man that he accepted the error on himself. "Not at all, Sir Maurice. It's a pleasure to meet you."

Winthrop clapped his hands together with a hearty laugh. "Capital! Maurice, Purefoy here is a reporter with *The Times*. He's going to be writing a piece about tonight's little soiree for the morning edition."

Newbury offered Purefoy a sly, knowing grin. "Indeed? And have you decided yet how you intend to approach your piece?"

Purefoy glanced awkwardly at Winthrop, who smiled at him expectantly. He cocked his head to one side in thought. "I don't believe I have, as yet. It rather hinges on what I think of the centrepiece." He paused, glancing around at the gathered crowd. "I'm sure it will be a spectacular revelation for us all."

Winthrop stepped forward and clapped him—a little overzealously—on the back. "Don't doubt it, dear boy! Don't doubt it for a minute. Now, I really must attend to Lady Worthington over there. She looks a little lost amongst the canopic jars. I'll leave you in the capable hands of Sir Maurice, here." He trailed off, his attention already on the other side of the room. Purefoy stepped aside to let him pass and smiled as Winthrop's genial voice boomed loudly behind him. "Lady Worthington! Over here, my dear."

Newbury leaned in towards Purefoy. He lowered his voice to a conspiratorial whisper. "Lovely old chap, but quite lost in his own magnificence, if you know what I mean."

Purefoy chuckled. "Precisely."

"Of course," Newbury looked momentarily troubled, "you won't print that, will you?"

Purefoy shook his head. "Indeed not, Sir Maurice. Your commentary is safe in my hands."

Newbury laughed. "Excellent to hear it!" He sipped his champagne. "Now, have they given you any notion about what's *really* going on in this room?"

Purefoy frowned. "I'm not quite sure I understand."

Newbury grinned. "I'll take that as a no." He beckoned

Purefoy forward. "Stand here for a minute. Tell me what you see."

Perplexed, Purefoy came forward until he was standing beside the glass cabinet that Newbury had been studying a few moments earlier. Newbury gestured to the crush of people. "Out there. What do you see?"

"I see a crowd of people dressed in finery, here to see the unrolling of a four-thousand-year-old mummy from Thebes."

Newbury laughed again. "I thought that's what you'd say."

"Why, what do you see?"

"*I* see a crowd of people desperate to be seen, all dressed up for an ancient dead man. I see no one who is truly interested in whatever it is they'll find under those ancient bandages, or the items on display in the cases in this hallway. No one here gives a damn about Egypt or Winthrop's expedition. London society is nothing but a game, Mr. Purefoy, and a dismal one at that. It's about being seen, about showing one's face at the appropriate functions. That's why all of these people are here tonight, and that's precisely why Winthrop invited them. He likes the pomp."

"Then why are *you* here, Sir Maurice, if you find it all so tiresome?"

Newbury smiled. "Ah, now that's a question. I could tell you that I'm here because I have an academic interest in the subject. Or that I'm very much intrigued by the reports I've seen filed at the British Museum about the expedition and exactly what it is they found out there in the hot sands. Or even that I enjoy the thrill of seeing ancient artefacts uncovered for the first time in millennia. But in truth, I'm sure I'm just as bad as the rest of them, here to drink my complimentary champagne and strut around before the gathered society commentators like a peacock."

Purefoy chuckled. "Now I know you're telling the truth."

Laughing, they both took another sip of their champagne.

"Now, see those three chaps over there, standing together in a huddle?"

Purefoy strained to see over Newbury's shoulder. "Ah, yes. I see." Three middle-aged men in top hats and black coats were standing by the doorway to the drawing room, gesticulating passionately, deep in the middle of what looked like a heated debate.

"Well, their story is something entirely different. Those are the other members of Winthrop's expedition. They were the men who helped him pull all of these wonderful things out of the ground, and I'll wager they're about to help him unwrap the old priest, too."

"Priest? I thought it was a pharaoh?"

Newbury raised an eyebrow. "Hmmm. It's clear from looking at a handful of the items on display here that the character beneath those wrappings was never a king. And what is more, I'm inclined to believe that there is a very good reason why the tomb had lain undisturbed by grave robbers for so long. I'm sure there must be something about the nature of the burial that Winthrop is not telling us. Anyway, we're about to find out. Here's our host now. . . ."

Purefoy turned to see Winthrop standing at the foot of the grand staircase. The man clapped his hands together loudly three times and a hush fell over the assembled crowd.

"Lords, ladies, and gentlemen. Welcome. I hope your glasses are all suitably charged. We are about to begin the process of unrolling the mummified remains of our Theban king. If you would care to take up a position in the drawing room, my associate Mr. Wilfred Blake"—at this, Winthrop gestured towards the three men Newbury had pointed out earlier—"will be delighted to explain the process to you as we perform the task. We begin momentarily. Thank you."

There was a brief smattering of applause, and then the room started to bustle again as people began making their way towards the large, white double doors that led into the drawing room. Purefoy turned to Newbury, who swiftly downed the last vestiges of his champagne and beckoned the reporter towards the door. "Come on. Let's make sure we get a good spot."

Tucking his notebook into his jacket pocket, Purefoy abandoned his unfinished drink on a small side table and followed Newbury around the rows of glass cabinets and on towards the drawing room. All the while, society veterans bearing dispassionate expressions milled around him, as though this next stage of the evening was just something that they had to grin and bear in order to carry on with their socialising and drinking. Newbury, on the other hand, seemed keen to get both himself and Purefoy to the forefront of things. When they finally crossed the threshold into the large drawing room, it did not take much effort for them to establish a position near the head of the table.

Purefoy took a moment to examine his surroundings. The curtains had been pulled shut against the twilight, and the room was dimly lit by an array of flickering gas lamps casting everything in a warm, yellow glow. Dark wooden bookshelves lined the far wall, filled with musty old tomes that Purefoy couldn't distinguish from one another in the half-light. People were forming a wide circle around a long, central table, whispering to each other in subdued voices. Purefoy savoured the moment as he took his place beside Newbury.

The item that dominated the room, of course, was the funeral casket of the ancient Egyptian laid out on the table. The large wooden coffin was shaped in the rough form of its occupant and was a truly wonderful sight to behold. Every inch of it was covered in the most intricate patterns and designs, and it was clear to Purefoy that the craftsmen who had tooled the object had been masters of their art, which was all the more impressive for the fact they had lived around four thousand years in the past. Gold leaf shimmered in the warm light of the gas lamps, whilst blue ink and inlaid precious stones finished the effect. Hieroglyphs were etched in long black columns over the torso and legs of the casket, and other, more unusual symbols had been painted on top of these in splashes of red, obliterating much of the original script. The red ink had faded somewhat, however, so it was clear that the markings were historical and had not been affected by Winthrop and his men during the course of the expedition.

Purefoy leaned in to examine the face that had been carved into the wooden lid. The eyes stared blankly at the ceiling, giving away nothing about the casket's occupant. It was so heavily stylised that he was unable to get any real impression of what the person had looked like in life.

Newbury leaned over to whisper in his ear. "Have you ever been to one of these things before?"

Purefoy shook his head.

"Well, I hope you're not squeamish. Fascinating stuff, though. Truly fascinating. I think we're in for a surprise." He raised his eyebrow once again and offered Purefoy a confident smile.

Purefoy glanced around. The other guests were huddling in behind them now, still clutching their drinks, their faces gleaming in the wan light. Purefoy folded his arms behind his back and waited.

A moment later, a hush rippled through the gathered throng as the four members of the expedition filed into the room. They had each shed their suit jackets and hats, rolled up their shirtsleeves, and donned leather gloves and smocks. Winthrop and Wilfred Blake were first to step up to the table. The others cleared a space for them, asking the audience to stand back to make room. Winthrop was carrying some sort of bizarre contraption, which proved to be a mechanical visual aid, like a pair of spectacles attached to a wire framework that fit neatly over his head. Lenses clicked down before his eyes, and he fiddled with a tool on either side of the device to adjust their focus. Thus prepared, Winthrop approached the casket, whilst Blake skirted around to the head of the table, readying himself to address the audience. He cleared his throat, and the susurrant voices of the crowd gave way to silence.

"I advise those of you with weak hearts or fragile constitutions to momentarily avert your eyes. Our first task will be to free the lid from the casket, and whilst we expect to find only another, smaller casket inside, we have no way of knowing how accurate our assumptions may be." His voice was thin and nasal, and he delivered his speech with impeccable precision.

Purefoy looked him up and down. The man was slim, drawn, and clean shaven, quite the opposite of the burly Winthrop. His blond hair was brushed back from his forehead in a neat side parting and his eyes were a piercing blue.

"There are many things about the burial of this ancient king that are inconsistent with other contemporary burials in the same region." Blake stepped closer to the casket and waved his hand to indicate the splashes of red paint that had been hastily daubed across the engraved hieroglyphs. "For example, we have no understanding of the nature of these red markings, but suspect them to be a magic ward of some type, a warning to anyone in the afterlife who may happen upon the spirit of the person contained within the casket. Of course, any such concerns are moot—nothing but superstitious nonsense—but it nevertheless serves to suggest that there may be more irregularities contained within the casket." He gave a dramatic pause. "None of our assumptions can be trusted. We hope to discover more as we proceed."

Newbury glanced over his shoulder at Purefoy with an unreadable look on his face.

Blake approached the casket, taking his place opposite Winthrop, who had moved around to the other side of the table. They both placed their hands on the lid of the casket and together proceeded to test the seal.

The two men worked the lid back and forth, but after a couple of minutes it became clear that it was stuck fast, warped with age, grime, and decay. Unperturbed, Winthrop took a three-inch blade from the pouch in the front of his smock and set about running the knife along the join, hacking away at the gummy seal in an effort to work the lid free.

Purefoy noticed Newbury wincing as flakes of gold leaf and four-thousand-year-old hieroglyphs fell to the polished floor by their feet.

It didn't take Winthrop long to complete his rather brutal assault on the seal. A moment later he resumed his position opposite Blake and they prepared to try to lift the lid again. Purefoy stepped closer, anxious to get a good view of whatever they would find inside.

Winthrop grunted as he wedged his fingers underneath the rim of the seal. There was a splintering crack, followed by a loud *sigh*, as the two men heaved the lid free of the base. They placed it hastily on the table. Dust plumed into the air from within the shell of the casket, which had been undisturbed for centuries. Purefoy wrinkled his nose. There was a dry odour from within the wooden coffin: the scent of ancient, foetid decay.

The other men from the expedition hurried forward to crowd around the casket. Purefoy found it hard to see what was going on as they gestured to one another excitedly, clearly animated by their find. He edged around the table, feeling uncomfortable, as the press of people behind him became more pronounced, each of the guests straining to see over the others. When he did finally manage to get a good look, he nearly gasped aloud. The contents of the casket were magnificent. Another coffin, decorated in shimmering black and gold, lay inside the outer shell like a Russian doll, perfectly designed to fit within the larger casing. The decoration was impeccable; beneath the thin layer of dust it was so bright and glassy it could almost have been new. The inner coffin had been carved out of a dark hardwood and inlaid with generous bands of bright yellow gold. The face was slimmer than the visage on the outer casket, and its eyes had been set with deep red gemstones that reflected the warm glow of the gas lamps. Once again, the torso was covered in a spidery pattern of white hieroglyphs and symbols that were as exotic as anything Purefoy had ever seen. He was more than a little awed by the experience.

He glanced at Newbury, who was leaning over the casket and studying the ancient markings. He looked thoughtful. Purefoy was just about to ask him what had caught his attention when Winthrop stepped back from the table and clapped his hands together to garner attention. "Lords, ladies and gentlemen! You are in the presence of a truly magnificent find!" Winthrop's excitement was clearly genuine. "The inner casket is like nothing we could have expected. The black-and-gold decoration is highly irregular. Please, take a moment to enjoy the sight before we continue with our unrolling." He urged the others back from the edge of the table and waved a handful of people forward to take a look. Blake and the other two members of the expedition—Purefoy realized he would have to elicit their names for his article by the end of the evening—moved away reluctantly and stood off to one side, whispering to one another with some urgency as many of the guests came forward to peer into the dead man's open casket.

Purefoy caught Newbury's attention, keeping his voice low. "So, tell me, Sir Maurice, do you know if this is quite as irregular as Lord Winthrop would have us believe?"

Newbury furrowed his brow. "Indeed so. It's quite the most singular casket I've ever seen. The black-and-gold decoration is most unusual. And the fact that the occupant has

been rendered anonymous, by virtue of the complete absence of any cartouches bearing his name on the inner or
outer caskets, is particularly strange. There's certainly nothing like it in the records of the British Museum." He smiled.
"Didn't I tell you we were in for a surprise?"

Purefoy nodded. "I can't deny it." He looked around.
People were beginning to mill around once again, and the
hubbub had noticeably increased. Newbury had been right;
most of the people in the room had feigned minimal interest
in the contents of the casket, but, left to their own devices, had
reverted to conversing with their neighbours. He searched
for Winthrop, and eventually spotted the lord by the fireplace,
deep in the middle of a heated discussion with Blake.

Newbury leaned closer, smoothing the front of his jacket
distractedly. "I suspect this has thrown them into something
of a quandary." He nodded in the direction of the bickering
men, who were still dressed in their leather smocks and
bizarre headgear. "I'd wager that Blake wants to halt proceed-
ings so that they may spend a little more time making a study
of the inner casket, whilst Winthrop is anxious to give his
guests a good show. If I know anything at all about the man,
he'll make a point of continuing with the performance."

"Yes, I think he'd sooner destroy the thing than allow his
guests to leave unsatisfied."

"Mr. Purefoy, I do believe you have the measure of the
situation. I wonder: do you . . ."

"Well, really, Winthrop! This is unbearable. I shall have
no further part in it!" Newbury was cut off abruptly when
Wilfred Blake, raising his voice above the din, exploded at

Winthrop, who was now leaning against the fireplace, his face unreadable behind the mechanical spectacles. The room was silent as Blake turned about and made a hasty exit from the drawing room.

Newbury and Purefoy looked at each other and nodded knowingly.

Winthrop stepped forward, his hands wide apart in a placating gesture. "Let us continue with the task at hand. Arthur?" He beckoned to one of the other men, who readily stepped forward to adopt Blake's place. Winthrop turned to the sea of faces. "We shall now extract the inner casket from the outer shell, before exposing the mummified remains of the king inside."

The two men closed in on the casket base and, reaching inside, fumbled around until they had a grip on the snugly fit inner coffin. Their eyes met, and Winthrop counted to three before they lifted the weighty coffin out, wheezing with the strain. There was a collective gasp from the audience as the true magnitude of the casket's beauty became evident. The two men carefully laid the object on the table, then set about giving themselves more room to work by replacing the outer lid on the larger casket and moving it to a spot on the floor behind them.

Winthrop ran his hands gently over the top of the coffin. There was no denying how impressive it was. The thing seemed to radiate an aura all its own, capturing the attention of the assembled guests, many of whom had forgotten their idle conversations and were now watching with apparent interest.

Winthrop looked up at Arthur. "Are you ready?"

Arthur nodded.

They both ran their fingers along the seal between the coffin lid and base. Then, with a brief glance at the gathered crowd, the two men slid their fingers into the gap and together lifted the lid. This time it came away easily, and Purefoy found he was holding his breath, transfixed.

In truth, what was revealed came as something of an anticlimax after the grandeur of their earlier find. As Winthrop and his man laid the casket lid carefully to one side, Purefoy was able to see into the coffin. There, amongst a bed of decayed reeds, was a human figure bound in yellowed linen bandages, only the very tips of his clawlike fingers exposed. The bandages were covered in an archaic scrawl that Purefoy did not recognise: black, faded markings that appeared to have been inked onto the linen before the body was wrapped.

Winthrop took no time to ponder his next move, or to concern himself with the decorum that Purefoy felt would have been appropriate in the handling of the dead. He reached directly into the coffin and scooped out the withered body, then placed it upon the tabletop as Arthur moved the coffin shell out of the way. He turned to Purefoy, smiling. "Now, let us see how our ancient king exited this world."

Taking up the same blade he had used to break his way into the outer casket, Winthrop slit into the wrappings along the right side of the mummy. Then, grabbing a fistful of bandages, he began to peel away the layers, discarding the wrapping casually on the floor. Purefoy was so appalled that he almost started forward to challenge the lord in his mistreatment of the ancient artefact, but remembered himself at the last moment and was able to bite his tongue. Layers of crumbling linen fell away.

Soon enough, Winthrop had exposed a large expanse of the mummy's waxlike flesh, which was partly decayed and browned with age. It had taken on the appearance of beaten leather, hardened with exotic compounds and age. Winthrop had also extracted a number of trinkets from within the wrappings: small jewels and talismans, a number of blue ushabti, and a disc of gold engraved with intricate hieroglyphs. All the while, Newbury stood on the sidelines, watching impassively.

A few moments later, Winthrop had unrolled everything but the head of the long-dead Egyptian. It was clear now that the body had been imperfectly preserved; the flesh had decayed around the ribs, exposing the corpse's bones, and the hands were nothing but bony protrusions with remnants of human tissue still attached. Sweating, Winthrop straightened his back and rubbed his hands together. It was clear he was now so involved in his task that he had almost forgotten about the multitude of people that stood around him, watching his every move. When he spoke, it was barely a whisper. "Now, we look on the face of our pharaoh for the first time in four thousand years."

He gripped a loose flap of linen and began slowly unrolling the wrappings around the mummy's head. After a moment it became evident that the cadaver still had wisps of thick black hair on the crown of its head; locks of the stuff fell loose as the bandages came away. No one spoke as the last few strands of linen were unravelled and the Egyptian's face was finally revealed.

As soon as it was, a woman screamed. Winthrop gave a visible shudder and stepped away from the mummy. Purefoy looked on in horror. There were shouts from the back of the drawing room.

The dead man's face was a twisted visage of terror and agony. He was screaming, his mouth wide open in a silent, millennia-long cry. His features had been perfectly preserved, his eyes stitched shut with coarse threads, his brow was furrowed in intense pain.

Newbury looked round at Purefoy, the shock evident on his face. "My God. He must have been mummified alive."

Purefoy felt bile rising in his gullet. He looked away.

Winthrop had removed his headgear and was standing back from the table, a deathly pallor on his cheeks. People were murmuring anxiously all over the room. One of the men from the expedition came forward and hurriedly covered the mummy with a white sheet. Arthur fetched Winthrop a brandy from a cabinet beside the fireplace. Guests began to spill back into the hallway, where the automatons were waiting with more drinks.

Newbury put a hand on Purefoy's arm. "Come along, dear chap. I think the party's over for tonight." They followed the other guests filing out into the grand hallway, Purefoy glancing back over his shoulder to see Winthrop shakily consuming his brandy in one long draw.

He turned to Newbury. "Not quite what I was expecting, I must admit."

Newbury smiled. "Nor I. Yet I can't help thinking that all of the clues were there. It was evident that there was something unusual about the burial, and now we have a mystery. There has to be a reason why that man was mummified alive." He met Purefoy's gaze, his eyes gleaming. "I do enjoy a good mystery, Mr. Purefoy."

Purefoy smiled. "Well, I think that's enough excitement for me, Sir Maurice. And I have an article to write for the morning edition." He glanced at his pocket watch. "I think I should be on my way, and I'm unlikely to get anything more from Lord Winthrop this evening."

Newbury nodded. "Very well, Mr. Purefoy. I suspect I shall as well. It's been a pleasure to meet you. I'll look out for your article in *The Times*." He extended his hand, and Purefoy took it firmly.

"Likewise, Sir Maurice. I do hope we meet again."

Newbury smiled. "Good evening, then." He turned and disappeared into the crowd.

Purefoy, an empty notebook in his pocket and a head swimming with images of the screaming dead man, straightened his jacket, took one last look around the thronging crowd, and made his way slowly towards the exit and the street outside.

It was still raining. He hunched against the downpour and set off for home. It was going to be a long night.

CHAPTER

2

The station concourse was bustling with people. Newbury watched as they rushed from pillar to post; men dressed in black and grey business suits and long, billowing coats, brandishing hats and folded umbrellas; ladies standing in little huddles under the shelter of the impressive roof, attempting to avoid the inclement weather that was gusting in through the open doors, spattering the marble floor with fat droplets of rain.

Newbury stood on the platform, a copy of *The Times* tucked neatly under his left arm. He tapped his foot impatiently. Around him, the air was infused with the sharp tang of oil, heated by the machinations of wheels and gears as trains screeched in and out of the station. Engines sighed easily on nearby platforms, their carriages slowly disgorging passengers onto the concourse. Steam hissed from pressure valves, fogging in the cold, damp air. He'd been there for thirty minutes, waiting for his quarry, and to his dismay had discovered a distinct lack of interesting distractions.

Whilst waiting, Newbury had been considering the events of the previous evening, mulling over the details of the things he'd seen and trying to ascertain what it was, specifically, that had made him uneasy about Winthrop's unrolling of the Theban mummy. It was certainly more than the revelation that the man had been mummified alive. And more, also, than the sheer lack of respect shown to both the dead man and the intricate craftsmanship of his casket. Newbury had been appalled by the manner in which Winthrop had attacked the unrolling like a stage performance, but this was nothing new or surprising; he'd seen any number of such events in the past and had chosen to attend the party anyway. No, it had more to do with the unfamiliarity of the decoration—the black-and-gold casket, the strange hieroglyphs—coupled with the manner in which the man had died. There was more to the dead man's story than was immediately obvious.

Newbury had pondered this for a short time before deciding that it was really far too early to be contemplating anything other than breakfast. Now, his stomach growling, he was growing impatient, keen to be done with his task. He checked his pocket watch. It was nearly half past seven. The train would be arriving soon.

He had made his way to Waterloo Station that morning to meet another agent, a man who was returning to London after spending a number of years undercover in St. Petersburg. He

had no idea what this agent looked like, or, indeed, the man's
real name. All he'd been given was a code name, "Caspian"; a
carriage number, 3B; and instructions to meet the man from
the train and escort him immediately to the Palace. It was
certainly one of the more sedate tasks he had been required
to carry out on behalf of the Crown, and he wondered briefly
why one of Her Majesty's footmen couldn't have performed
the task to equally adequate effect. Yet, he admitted to himself begrudgingly, he *was* intrigued to discover more about
the mysterious man. It was certainly no surprise to him to
learn that Her Majesty had been managing agents abroad, in
territories outside the Empire, but he had no notion of why
the man's identity had to be kept so secret, especially from
another agent. Not only that, but it perplexed Newbury that
the man would choose to travel so far by rail, rather than airship. It must have added days, if not weeks, to his journey,
and caused it to be spent in cramped, noisy accommodations.
Perhaps that was what the man had grown used to in Russia,
living undercover and shrugging off the veneer of wealth. He
wondered how difficult the agent would find it to readjust to
life back in London after so many years away, steeped in the
routines and society of another culture.

He looked around, sighed, and took his copy of *The Times*
from beneath his arm. He shook it open and gave the head-
lines a cursory glance. Smiling, he realised what he had
failed to spot earlier that morning when he had scooped the
paper up off the silver tray in his hallway. The main headline
read THE MYSTERY OF THE SCREAMING MUMMY,
and the article beneath it was attributed to Mr. G. Purefoy.

The front page! Newbury chuckled to himself. Purefoy had done well.

He gave the article a brief scan. The slightly sensational tone of the piece grated against his more literary sensibilities, but he could tell immediately that it was an excellent example of the journalistic art. It was insightful and made many of the same observations that Newbury himself had noted during the course of the evening. He was impressed by Purefoy. The boy appeared to have an eye for detail. He could make a good agent one day. Newbury resolved to mention it to the Queen next time he had an audience with her. Not that he had time to take on an apprentice.

He looked up from his newspaper to see the train screeching into the station. He folded the paper under his arm once more and watched as the enormous green engine shuddered to a halt before the buffers, the carriages clacking together noisily as the train slowly came to rest. He edged along as the thin wooden doors of the carriages began to swing open, spilling passengers onto the platform. The agent would be waiting for him in the appointed compartment.

Dodging the sudden press of people clamouring to take their leave of the platform, Newbury paced alongside the row of carriages until he located the correct number. It was a first-class carriage, near the front of the train. He could see little through the grimy windows, which had been spattered with mud and dirt during the course of the journey. Dark shapes moved around inside as people tried to find the quickest route off the train. After allowing a young lady in a flowing yellow dress to step down onto the platform,

Newbury mounted the step and hauled himself up into the carriage.

The lobby area was small, and the carriage itself was divided into three separate compartments that branched off from a long passageway, each of them with their own windows and interior doors. The carriage was panelled in a dark wood, and whilst it appeared comfortable enough, there was a sour odour in the air that Newbury found difficult to place. Bringing the back of his hand to his face to stifle the smell, he shuffled along the passageway, glancing in at an empty compartment as he passed by. He assumed this was the room that had been occupied by the lady in the yellow dress. He wondered what she had made of the smell.

Beside the empty compartment was another identical one, although the blinds had been lowered over the windows and glass-panelled door. Newbury double-checked the small brass plate beside the door handle. The legend read 3B. He rapped his knuckles loudly on the wooden frame. There was no reply. He tried knocking again, then turned the handle and pushed the door open to step inside.

"Hello?"

The small room appeared to be empty, save for two long leather seats that faced each other across the compartment and two overhead racks for storing luggage. Both were vacant. Newbury glanced from side to side, wrinkling his nose. The smell he'd encountered upon entering the carriage was much stronger here, a lingering stench like foetid, rotten meat. It made him gag involuntarily and reach for the handkerchief in his jacket pocket. He used it to cover his mouth and nose, but it did little to disguise the overwhelming smell. He wondered what could have caused such a foul odour. It was as if a dead animal had been left in the compartment to rot, or had only just been removed upon arrival at the station, its musty stink still circulating in the stale air.

Newbury inched further into the small room, looking for any obvious sign that he had somehow missed the man he had come to the station to meet. There were no notes or items left behind for him to collect. He wondered if the man had already found his way off the train and was waiting on the platform. That would be a distinct break with procedure, but the man *had* been working alone in Russia for a number of years. He could hardly be expected to follow protocol to the letter. Whatever the case, if Newbury did find the man waiting for him on the platform, he hoped that he wouldn't have to spend long in his company if he were carrying the article that had generated such an offensive smell.

Shrugging his shoulders and coughing into his handkerchief, Newbury stepped out into the passageway and pulled the door shut behind him. He was relieved to get a measure of fresh air, although the foul stench had left a thick, cloying taste at the back of his throat. Sputtering, he made his way back to the lobby area, hopped down to the platform, and glanced from side to side in search of the other agent. The concourse was nearly empty. A few stragglers were still edging their way towards the station exit, porters humping luggage behind them as they drifted towards the row of waiting cabs on the other side of the main doors. Rain was drumming loudly on the roof overhead.

Newbury paced up and down, growing increasingly infuriated. There was no sign of the man known as "Caspian," no note left in the compartment, no luggage, and no clues as to what may have become of him. Her Majesty would not be amused. Newbury could only assume he'd somehow missed the man, who had then decided to make his own way back to the palace.

Frowning, but resigned to abandoning his abortive mission, Newbury quit the platform and walked briskly along the concourse. The rain was still blowing into the station on a fierce wind, and he cursed himself for forgetting his umbrella. Using his copy of *The Times* to shield his head from the worst of the weather, he dashed out into the street in search of a hansom cab, intent on making his way to his office at the British Museum. There, he would construct a brief missive to the Queen, detailing the bizarre circumstances of his morning and seeking clarity on what his next move should be, if any. And then, he promised himself, he would finally make time for breakfast.

CHAPTER

3

M orning, Watkins."

"Good morning, sir."

Newbury, still damp from being caught
in the rain, nodded politely to the doorman as
he made his way up the steps at the front of the
British Museum. The building was a magnificent edifice of grey stone, reminiscent of a clas-
sical Greek structure, with towering Corinthian
columns and bizarre effigies carved in relief
along the roofline in long decorative friezes. The
dreary morning didn't show the wonderful architecture to its best advantage, Newbury thought,
as he looked up to note with dismay that the sky
was almost as grey as the building itself. It was
going to rain again shortly.

Watkins held the door open for him, and Newbury smiled as he slipped inside.

It was still too early for the public to be milling around the exhibits, so the place felt deserted as he crossed the lobby, his shoes clicking loudly on the polished marble floor. He'd abandoned his copy of *The Times* in the back of the cab, but his fingers were still stained with streaks of dark ink from when he'd used the newspaper as a shield against the rain. He'd have to wash and dry off before he prepared his note for the Queen. He coughed, still hacking on the grotesque smell that had lodged in his nostrils and throat following his experience on the train. He hoped a pot of Earl Grey would help to clear out the disgusting scent.

Newbury made his way to the private staircase that led down into the bowels of the enormous building, where his office was hidden between the dusty stacks of the archives and the museum's administration offices.

A few minutes later, having passed through a network of winding corridors, he came to the door to his office. He straightened the front of his jacket and turned the handle. The door swung open to reveal a small room, lit by a series of hissing gas lamps. He stepped inside, pulled the door shut behind him, and began shrugging off his damp jacket so he could hang it on the coat stand in the corner.

"Ah, Sir Maurice. I trust you had a pleasant evening?"

Newbury turned to see his secretary, Miss Coulthard, emerging from the adjoining room, where he and his assistant, Miss Veronica Hobbes, kept their desks. Miss Coulthard was a diminutive woman in her early thirties, with dark brown hair tied up in a tight bun. She was dressed in a long grey dress and matching woollen cardigan. She was one of the most reliable people that Newbury knew, and he admired her for her dedication and resolve.

"Pleasant enough, thank you, Miss Coulthard. An interesting diversion." He draped his jacket on the coat stand and rolled his shirtsleeves up to his elbows, leaving dirty smears of ink on his white shirt. "I fear this morning has been less successful, however." He sighed.

Miss Coulthard gave him an appraising look. "Tea?"

Newbury laughed. "It's almost as if you can read my mind, Miss Coulthard. Thank you. Tea would be delightful." He turned, heading towards the other room, then stopped by the edge of Miss Coulthard's desk. "May I enquire as to the health of your brother, Miss Coulthard? Is he making a smooth recovery?"

Miss Coulthard nodded. "As expected, Sir Maurice. The doctor says he'll need a few more weeks to get his strength back, but his memory is returning, slowly but surely."

Newbury smiled. "Delighted to hear it." He glanced at his hands. "Ah, excuse me for a moment." He crossed to the sink in the corner of the room and, taking up a cake of soap, began scrubbing away the newspaper ink stains. Then, grabbing a towel from the rack beside the sink, he made his way to the adjoining room, leaving Miss Coulthard to set to work with the kettle.

Newbury hovered on the threshold of the inner office for a moment, watching his assistant work as he dried his hands. She was lost in a stack of papers, a look of concentration furrowing her brow, and if she was aware of his presence she was choosing not to let it distract her from her task.

Miss Veronica Hobbes had been working with him for over three months now, and had already saved his life on more than one occasion, both physically and emotionally. She was a most excellent woman, full of the energy and spirit of the modern age, an embodiment of progress, of equality, and of the future. She was pretty, too: a brunette, in her early twenties and full of life. Her features were well proportioned and feminine, and her eyes were a deep, arresting blue. She had a sharp mind, and an even sharper tongue.

Newbury cleared his throat. "Good morning, Miss Hobbes. I see you're still hard at work on that mystery of yours."

Veronica looked up, gave him a warm smile, and then returned to her reading. She spoke whilst her eyes followed the lines on the page before her. "Indeed. I believe that I'm making good progress, too. I have a potential suspect."

"Excellent. I look forward to hearing all about it. Just as soon as we have tea and I've dashed off a short missive to Her Majesty."

At this Veronica looked up again, leaning back in her chair to regard him. She seemed to see him properly for the first time. "You're damp, Sir Maurice. But tell me—did this morning's outing progress as planned?"

Newbury shook his head. "I fear not. In fact, I'd go as far as saying it was an unmitigated disaster. The gentleman I was tasked with escorting to the Palace did not arrive for our rendezvous. The circumstances were most peculiar. But I won't go into it now. I'm much more interested in hearing your news." He dropped the towel on the edge of his desk and moved around to find his chair. "Now, where did I put those notecards . . . ?" He fumbled with the many piles of paper that cluttered his desk.

Veronica laughed. She opened her drawer and withdrew a sheaf of small white cards. "Here. Take one of these."

Newbury smiled and accepted the proffered stationery. "My thanks." He lowered himself into his chair, took up a pen and inkwell, and began to write:

> *Majesty,*
>
> *Agent by codename "Caspian" did not attend rendezvous as expected. Please advise if further action is required.*
>
> > *Yours,*
> > *Newbury*

He gave the note a cursory glance, considering whether he should elaborate on the strange circumstances and the disturbing smell he had found lingering in the appointed compartment. He decided against the idea. After all, it was clear that Her Majesty knew more about the situation than he did, and he knew that she would just as soon summon him to the Palace if she had any cause for concern. He resolved not to make any plans for the following morning. He'd likely have to cancel them, anyway, when the summons from the Palace arrived. He folded the card into an envelope. Then, still holding the note in his hand, he leaned back in his chair and stared thoughtfully at the wall.

"I take it you've seen this morning's edition of *The Times*, Sir Maurice?"

Newbury grinned, blinking away his reverie. "Yes, indeed I have. I've just washed half of it down the sink." Veronica frowned, not catching his meaning. He chose not to elaborate. "I met the reporter at Winthrop's place, actually. Decent sort of chap. The piece was a little sensational for my liking, though."

"It certainly sounds as if it was an interesting evening, whatever the case. Are you planning to involve yourself in the mystery? Of the screaming mummy, I mean." Veronica delivered this with her usual casual aplomb, but it was clear to Newbury that she was fishing for something.

He smiled. "I doubt it's a case for the Crown. I did think I might call on old Peterson this afternoon, just to run a few things past him and make doubly sure it's not of interest. But I suspect Winthrop can take care of it. I never was an expert on the Egyptian arts, anyway." He searched Veronica's face for signs of disapproval. There were none. "I doubt Peterson will have much to add, either. He's more of a traditionalist. If he'd been interested in the find he'd have been there last night alongside me."

Veronica laughed. "Come now, Sir Maurice! Admit that you're rather taken with the whole affair. It sounds as if there's some fun to be had from it. Or you could write a paper on it."

"Well, I . . ." There was a high pitched whistle from the adjoining room. Newbury slapped a hand on his desk. "Ah, good. Time for that pot of Earl Grey." He stood, brandishing his letter to the Queen. "I'll ask Miss Coulthard to have this delivered directly to the Palace. And then you can tell me all about these missing women."

Veronica nodded, clearly amused. Newbury felt his cheeks flush. He circled his desk and went in search of Miss Coulthard. He needed his morning tea. And, he reminded himself, he still hadn't had any breakfast.

"So tell me about your suspect, Miss Hobbes." Newbury was sitting behind his desk once again, sipping his tea. He was watching Veronica intently. She placed her sheaf of papers on the desk and folded her arms. She met his gaze, her face serious.

"*Potential* suspect, Sir Maurice. The man might not have done anything wrong."

"So it is a man?"

"Yes."

"And?"

"And he's a travelling stage magician. He operates under the disappointingly unoriginal nom de plume The Mysterious Alfonso."

Newbury smiled over the rim of his teacup. "Oh, dear, that *is* rather fanciful. So tell me, how is this travelling magician associated with the missing women?"

"He's not. Well, at least not directly. But there are a few too many coincidences to easily rule out his involvement. Firstly, the dates and locations of his travelling stage show coincide exactly with the dates and places that the young women went missing. And secondly, many of the families of the missing women reported that the last thing they did before they disappeared was attend a travelling show."

Newbury studied Veronica's face. She was clearly passionate

about bringing the case to a successful conclusion. She'd been on the trail of the missing women ever since Sir Charles Bainbridge, Chief Inspector at Scotland Yard and a close friend of Newbury's, had brought the case to their attention.

A string of young females, aged between seventeen and twenty-three, had been disappearing from towns all over the Home Counties, and no one had been able to piece together any pattern as yet. It had been going on since Christmas, and the disappearances showed no signs of abating. There were at least nine reported cases to date. Many of the families were claiming that witchcraft had been involved, and it was for this reason that Bainbridge had stopped by to seek Newbury's advice. Newbury, however, had felt that there was no evidence of supernatural wrongdoing, and was already engaged with an entirely different case involving an infestation of spirits at Huntington Manor in Cambridgeshire. Veronica had been aiding him on the case, of course, but had been unable to put aside her desire to help Bainbridge solve the mystery of the missing women. She agreed with Newbury that there was nothing supernatural about the case and had set to work looking for patterns in the web of disappearances. Since the successful conclusion of the Huntington case, she had spent almost every waking hour at her desk, looking for clues in the statements and police reports. Newbury, of course, had been given other assignments to contend with, but he had allowed Veronica to pursue her quest. Now, it seemed, she had finally found something that resembled a lead.

"Are you planning to call on Sir Charles?"

Veronica frowned. "Not yet. Not until I know that the

man is definitely involved. It wouldn't do to set Scotland Yard on him unnecessarily."

Newbury placed his teacup down on its saucer with a clatter. "I'm not convinced that's the wisest course of action, Miss Hobbes. We can't have you putting yourself in any danger. This is a police matter. How do you intend to go about proving this magician fellow is actually involved, anyway?"

Veronica smiled. "That's easy. He's here in London. It's my intention to attend his performance this evening."

Newbury looked thoughtful for a moment. Then his face cracked into a wide grin. "Well, Miss Hobbes, you find me at your disposal. I fear I am without a dinner date this evening, and I've always enjoyed the theatre. Would you mind terribly if I escorted you to the show?"

Veronica laughed. "Indeed not. I have two tickets." Her eyes glittered. "If you can bear to tear yourself away from your ancient Egyptian mystery, it would be a pleasure to be escorted to the event."

"Then we shall take it in together. A most satisfactory resolution." He glanced at his pocket watch. "But now, I suspect old Peterson will have found his way to his desk, and I rather think it would be opportune to catch him before he wanders off again."

Veronica laughed. "I knew you wouldn't be able to resist looking into it!"

Newbury shrugged. "Well, we can't just leave that young Mr. Purefoy to sensationalise the whole affair in the national press, can we? Someone is going to have to set the record straight. I doubt very much it will be Winthrop." He got to his feet. "Until this evening, then?"

Veronica nodded. "Until this evening."

Smiling, Newbury set off to find Claude Peterson, one of the British Museum's foremost experts on ancient Egyptian ritual. He had a notion to question the man on the strange carvings he had seen on some of the ushabti the previous evening, and to see if Peterson found any significance in the red markings on the outer casket of the mummy.

Then, later, he would return to his Chelsea lodgings to prepare for an early-evening trip to the theatre. He wondered what bizarre treats The Mysterious Alfonso would have up his sleeves and whether he would be forthcoming in his interview. The case of the missing women was certainly disturbing and had entirely consumed Veronica these last few weeks. He hoped, for the sake of all involved, that she had finally found her man, and that they would soon be able to bring the episode to a tidy conclusion. Most of all, he hoped that whatever it was that had caused Veronica to become so emotionally embroiled in the case would be resolved at the same time. She was clearly pained by the plight of these missing women, and he hated to see her suffer.

CHAPTER

4

The Archibald Theatre in Soho was rather more bohemian than Newbury had been expecting. In fact, it was so far removed from the austere splendour of Drury Lane that he could hardly bring himself to consider it a theatre at all. Nevertheless, there was a stage—which, considering the condition of the rest of the building, he assumed had been erected specifically to accommodate the new show—and an auditorium to seat the raucous crowd. The rest of the facilities were basic, to say the least, and it was clear the interior decor had seen better days. The floor was sticky, the seats uncomfortable, and the smell almost as unpalatable as the stench he had encountered at the train station earlier that day. The space was dimly lit by a series of gas lamps mounted in a row along the rear wall, and whilst the venue was sizeable enough, it still felt cramped and uninviting.

With a sigh, Newbury surveyed the audience around him. The crowd was comprised of men and women who had spilled out of the factories and cookhouses just an hour or so before and were now engaged in quaffing extraordinary amounts of gin and heckling the magician with a variety of jibes and cheers. For his part, though, the magician appeared to revel in all of the attention, responding to the cheers of his audience with increasingly impressive sleights of hand. So far the audience had seen a host of elaborate illusions, ranging from a bouquet of flowers pulled out of a sleeve, to card tricks, to doves disappearing and reappearing beneath a red silk sheet. The Mysterious Alfonso was a consummate performer who had clearly spent years perfecting his act, and even longer learning how to engage the crowd. His thick Italian accent added a sense of the exotic, and his little flourishes at the end of each trick—a roll of the arm followed by a brisk bow to the front row—clearly showed that he understood how and when to give his audience a cue to applaud. Duly, they showered him with praise.

Newbury leaned back in his uncomfortable seat. The show was impressive, yet it offered him nothing that he had not seen before. As he sat in the midst of the noisy audience, jostled from side to side by the people around him, he found himself growing impatient. He was keen for the show to be over so that he and Veronica could try to get backstage and interview the showman about his possible connection to the missing women. He shook his head.

He studied Veronica for a few moments. She appeared to be increasingly enraptured by the magician's trickery and had allowed herself to be carried along by the audience, applauding loudly at each appropriate juncture and generally accepting the show for the entertainment it was. Newbury envied her that. He simply didn't have the sort of mind that would allow him to enjoy such trivial pursuits without first attempting to analyse exactly *how* the trick had been carried out, what the basis of the illusion was, or how his eye had been tricked into believing something contrary to what had really occurred. There was nothing truly mysterious, arcane, or occult in what he was seeing on the stage. He was also surprised that Veronica could engage with the show so deeply, given their reasons for visiting the theatre—unless, of course, she was feigning enjoyment as a means of gaining access to Alfonso after the show.

Newbury's attention was pulled back to the performance. Alfonso had wheeled out a large, coffin-shaped contraption on a trolley and placed it in the very centre of the stage. It reminded Newbury of the ancient Egyptian casket he had seen the previous evening, although this contraption was hewn from plain wood and lacked the gaudy decoration of the Egyptian artefact. Not only that, but Alfonso's box also had a series of thin slits cut into it at regular intervals along the sides and lid.

The magician moved around to stand behind the box, lifted his top hat, and gave a dramatic sweep of his arm to silence the audience. A hush settled over the theatre. Newbury glanced at Veronica, whose eyes flashed in the low light.

"Ladies and gentlemen! The time has come. This is what

you have come from miles around to see, no? The Mysterious
Alfonso offers to you his death-defying sword box!" The magician smiled a toothy grin as the crowd began to cheer again,
loudly. He waved them quiet once more. Slowly, as if to
punctuate his next few words, Alfonso began to tug his white
gloves from his hands, extracting one finger at a time, keeping
a watchful eye on the audience all the while. "Now . . . do I
have a volunteer?"

A few tentative hands went up around the room. Alfonso
appeared to consider his options, scanning the audience
with his outstretched finger. After a moment he settled on a
woman in the second row. She was young, blonde, and wearing a pale blue dress. The men to the left of her all stood to
allow her to pass. She made her way slowly through the row
of seats and approached the stage. Alfonso came forward
and took her hand as she mounted the steps, helping her
up to take her place beside him. He twirled her around,
showing her off with a wide smile, as if to demonstrate that
she wasn't a plant and that there was nothing unusual
about her. The crowd clapped appreciatively. Next, Alfonso
led the woman forward, towards the coffin-shaped box at
the centre of the stage. He left her there for a moment
whilst he fetched a small stool, which he placed on the
wooden boards before her. Then, lifting the lid to reveal the
interior of the box, he stood back and encouraged her to
climb inside.

The woman looked nervous. She peered over the lip of
the box as if she suspected there might be something hiding
within. Then she glanced back over her shoulder, searching out the face of her companion in the crowd. Newbury

watched the man wave at her to continue. Hesitating, the
woman stepped up onto the stool. Holding her skirt so as
not to trip, she lifted first one leg and then the other into the
box, until she was standing inside it, towering above Alfonso
and shaking visibly. Newbury wondered what was going
through her mind. Gulping at the air, clearly terrified, the
young woman sank to her knees and then lay down inside the
open casket, disappearing from view. Alfonso acted quickly.
He took the lid he had removed just a few moments before
and lifted it back into place, being careful to ensure a snug
fit. The audience was almost silent with anticipation. Even
Newbury found himself leaning forward in his seat, straining
to see what Alfonso would do next.

The magician moved off to the left-hand side of the
stage, where a young female stagehand—dressed in a revealing costume of feathers and sequins—had wheeled on a large
wooden rack filled with glittering swords. Alfonso stepped
up to the rack and drew one of the blades. He held it high
above his head, showing it off to the crowd. It glinted brightly
in the light. Then, moving back to stand before the box
containing the woman, he slapped the flat edge of the blade
against the casket, causing it to clang noisily. Next he took
the sharp end of the blade between his thumb and index finger and held it aloft, trying to flex the metal. The audience
watched, enraptured.

Alfonso moved the casket around a little so that the crowd
could see what he was about to do next. He took the point of
the sword, found one of the thin notches that had been cut
into the sides of the box, and thrust the blade into it with all
his might. The tip of the sword exited the box on the other

side through another of the precut slits. Alfonso pushed the blade home until the hilt of the sword was resting against the side of the box.

There was a gasp from the audience. Alfonso didn't hesitate to soak up their admiration. He went back to the rack of swords, took another blade, and repeated his actions, first proving to the crowd that the blade was real and then pushing it through the box—and, supposedly, the woman inside—until its tip was clearly protruding from the other side. He did this again and again until the rack was almost empty and there were at least ten blades perforating the box. Finally, frenetic and short of breath from the exertion, he mounted the stool, placed the tip of the last blade against the lid, and thrust it downwards through the last hole so that it slid through the box and burst out of a matching hole in the base. There was no way the woman inside the box could have survived.

Alfonso climbed down from the stool and stood before the audience. Panting, he rolled his shirtsleeves up to his elbows. The audience was silent and agog. Smiling, Alfonso kicked the stool away and grasped hold of one end of the box, which was still resting on the low trolley he had used to wheel it across the stage. He spun it around for the audience, offering them a view of the casket from all sides. Newbury frowned. It was not at all clear what had happened to the woman. There were no obvious trapdoors in the base of the box, and if she *had* dropped out through a small hatch in the bottom, she would have been easy to spot. The only explanation was that she was still inside the box, but Newbury found that hard to believe. The swords had certainly looked real enough, and he couldn't see how Alfonso could have missed her when he inserted the blades, no matter how much precision he had used when cutting the guide holes prior to the event.

"Impressive, isn't it?" Newbury turned to see Veronica leaning in towards him, smiling.

"Most definitely. I'll admit I was growing a little impatient with the performance until this most recent development. I haven't any notion how he has effected the woman's escape from the box. It's really quite intriguing."

Veronica laughed. "Perhaps there will be a chance to ask him after the performance has finished. If we're not taking him into custody, that is."

Newbury nodded. "Quite so." He paused. "Look, he's about to get her out again."

They both turned back to see Alfonso removing the swords with abandon, sliding them out of the box and dropping them noisily to the stage. It took him only a moment before all of the blades had been extracted. He hesitated before the box. Then, with one last, grand gesture, he swept the lid from the top of the casket and stepped back, allowing the final scenes of the trick to play out before him. There was a gentle cough from within the box and then the woman sat up, looking around at the audience, her eyes wild with disorientation. There was a roar from the crowd. The front rows stood. The applause was deafening. Newbury smiled as he watched Alfonso enjoying the adoration of his fans. The man was definitely growing on him.

Alfonso returned the stool to its place beside the box and helped the young woman step down, then saw her back to her seat in the second row. The female stagehand returned to the stage and began collecting the swords, sliding them back into their housings in the wooden rack. When she had finished, Alfonso, nodding his appreciation to the audience and smiling, crossed to where he'd left the open casket on the stage. He replaced the lid and then pushed it off to one side, allowing it to roll away on its casters.

Then he turned to the crowd. "One more?" They roared again, loudly. Alfonso waved at them to quiet down. "I shall warn you, though. This is no trifling feat of illusion." His voice dropped to a stage whisper. "This time I offer you the chance to glimpse some real magic." There was another cheer. Alfonso approached the front of the stage. He threw his arms wide. "Then I find myself in need of another volunteer."

This time hands shot up all across the theatre. Newbury turned to Veronica and was appalled to see that she was offering herself up as a volunteer, her hand raised high above her head. "Miss Hobbes! I feel strongly that this is not the safest course of action to pursue. We came to this place expecting to find a villain."

Veronica turned to meet his gaze, but kept her hand raised. "And that is exactly what I intend to do, Sir Maurice. We need to get close enough to see how his illusions work." Her whisper was strained. She clearly didn't want to be pressed further. Nevertheless, Newbury felt he had no choice.

"Really, Miss Hobbes. I must insist that you lower your hand. I cannot sit by and allow you to put yourself forward for such a dangerous enterprise, especially given the fact that you yourself are investigating this very man in connection with a series of missing women. I would be foolish to allow it. I quite understand your desire to bring this matter to a close, but I will not be responsible for allowing *you* to become one of your suspect's many victims. Will you desist?"

Veronica drew a sharp breath and lowered her hand. "I will." Her voice trembled with barely contained anger. She broke his gaze and returned her attention to Alfonso, who, whilst Newbury and Veronica had been debating, had chosen a volunteer from the audience and was in the process of helping her up onto the stage. Newbury glanced at Veronica once more, unsure what her reaction meant. Her hands were balled into fists by her sides. She was clearly furious with him. Unsure what he could do to remedy the situation, he leaned forward in his chair to continue in his observation of the goings-on at the front of the theatre.

The volunteer was once again a young woman, this time with raven hair and a lilac dress. She seemed more confident than the previous volunteer, and, from what Newbury could gather from her manner, happy for the attention she was receiving. Alfonso stood her in the very centre of the stage and bade her to remain still. Then he circled her, looking her up and down from all angles, as if studying her carefully, weighing her up with his eyes. He glanced up, catching sight of his stagehand standing off to one side, and beckoned her forward. She hurried over, handed him a red silk sheet, and then moved away again, smiling at the audience as she disappeared from view.

Alfonso turned to the audience. "Watch closely." He unfurled the large red sheet and draped it over the woman, spreading the edges out neatly so that they pooled on the floor around her, covering her from head to toe. Then, with barely a moment to catch his breath, he snapped his wrist and swept the sheet away again, flicking it up into the air in a bold dramatic flourish.

The woman was gone.

The crowd took a moment to react. The woman had completely vanished. There was not a trace of her to be seen. One minute she had been there, clearly evident beneath the thin silk sheet, the next she had entirely disappeared. There had been no sound, no sign of any movement. It was as if she had simply been swept up into the ether like an errant spirit.

Someone started to clap. Others followed. Soon the entire audience was standing and applauding the magician, who lingered just a moment longer on the stage before giving a sweeping bow, collecting his hat, and exiting stage left. The audience continued to clap, even after the final curtain fell.

Newbury turned to Veronica. He had to shout to make his voice heard over the clamour of the audience. *"Now* I'm impressed."

Veronica nodded, a knowing look in her eye. "It's what happens to her next that concerns me."

Newbury smiled. "That, Miss Hobbes, is what we are here to find out." He glanced over his shoulder. "Come on, let's see if we can make our way around this crowd. I can't imagine it will be too difficult to find our way backstage."

Veronica rose to her feet. She was smiling. "Thank you, Sir Maurice. For coming here with me, I mean."

Newbury grinned as he offered her his arm. "Always a pleasure, Miss Hobbes. Always a pleasure."

CHAPTER

5

As Newbury had anticipated, it was not difficult for the two of them to find their way backstage. Newbury was without a doubt the best dressed man in the house, and after speaking in hushed tones with the wizened old man who was standing sentrylike at the artists' entrance, the two Crown investigators soon found themselves admitted to the area behind the stage.

The Archibald Theatre was a small venue and it was soon clear to Newbury that most of the space had been reserved for the paying guests. The conditions behind the scenes were cramped and dirty, and if the front of the house was dilapidated, the backstage area was ready to be condemned.

Newbury and Veronica found themselves in a short, narrow corridor, which terminated in an exit to the street behind the theatre. A number of mildew-stained doors opened into dressing rooms along either side. The wooden floorboards creaked alarmingly as they walked. Newbury noticed that Veronica was lifting the hem of her yellow dress ever so slightly so that it wouldn't trail on the dirty floor. Crossing to one of the open doorways, he peered into an empty dressing room with a grimace. The room had not seen use for some time and had been allowed to become rundown and mouldy. The walls were slick with damp, the floorboards were peppered with rodent faeces and the now-rotten remnants of abandoned food, and the furniture had been piled up in one corner and was covered in a thick film of dust.

"It astounds me that the theatre can function in such a decrepit state." Veronica wrinkled her nose as she joined Newbury in the doorway of the abandoned room. Her eyes were shining in the low light. She was full of energy and life, excited at finding herself in the midst of another adventure. Newbury couldn't help but smile; the thrill of the chase was upon her.

He nodded. "Quite. I fear the halcyon days of this particular establishment are long gone."

A sound of coughing from one of the other rooms along the corridor prompted Veronica to turn her head and Newbury to look over her shoulder. There was no one in the doorway, but it was clear which room the sound had come from; the door had been propped open and light was spilling out into the corridor, causing shadows to flicker ominously up and down the walls. They made their way towards the light. Newbury hesitated in the doorway and rapped loudly, three times, on the frame. He couldn't see the occupant from where he was standing, but what he could see of the room suggested it saw more frequent use than the dressing room they had been in a moment before. Gaudy posters advertising events that had long since moved on to other, more savory venues were posted all over the walls: strongman acts, dancing girls, magicians from the Far East. A dressing table was pushed up against one wall, a sepia photograph of two women was tucked into one corner of the discoloured mirror and a top hat rested before it. An uncomfortable-looking dove fluttered its wings in a domed cage hanging from the ceiling.

"What is it?" The man's voice was gruff and unexpectedly English.

Newbury stepped across the threshold and into the room. Veronica followed behind him. The man—whom Newbury immediately recognised as Alfonso—was lounging in a chair, dressed in his shirtsleeves and trousers and puffing luxuriously on a long cigarette. Smoke plumed from his nostrils. He looked up at Newbury, a dour expression on his face. "The show's over. I think you must have taken a wrong turn." He returned to studying his boots.

Newbury smiled. All traces of the man's Italian accent had gone, replaced by a home counties drawl. "On the contrary. I sought you out in order to offer my compliments, Mr. Alfonso. My name is Sir Maurice Newbury and this is my associate, Miss Veronica Hobbes."

At this mention of Newbury's honorific, the magician snapped to attention. He glanced at Veronica, seeing her properly for the first time. "Sir Maurice. Please forgive me.

I'm sure you will understand that a venue such as this does not frequently attract clientele of the genteel variety." His face cracked into a wide grin. He shifted his feet from where they were perched on a stool and stood, offering Newbury his hand. Newbury took it and shook it firmly. "So, what on Earth attracted you to the Archibald this evening?"

"You, Mr. Alfonso. I hear your show has been causing quite a stir in the home counties and wanted to see it for myself."

"Really? Well, thank you for taking an interest. And how did you find it? I hope it wasn't a disappointment?"

"No. Not at all. It was most impressive. I was particularly taken with the card tricks. I've been studiously attempting to work out how you managed to affect them all so easily."

Alfonso grinned. "Ha! Parlour tricks. It surprises me that a man of your distinction should be so taken with such trivialities."

Veronica laughed. Newbury was pleased to see that she had taken his cue. "Well, I, for one, was struck by how successfully you made that young woman disappear. I am quite in awe of you, Mr. Alfonso. She appeared to vanish in a puff of smoke!"

Newbury feigned ignorance. "Yes, indeed! But tell me, what happened to the poor girl? You didn't make her reappear again afterwards! I do hope she hasn't disappeared forever. How did you pull it off?"

Alfonso smiled, shaking his head. "Sir Maurice, I'm sure you don't really expect me to give away my secrets, do you? I've worked for many, many years to develop my act. Many have tried to impersonate it. So far, none have succeeded. I intend to carry my secrets to the grave."

Veronica frowned. "But what of the girl?"

Alfonso laughed. "The girl? She's probably on her way home by now. My assistant will have given her the fare for a cab." He waved his cigarette. "Now, I'm afraid I really must press on. I have another show on the morrow to prepare for, and the act rather takes it out of me." He looked from Newbury to Veronica and back again. "I appreciate your kind words."

Newbury nodded. "Of course." He took Veronica's arm as if to lead her from the room. Then, just as they were about to turn their backs on the magician, he paused. "How long do you intend to continue your run at the Archibald, Mr. Alfonso?"

"Another week, Sir Maurice. Then I'm taking the show north to Manchester."

Newbury met his gaze. "Excellent. In that case, I'm sure we'll meet again. Good night."

"Good night."

The two investigators took their leave.

Outside, the fog had descended on the city like a thick woollen blanket, smothering the streets and diffusing the light so that everything lost its definition, becoming hazy and soft around the edges. Newbury sniffed. The air was damp with the grey miasma. He adjusted his hat and scarf, then offered Veronica his arm.

The two investigators stepped out onto the cobbled road, pausing to close the door behind them. The artists' exit opened directly onto the street at the back of the theatre and they had taken advantage of the private door, slipping out in order to avoid the crush of people who, even now, would still be spilling out of the front of the theatre.

Newbury glanced from side to side. He could hear horses whinnying in the murky fog, somewhere off to the left. It was likely there were still a few hansom cabs patrolling the area, hoping to pick up fares as the theatregoers stumbled into the night, drunk and in need of transportation home.

He looked to Veronica, who was bracing herself against the cold. She shivered. "Well, The Mysterious Alfonso wasn't quite the wretch I had anticipated. What did you think?"

He shook his head to indicate the conversation was better left until they were safely out of earshot. "I think that, in places such as this, even the walls have eyes and ears. Let's find ourselves a cab."

Huddling against the chill, Veronica nodded her assent. They inched along the road, following the kerb to make sure that they didn't wander too far off track in the thick, wintry fog.

There was a sob from somewhere just to the right of them. A woman's sob, soft and stifled.

"Hello?" Veronica broke away from Newbury, trying to locate the source of the crying. "Hello?"

Newbury followed her. The sobbing sound came again. "Veronica. Over here." He approached the shape that loomed in the fog and slowly resolved into the form of a young woman leaning against the wall of the theatre, clearly distraught. He stepped closer, putting a hand on her arm. "My dear. Whatever is the matter?"

The woman looked up. Newbury almost started in surprise.

She had a spill of long dark hair and was wearing a lilac dress. She was young and pretty and her cheeks were stained with tears. It was the girl from the theatre, the woman who had disappeared during the show. She looked confused, her eyes searching Newbury's face for the answer to some undisclosed question. When she spoke it was with another sob. "Where am I?"

Veronica, who had moved to stand beside Newbury, gave her a concerned but quizzical look. "You're outside the Archibald Theatre. You were there to see a show, a magician. Don't you remember getting up to go on stage?"

The woman bit her bottom lip apologetically and shook her head. She sniffed and wiped her eyes with the back of her hand. "I'm . . . I'm not sure. I don't remember." Her voice was a whimper. Her accent was thick and telling; she was from the East End.

Newbury leaned closer, trying to catch the scent of gin on her breath. He wondered if she were simply drunk, but she didn't smell of alcohol. She seemed sober, but terribly confused. And there was the hint of something else, some chemical he found difficult to place. He frowned. "Are you able to recall your name?"

She nodded. "Miss Annabel Myers."

"And did you have an escort this evening, Miss Myers?"

"Yes." She gave another sob. "My brother, Jimmy. He should be around here . . . somewhere." She looked from side to side, but it was difficult to make out anything in the cloying fog.

Veronica smiled warmly. "Miss Myers. Do you have an address we could see you to? I suspect that even if your brother is searching for you now, he won't get far in this fog. If we were to see you home, I'm sure he would be relieved to find you there upon his return."

The woman stifled her tears. "Yes." And then, more resolute, "Yes, that sounds like a good idea. I live at my father's house at 26 Nelson Street, Shoreditch." She looked down at the palm of her hand, then held it up towards Veronica. Resting there was a smattering of small coins. "I think someone handed me this for my fare. I'm sorry. . . ." She hung her head. "I'm so confused."

"Put your money away, Miss Myers. I'll fetch us a cab."

"Thank you . . . ?"

"Sir Maurice Newbury. And this is my associate, Miss Veronica Hobbes."

"Thank you, sir." Miss Myers looked utterly bemused.

"Don't mention it, Miss Myers. I shall return momentarily with a cab." Newbury moved towards the sound of horses, somewhere up ahead of them by the side of the road. Behind him, the two women were soon enveloped by the thick, tubercular blanket of smog.

The house in Shoreditch was everything that Newbury had been expecting: rundown, dirty, a pile of red bricks leaning awkwardly against its neighbour for support. The cab ride had proved uneventful. Miss Myers had been able to tell them very little about Alfonso and the method by which he had caused her to disappear on stage. Her memory of the event was erratic and impressionistic. All she could tell Newbury and Veronica was that she was terribly confused and remembered feeling as though she had somehow been squeezed into a box that was too small to contain her. Her next vague recollection was that someone had pressed money into her hand and turned her out into the foggy street, where she was found by the two investigators.

Newbury had waited in the cab whilst Veronica had shown Miss Myers to her door, then they set out for Kensington so that Newbury could escort Veronica to her rooms just off the High Street. With all this talk of missing women and the continuing threat of the revenants prowling the streets, Newbury was keen to ensure that his assistant made it back to her home in safety. He was also keen to discuss her impressions of the evening's events.

After she had said her piece, he glanced at her, watching as the motion of the cab caused her to rock from side to side in her seat. "I think our Mysterious Alfonso was every bit of the wretch you anticipated him to be."

Veronica frowned. "So you believe him to be guilty, then?"

Newbury shrugged. "All the evidence suggests not. The girl was fine—if a little confused and disoriented by her experience—and he had provided her with the cab fare home as he suggested. But I do feel there is more to the man than meets the eye. I'd like to know what sort of trick he's using to pull off that disappearing act, and what's more, why it should leave the volunteer feeling so lost and unwell. I have a suspicion she was rendered unconscious, probably with some kind of chemical compound. It certainly bears more investigation."

Veronica nodded. "Indeed. I wonder if it is the process

itself that is causing the women to go missing. By that I mean, do they stumble out of there disoriented and with no memory of the preceding events and then wind up getting themselves lost, or worse?"

Newbury looked thoughtful. "Or perhaps some of them are simply rendered unconscious during the process and then don't wake up at all. But we must also consider the possibility that Alfonso, or whatever his real name is, may not be to blame. There is always coincidence to consider."

Veronica raised an eyebrow in a parody of Newbury. "Hmmm. Coincidence indeed? I've heard you argue on more than one occasion that coincidence is the last resort of the inept detective."

Newbury laughed. "Yes, you have me there, my dear Miss Hobbes." He glanced out of the window. Kensington loomed out of the fog. "Shall we talk further in the morning?"

Veronica nodded. "I'll wait for you at the office." The cab juddered to a halt as the driver reined in the horses. Veronica got to her feet. "Did Peterson have any thoughts on your mysterious screaming mummy, by the way?"

"Very few. He suggested it was probably some sort of elaborate punishment, that the poor chap was probably mummified alive for some terrible crime he'd committed. Other than that, the markings are unlike anything he's seen before."

Veronica smiled. "Well, I'm sure tomorrow will bring some fresh ideas." She pushed open the cab door and moved to step out.

"Oh, and Miss Hobbes?"

She turned to look over her shoulder and was framed for a moment by the open doorway of the cab. Newbury couldn't help but feel stirred by her beauty and had to fight the impulse to reach out to her.

"Yes?"

"Assure me you won't place yourself in any unnecessary danger."

She nodded. "I won't. Good night, Sir Maurice."

"Good night, Miss Hobbes."

The door shut behind her, and a moment later Newbury rocked back in his seat as the cab rolled away towards Chelsea and home.

CHAPTER

6

Morning brought with it a laudanum fugue that would have proved debilitating if not for Mrs. Bradshaw's revitalising breakfast of bacon, eggs, and Earl Grey tea. Newbury, wrapped in his blue velvet dressing gown, sat heavily at the table, wincing at the sunlight that was streaming in through the dining room window. Outside, a frost had settled, clearing the fog, and people were already beginning to bustle along the streets, carriages creaking loudly, animals yapping and chirping, steam engines firing noisily as they powered ground trains, and other, stranger, steam-powered vehicles. The last two months had seen a proliferation of new devices: bizarre, single-person carriages that barrelled along at great speed, bowling over everyone and everything in their wake. They were smaller than hansom cabs, but far larger than bicycles; squat, fat little cockpits on three or four wooden wheels, with rear ends that housed a small furnace and water tank, like miniaturised versions of the steam-powered hansoms which Newbury used frequently. The driver lowered himself into the cockpit, leaving his head and shoulders exposed to the elements and his hands near a series of panels and pulleys which he would use to operate the steering mechanism. Early on, Newbury had considered obtaining one of the strange vehicles, but *The Times* had reported a growing number of fatalities involving the contraptions. Over time, Newbury had lost the mounting temptation to adopt the new form of transportation and grown to see them as a menace. Newbury was a huge supporter of progress, but he didn't believe the city was ready for the coming transport revolution that these new devices seemed to foreshadow. Aside from that, they were damn ugly, and a nuisance, too. Perhaps Veronica was right after all, in her frequent assertions that things were getting out of hand. Perhaps there was a very real need to slow things down, to stop the world from rushing too hastily towards the future. Or perhaps he was just feeling dour and hungover.

He been taking more risks with the laudanum recently, and he knew he was playing a dangerous game. He'd even visited an opium den the prior week, a place at the back of a coffee-house known to its clientele as Johnny Chang's. It was a nauseating place, full of Chinese sailors and fallen gentlemen, but the heady aroma of the opium and the promise of relief at the end of the pipe had proved too tempting, so he had allowed himself to wallow there for most of an afternoon, buried in a sea of silk cushions. Chasing the dragon was something new to him. Until that episode, he had only used laudanum, measuring it out into glasses of red wine and imbibing it in the comfort of his own home. The ritual of the pipe was exotic, bewildering, and somehow more appealing, but he preferred to indulge himself in private. The only solution was to purchase one of the devices for use in his apartments.

Newbury understood that others could not appreciate his craving for the opiates; that both Charles and Veronica saw it as a weakness to be overcome. But to Newbury it was much more than that, more than just the need for physiological intoxication. It helped him to think, to see the world from a different perspective. It was during his opium hazes that he often found the solution to a case, or made a connection where previously he had seen none. The drug allowed him to retreat into the crevices of his own mind, and what he found there was often illuminating. It lifted the shades of perception, opened his eyes to things that others would deem impossible. It enabled him to trust his instincts. He feared he would not be half the detective he was without the drugs, and that troubled him beyond regard for his physical well-being, so he continued to indulge, keeping his practises hidden from the world. The drugs were at the epicentre of a maelstrom of need and desire: fuel for his mind but poison for his body.

For a moment, Newbury considered going back to bed. He allowed himself to entertain that fantasy for a few minutes, knowing full well that it was never truly an option. He had to meet with Veronica, for a start, and besides, he was fully expecting to receive a summons to the palace to discuss the missing agent, "Caspian," and determine whether or not Her Majesty had any intention of pursuing the matter further.

His mind was also exercised by the mystery surrounding the Theban mummy. He'd spent the evening reading through his library of occult tomes, searching out any references to irregular mummification practices in ancient Egypt, but had found nothing to help him identify what Winthrop had uncovered in Thebes. Unperturbed, he had dashed off a note to Aldous Renwick, a longtime correspondent and a master of occult literature, describing the circumstances and asking his friend to examine his own library on the off chance that he might be able to come up with something.

For the time being, then, both of Newbury's mysteries had stuttered to a halt. Whilst he waited on answers, he would do all he could to help Veronica bring her own matter to a close. Downing the dregs of his tea, Newbury forced himself to stand, flinching as the movement caused a brief explosion of pain in his temples. He sighed, cursing under his breath. Then, snatching up another piece of toast from the rack, he made his way towards the washroom, where he planned, if at all possible, to make himself reasonably presentable.

A short while later, following a wash and a shave, Newbury got dressed and began feeling more like his usual self. He had donned a black suit with a white collar and red cravat, but he knew from catching a glimpse of himself in the cheval glass that the black rings beneath his eyes betrayed his tiredness, if not the reason for it. He hoped he could hide it from Veronica. He couldn't bear to think that she could consider him weak.

It was just after nine o'clock and Mrs. Bradshaw had cleared away the debris from breakfast, leaving a small silver tray containing his post for the day. He eyed it from across the room, immediately recognising the heavy vellum envelope that lay atop the pile. So, he'd been right about the summons. He collected the small pile of letters and took them to the drawing room, which adjoined the dining room through a single door. In the corner of the room, atop its little wooden perch, a brass owl that he'd inherited from Lord Carruthers trilled noisily and fluttered its metallic wings.

Casting the rest of the pile on the coffee table, Newbury searched out his letter opener and slid it underneath the gummed fold of the envelope from the palace. The paper tore readily, and inside there was nothing but a small note card, printed neatly in the perfect handwriting of one of Her Majesty's administrators. He withdrew it and held it up to the light.

> *Newbury,*
>   *You are expected at the palace forthwith.*
>   *Victoria R.*

He turned the card over in his hand, smiling. Perhaps now he'd find out a little more about "Caspian" and the reason for the man's failure to rendezvous at the station the previous day. Miss Hobbes, he feared, would have to wait a while longer. He placed the card on the bureau beside the letter opener. Then, taking a moment just to steady himself, he fetched his coat and hat from their place in the hallway and set out to see his employer, Her Majesty the Queen.

"Well, Newbury?"

Her Majesty did not keep him waiting long. He had taken a cab directly to Buckingham Palace, one of the loud-but-fast steam-powered vehicles that Veronica so detested. Sandford, the aged butler who now waited on the Queen's small coterie of field agents, had been waiting for Newbury by the side entrance and guided him in, taking his coat and hat and hurrying him along the secret passageway to Her Majesty's audience chamber.

Newbury stood before the monarch now, trying to make her out in the shadowy half light of the room. She was sitting, as ever, in her life-giving chair, the pumps and bellows wheezing noisily as they artificially inflated her lungs, heaving her chest in and out alarmingly as they forced her to breathe, artificially sustaining her life. Tubes coiled down from the bags of strange-coloured fluids that were attached to a metal frame above her head, pumping preservatives, saline, and other, more unusual compounds, into her bloodstream. Her chest was covered by a swath of black silk, but Newbury could see where the tubing snaked from the tanks at the back of her chair, up under her arms, and into her chest. Victoria was empress of half the world and she clearly wasn't going to give it up without a fight. At least, not whilst she had the marvellous machines of Dr. Fabian to keep her alive indefinitely.

When she spoke again, her voice was a husky, gritty rasp. "Where is our man, Newbury?" She gave him a reproachful look.

Newbury took a deep breath. "Your Majesty, I attended the rendezvous as directed. The agent code-named 'Caspian' was not in the appointed carriage, nor did he make himself known to me on the platform. All I was able to glean from the experience was that the person who had inhabited compartment 3B was carrying with them some item or creature that smelled distinctly as if it were carrion."

Victoria raised an eyebrow. She wheeled forward in the chair, the wooden rims creaking against the marble floor. Her hands were shaking with the effort. "Newbury, let us make the situation clear to you. You must locate this man, 'Caspian,' and bring him to the palace forthwith."

Newbury tried to hide his exasperation. "As you wish, Your Majesty. I fear I will need some more of the details to do so, however. . . ."

Victoria laughed, a wet, spluttering laugh. "Very well." Her face became serious. "This is a difficult assignment, Newbury. It may have repercussions for both you, personally, and for the Crown."

"How so?"

"That will no doubt become clear as you continue. For now, all you need to know is that the man you are looking for was once an agent named William Ashford."

Newbury frowned. "Ashford? I thought he died years ago, before my time. I've heard stories of the man."

Victoria gave an approximation of a shrug. The machinery groaned with the movement. "It was all a long time ago,

Newbury. Ashford *was* killed, five years ago, in a manner of speaking. But he was rebuilt by Dr. Fabian as an instrument, and a blunt one at that. He has been living undercover in St. Petersburg, but now he has returned for some reason, contrary to our instructions. Another agent in Russia was able to warn us of his intended return."

"So Ashford is rogue? Why would he risk returning to London, and why should he travel so far by train rather than airship?"

"Ashford is no longer a man, Newbury. Not in the sense that you would understand. He is an anomaly, neither living nor dead, but trapped somewhere in between and full of vengeance. His sense of what is right and wrong no longer equates to our own. We believe he has returned to seek revenge on those who plotted his downfall. He travels only by land and sea, for the altitude of an air-going vessel would affect the workings of the machines that sustain him." She paused, meeting Newbury's gaze. "You must find this anomaly, Newbury, and bring it to heel. One does not allow such things to travel freely about the capital."

"Quite so, Your Majesty. Quite so. I shall attend to it directly."

"See that you do. Put all else out of your mind. Ashford must be foremost in your thoughts."

Newbury nodded. "There is just one other thing, Your Majesty, that I would prevail upon you for."

Victoria nodded her consent and he went on.

"A boy. George Purefoy. He's a reporter for *The Times*. I have a notion that he deserves our attention. He might make an excellent agent, given some time."

Victoria waved a dismissive hand. "Later, Newbury, later. There will be time enough for taking a young apprentice under your wing, perhaps when the Ashford matter has been resolved. For now, we urge you to focus on the task at hand. Go to it."

Newbury watched as the Queen rolled backwards in her strange mechanised chair and the darkness enveloped her. He turned to leave.

"Oh, and the Hobbes girl?" Her voice called out from the shadows.

He looked back, but Victoria remained shrouded in darkness. "Veronica?"

"No, the younger one. We have considered your request and have decided to oblige. She will be moved to a new facility. More information will be forthcoming. We suggest you do not tell the family until arrangements have been made."

Newbury grinned. "Thank you, Your Majesty. That is most excellent news."

Victoria's hissing laugh echoed around the dark cavernous room. "We do what is necessary. As should you, Sir Maurice." She coughed. "Now go and deal with Ashford."

"As you wish."

Newbury crossed the room and stepped through the door into the passageway that would lead him back to Sandford, the waiting room, and the cold London morning outside.

Whilst Her Majesty had given him a little more to go on, Newbury still felt he was only hearing half of the story, and that if he were to uncover a little more information about Ashford, he'd be able to bring the case to a much swifter resolution. Not only that, but Victoria's talk of Newbury's personal stake in the assignment had left him feeling more than a little uncomfortable. He had no idea how an agent from five years ago could have any bearing on him, or the nature of the 'repercussions' that she had referred to. But he did know someone who might: Sir Charles Bainbridge. Charles had been an agent for many, many years and would likely remember Ashford. He may even have worked with the man on a number of assignments. Whether he knew the truth, or, like Newbury, had been led to believe that Ashford was dead, Newbury had no idea. But he knew that he needed to find out. He would head directly to Scotland Yard and speak with Charles. For now, it was the only lead he had.

CHAPTER

7

"Ashford, you say? It's a long time since I last heard that name." Sir Charles Bainbridge, Chief Inspector at Scotland Yard, moved about behind his desk, shuffling papers with a flustered expression. He was older than Newbury, just over fifty, with greying temples and a big bushy moustache. He was dressed in a grey suit with a white starched collar and black necktie. He glanced up at Newbury, who was sitting in a chair off to one side, watching his friend. "Why do you ask?"

Newbury stroked his chin thoughtfully. He hadn't really decided how to put it yet. "Her Majesty has asked me to find him."

Bainbridge dropped the stack of papers in his hands into a heap and looked back at Newbury before lowering himself into the chair behind his desk. "Newbury, William Ashford has been dead for over five years. What on earth are you going on about?"

Bainbridge clearly wasn't aware of Ashford's remarkable second life. "Indeed. That, apparently, is the received wisdom on the matter. But it transpires that there is more to Ashford's death than meets the eye."

Bainbridge looked confused. "Stop talking cryptically and get on with it, Newbury."

"You start. What can you tell me about Ashford? What sort of man was he and how did he die?"

Bainbridge sat back in his chair. "He was a good man, I'll venture that much. I knew him fairly well. He was married, with two children. A boy and a girl, if I remember correctly. He was a good agent—did what was necessary. He always had the best interests of the Empire at heart."

Newbury nodded, glancing out the window. In the yard below, a group of uniformed men were readying a police carriage. He turned to meet Charles's gaze. "So how did he die?"

"It was a nasty business, Newbury. Not something I care to remember."

Newbury furrowed his brow. It was unusual for Bainbridge to be so reserved. "Come on, Charles! This is important." He banged his fist on the table with impatience.

Bainbridge sighed. He leaned forward in his chair again. "What do you know of Dr. Aubrey Knox?"

"Not a great deal. Former agent. Lost in action about the same time as Ashford. It's never really come up."

"Well, it's never come up for a reason."

"Go on."

"Knox was a genius. A brilliant man who, like you, had a fascination with the occult sciences. He was one of the shining lights of Her Majesty's secret circle. He had proven himself a reliable, loyal subject for over ten years, and his service record was impeccable. He took on many of the same sorts of cases that you do now: anything strange, psychological, paranormal, supernatural. He had a depth of knowledge surpassed by none in the Empire, yet he didn't crave personal recognition. In many ways he was the perfect agent: quite brilliant, but quiet, effective and unassuming."

"What happened to him? Is it all tied up with Ashford?"

Bainbridge nodded. "It was midway through 1896. June, I think. There was a botched assignment. I'm not sure of the details but something went wrong. Something that everyone expected to be an easy job. Somehow, in the aftermath, it was brought to Her Majesty's attention that Knox had been pursuing his own interests. He'd become obsessed with the practise of the occult. Agents were sent to his laboratory in Ladbroke Grove. They discovered that he'd been experimenting on human subjects: waifs, whores, paupers. No one knew what he was trying to do but we were all appalled by it. It wasn't just the work of an enquiring mind. You should have seen the place, Newbury. It's burned into my mind. The things he'd done . . . he should be damned to hell for all eternity.

"Anyway, a warrant was issued for his arrest. Ashford was given the case and told to find Knox and bring him in, whatever the cost." Pausing, Bainbridge stood, crossed the room, and collected two brandy glasses from a shelf by the door.

He reached into a cupboard and searched out a plain glass decanter, from which he removed the stopper and sloshed an ample measure of brandy into each glass. He returned to his desk and handed one of the drinks to Newbury. He looked pale. "Bit early, I know, but . . ." He shrugged.

Then his tone changed. "Now, Newbury, you must understand that Ashford was very much unlike you or I. His disposition was entirely different. Put him in a room with a foreign agent and he'd make them talk without even batting an eyelid. He was the sort of man who could bring down a network of criminals with sheer brute force. Simple, but effective. 'A tool,' Her Majesty would call him, for when we needed 'something a little stronger.' But he had no experience of the occult, no sense of what he was getting himself into with Knox. And Knox, for his part, knew how to play him." Bainbridge sighed.

"Ashford tracked Knox across the country for months, finally cornering him back here in London. But Knox was expecting him, and had laid a trap. No one is sure exactly what happened to Ashford, but his body was found mangled in an abandoned warehouse near the docks. He'd been torn open like a doll. Knox was never heard from again."

"So he got away? No one went after him?"

"Plenty of people went after him. But no one ever found him. He disappeared. I wouldn't be surprised to learn that Her Majesty still had people looking for him now, all over the world. But poor old Ashford was buried a few days later, and I'd had to break the news to his wife. It was a sorry business indeed."

"So why have I never heard about this before?"

"Because, Newbury, you were brought in to replace Knox. In many ways you're the same sort of man: brilliant, dedicated, effective. But even the very best of men is fallible. Don't think I don't know about your fondness for the laudanum, for a start."

"Let's not get into that."

Bainbridge took a long draw on his brandy. "The Queen is worried. Not because she doubts you, you understand, but because she's seen it before. Knox left a bad taste in her mouth. In all our mouths. She's concerned that, one day, you may drift too close to the line; that the allure of the occult is too strong. Not just for you, but for any man."

Newbury gripped the arms of his chair. "Goddamn it, Charles! That's ridiculous. How can she equate me with a man like that? I have a mind to head back there now, to have it out with her myself!"

Bainbridge slammed his drink down on his desk. "Don't be a fool, Newbury! Didn't you hear what I said? It's precisely that sort of behaviour that Her Majesty is trying to avoid." He stood, looking down at his friend. "Newbury, we've been friends for a long time. Listen to me when I tell you: stay away from this business. It'll do you no good. Ashford is dead, Knox is lost, and you, my friend, are one of the finest men I know. It wouldn't do to mix yourself up in this business. The Queen has nothing to fear. I've told her that myself. She's simply trying to protect you."

Newbury looked up at Bainbridge, resignation in his eyes. "I'm afraid it's not that simple, Charles. Ashford isn't dead. At least not in the way you think he is."

"What?"

"The Queen told me herself, just this morning. It's all starting to make a horrible sort of sense. After what happened at the docks—after they found Ashford's shredded remains—Dr. Fabian took his body to his laboratory and *re-built* him. He's still alive, but he's barely human. Her Majesty said he was 'a blunt instrument' and 'no longer a man in the way that I'd understand it.' He's been living undercover in St. Petersburg for five years. Now, for some reason, he's gone rogue. He's probably somewhere in London as we speak. Her Majesty thinks he's returned to wreak vengeance, and that he's probably half mad. She's charged me with bringing him in."

Bainbridge flushed red. He looked flustered. "My God . . ." He grabbed his glass and downed the rest of his brandy in one long gulp. "It seems that I don't know everything after all."

"I'm beginning to think it's an epidemic." Newbury took a pull on his own brandy. "Do you think he's come looking for Knox?"

"Perhaps. I don't know. Knox hasn't come up in years. There could be other reasons."

"Such as?"

Bainbridge shrugged. "All I know is that the Ashford I knew would never go rogue. Not without a damn good reason. Perhaps he's on to something. Perhaps he's following a trail. Or perhaps he really has lost his mind."

Newbury nodded, slowly. "Perhaps. Being half dead for five years, trapped in Russia without his family. No one could blame him." He placed his empty tumbler on the edge of Bainbridge's mahogany desk. "Will you help me, Charles? I don't even know where to begin."

The chief inspector looked pained. "Newbury, I wish I could, but . . . I can't. I have no time. I'm about to head out to the scene of a murder. A high-profile one, too. A lord has been found dead in his home. I need to attend to it before I can think of anything else."

Newbury smiled. "Of course. Can I ask what the circumstances are?"

"It's all rather rum. Lord Henry Winthrop was found dead in his drawing room at Albion House. He held an extravagant soiree on Tuesday evening, something to do with a mummy unrolling. He'd just returned from an expedition to Egypt. It looks like a bungled robbery, according to the chaps on the scene. The burglar may have been interrupted by Winthrop; there's not a great deal missing. We're wondering if someone scoped the place out during the party and tried to come back the next day."

Newbury was already on his feet. "Charles! I was there. Two nights ago, at the party. I spoke to Winthrop. My God."

"What? Then you could be of use to me on the scene. Can you talk me through what happened there?"

"Of course. I may even be able to point you to a suspect. There was a heated exchange at the party between Winthrop and a man named Blake. Wilfred Blake. He left under a heavy cloud."

"Good man! Come on, grab your coat. The carriage should be ready and waiting. Once we've got this nasty business out of the way I can help you with Ashford, assuming he doesn't

show his hand in the meantime." Bainbridge strode over to
the coat stand in the corner and collected his overcoat, gloves,
and cane. Newbury followed suit. So, Winthrop had been
murdered, the very night he had revealed his Egyptian mystery to the world. Newbury wondered what to make of it. But
this was not enough of a distraction to quell the rising feeling
of disquiet that gripped him tightly in the chest every time he
considered Bainbridge's words: "The Queen is worried . . .
even the very best of men is fallible."

He knew that concern only too well himself.

Together, the two men set out for Albion House.

CHAPTER

8

Veronica stood on the gravel path at the
foot of the sanatorium and tried to will
herself to smile. It was midmorning and
the journey to Wandsworth had been fraught
with chaos. The progress of her hansom had
been impeded by a terrible accident, in which
a small, steam-powered vehicle had exploded,
sprinkling the driver in a bloody mess across a
residential square. Debris was scattered over
the road and frightened horses bolted in every
direction. Many cabs, including her own, had
been dragged halfway across the neighbour-
hood, and Veronica would not have been surprised to learn that these errant vehicles had
themselves been the cause of further accidents.

Thankfully, her driver had been quick to get his spooked horses under control, then took a swift detour to avoid the inevitable delays that awaited them in the other direction.

In truth, however, Veronica knew it was not this that had left her feeling so dejected. Sir Maurice had failed to make their appointment once again that morning, and whilst she knew that she shouldn't blame him—he had his own affairs to attend to, after all—she couldn't help but feel a little slighted by his lack of attention. Particularly as there were missing women to consider.

Then, of course, there was Amelia. The last time she had visited her younger sister, a week earlier, Veronica had found the experience almost unbearable. Amelia was growing weaker and frailer with every passing day. It was as if her sporadic seizures were somehow draining the life from her, stealing her vitality, like some kind of wasting disease was slowly dragging her towards death. Veronica couldn't bear to stand by and watch that happen. She cared for Amelia too much.

She stared up at the building. It looked foreboding, deserted. The airing courts were empty, and a thick, rolling mist lay heavy on the gardens. The clock tower disappeared into the milky sky above the entrance. But she couldn't put it off any longer. Sighing, Veronica walked decisively towards the sanatorium, her boots crunching noisily on the loose gravel.

Inside, the reception area was a remarkable counterpoint to the misty solitude of the sanatorium grounds. Here, there were signs of life in plenitude. A nurse sat behind the reception desk, a vacant expression on her face; a doctor strolled purposefully along the corridor; and the patients in their rooms suffered audibly from any number of terrible mental afflictions. Veronica always felt disconcerted by the sounds of the inmates. Their keening, shouting, wailing, and babbling was a constant background noise, disturbing and inescapable. It left her feeling edgy, as if she was surrounded by fear. It was this above all else that made her wish she could find Amelia a more salubrious environment in which to heal. She was certain that her sister's surroundings were adding to her slow decline. Veronica blamed her parents for washing their hands of the "embarrassment" and insisting on having Amelia committed. What she needed was love and to be treated like a real person, not to be hidden away from society like a shameful secret.

Distracted, Veronica turned to see Dr. Mason, Amelia's physician, approaching across the reception hall. He looked tired, worn down by his work. He was dressed in a smart black suit with a white collar, although he had evidently removed his tie and forgotten to replace it. He was in his fifties, swarthy, with dark hair swept back from his forehead. When he spoke, his voice was filled with relief. "Miss Hobbes, I'm glad you've come. I've been trying unsuccessfully to reach your parents for a week now."

Veronica frowned. "Dr. Mason, I do not pretend to follow their movements. I fear I am no better equipped to locate them than you. Perhaps they are visiting Father's cousin, in Paris." Her expression softened to one of concern. "Why? Is there news of Amelia?"

Dr. Mason looked pained. It was evidently bad news. "Your sister is gravely ill, Miss Hobbes. I fear you must prepare yourself."

Veronica sighed. *Prepare herself . . .* Then things had become even more desperate for Amelia. Quickly, she gathered her composure, but her voice was thin and reedy when she spoke. "How long?"

Dr. Mason shook his head. "I cannot answer that, Miss Hobbes. Two or three months would be my estimate, judging by the rate of her deterioration."

Veronica realised she was clenching her fists so hard that her fingernails were biting into the flesh of her palms. "Is there nothing you can do?"

The doctor looked sheepish. "I can make her comfortable." He wouldn't meet her eye.

Veronica blinked away stinging tears. "Can I see her?"

"Yes, I'll take you to her." He set off along the corridor, Veronica trailing behind him. She dabbed at her eyes, trying to regain her composure.

A few moments later, after following the doctor through a seemingly endless warren of blank, sterile passageways, they stopped before a door. "She's in there. She may be asleep." He turned, glancing back the way they had come. "I'll give you some time alone. Try not to tire her too much. And do your best to stay buoyant." He coughed once into his fist and then, smoothing the front of his suit, he left her there, standing outside the door. In a moment his echoing footsteps had dissolved into the ever-present cacophony of voices.

Steadying herself, Veronica reached for the handle and

pushed the door open, stepping into the room. It was small, with space for only a bed, a chair, and a bedside table. It was lit by a single lamp, and the curtains were drawn shut over the window.

Her sister was slumped on the bed, almost entirely subsumed by the pillows and blankets. Her raven hair spilled out all around her face and she looked painfully thin, emaciated by her inability to eat. Her eyes were sunken pits and her face was gaunt. She was only nineteen years old but could easily have passed for a woman twice her age. To Veronica, though, she was still beautiful. She gave her brightest smile as Amelia turned to look at her, startled by the sound of the door clicking back into place.

"Hello, sister. Put away that fake grin. Don't think I don't realise what people see when they look at me. I've looked in the mirror." She gave Veronica a hard stare. "I'm dying. Degenerating. And the doctors don't understand why." Her face softened.

Veronica crossed to her bedside. "I wouldn't hide anything from you, Amelia."

"Then why are you standing there trying to pretend that everything is normal?"

"You know why."

Amelia shrugged. "I'm not scared, Veronica. It's nothing new. People die every day. It's the same for us all. Life is simply one long fight towards death. I've come to realise that all we learn from life, all we truly learn, is how to die with dignity. I intend to do just that."

"My God, Amelia . . ."

"Do you believe in God, sister? I mean, really, truly believe in him?"

Veronica hesitated. Her voice was a breathless whisper. "I . . . no. I don't. At least not in the conventional way. I—"

"It's alright," Amelia cut in, her voice faltering. She turned her head on the pillow so that she was looking at the panelled door. "Neither do I. I don't have the capacity to imagine an afterlife."

Veronica sucked in her breath. "Amelia, that's a terribly stark view of life."

"It's a terribly *honest* view."

"And that's what you want? For everything to end?" Veronica couldn't keep the scorn out of her voice.

Amelia tried to sit up. She turned to meet her sister's gaze. "No! That's not what I want. Quite the opposite. I *want* to live. I'm not ready for it all to end. Not yet. But all the same, I recognise the end is near."

Veronica shook her head. "Don't you dare stop fighting this, Amelia!"

Amelia smiled and allowed herself to sink back into the the pillows. "Veronica, I have no intention of giving up without a fight. Now," she beckoned her sister closer, "will you come here and let me look at you properly? I want to hear all of your news."

Veronica stifled a sob. She knew she needed to be strong for Amelia. Later, when she was at home, in the darkness, she could allow herself to cry.

She perched on the edge of the bed, taking up her sister's hand and realising, surprised, that in the intervening seconds

Amelia had drifted off into unconsciousness. Sighing, she brushed Amelia's long dark hair away from her forehead and watched her breathing, an overwhelming sense of sadness in her heart.

"Amelia, I have to go. I have to be somewhere. But I'll be back soon, I promise." Veronica's voice was a gentle whisper. She had sat by her sister's bed for over an hour, and it was only now that Amelia had begun to stir.

Amelia blinked up at her sleepily. "The missing women?"

Veronica gave her a quizzical look. "Yes. How did you know that? Have you started to remember the content of your visions?"

Amelia gave an almost imperceptible nod. "A little." She propped herself up on her elbow, yawning. She suddenly looked serious. "Veronica, I've seen terrible things. Nightmar-ish things. A man with no face, looming out of the darkness. Horrible screeching sounds. And spinning. Always spinning, around and around, like I'm trapped on a carousel, unable to focus. I have no idea what it means."

Veronica couldn't bear to look Amelia in the eye. She studied her own hands instead, turning them over, following the map of folds and tributaries described by her pale skin. "It may not mean anything, Amelia. It may be your mind trying to heal itself, is all."

Amelia clenched her fists dramatically, gathering bundles of the bedsheets. When she spoke, her voice was hot with anger. "Not you, Veronica. I couldn't stand it if you began spouting their rhetoric, too. You know better than that. Tell me you don't think that."

Veronica placed a placatory hand on her sister's arm. "I don't think that, Amelia. Not for a minute. But I hate what your . . . condition is doing to you."

Amelia nodded, silently.

"I really have to go now, sister. I'll come back as soon as I'm able."

Amelia smiled. "I know you will."

Veronica placed Amelia's hand carefully on the bed and got to her feet. "Take care, Amelia."

Without looking back at the thin shadow of a woman who lay on the bed behind her, Veronica opened the door and stepped into the hall. Dr. Mason was nowhere to be seen. It was probably for the best. Veronica couldn't imagine dealing with the man now. Instead, she needed to throw herself into the case. Crying wouldn't help her sister. And out there, somewhere, were missing women that she *could* help. She needed to do that, for herself, and for Amelia.

Drawing her coat around her, Veronica set out. Whether she could count on Sir Maurice's assistance or not, she would solve this case. And in the meantime, she would consider how best to aid her dying sister.

CHAPTER

9

The police carriage pulled to a sharp halt. Newbury looked out the window.

Albion House was once again bustling with people, but it was an entirely different sort of bustle than the one he had witnessed just a couple of evenings before. Gone was the impressive flock of lords and ladies who had fluttered around on the front steps like preening birds, all dressed in their elaborate finery; instead he saw an army of uniformed constables with grey, tired faces and expectant looks.

A large crowd of onlookers had gathered on the pavement outside of Lord Winthrop's house, each of them trying to catch a glimpse of whatever gruesome mystery was hidden behind the shuttered windows. The bobbies were doing their best to marshal this unruly crowd, keeping them back from the scene and ignoring their pleas for information. Newbury guessed there would be half a dozen reporters in the mob. He wondered if one of them was Purefoy.

Newbury edged forward in his seat, leaning over to open the carriage door. Before he could do so, it swung open and a man peered in. He was wearing a full black beard and his eyes were a shining sea green. He looked smart in his grey woollen suit and bowler hat. Newbury gave him a wide, welcoming grin. "Inspector Foulkes. How unfortunate that we seem only to meet on occasions such as this."

The man glanced at Newbury and nodded sullenly. "Indeed, Sir Maurice. Unfortunate is the word. My job would be so much easier if people would only stop killing each other." His moustache twitched. He glanced at Bainbridge. "Sir Charles, we haven't touched anything inside. What would be your preferred course of action?"

Bainbridge sighed. "I'd *prefer* to be back in my warm office shuffling papers. But I suppose we should get to it. We'll go inside and take a look." He climbed to his feet, leaning heavily on his cane and muttering beneath his breath. "This cold weather will be the death of me."

They stepped down from the carriage and into the crisp London morning. The horses were sweating profusely, their breaths fogging in the cold air. Newbury looked up at the house. It seemed quiet. Different, somehow. Now it seemed cold and dreary, and Newbury knew that all that awaited him inside was the stink of death and corruption. His mood darkened. Winthrop had been rather a buffoon—a buffoon with a great deal of money to throw at his hobbies—but whatever had happened to him in there, it was unlikely that he deserved it.

Glancing back at Charles and Foulkes, Newbury mounted the steps towards the grand entrance. There was no butler to show him in this time, but one of the uniformed officers pushed the door aside and let him pass. Newbury nodded his thanks and stepped onto the portico. Nothing there had been obviously disturbed and there were no signs of forced entry. The stained glass panels of the inner frame were still perfectly intact, beautifully refracting the light. He turned the handle on the inner door and pushed it open, stepping through into the grand hallway on the other side.

Once there, he could immediately tell that something devastating had occurred. Where there had previously been an arrangement of tall glass display cases, perfectly placed to allow people to move easily amongst them, there was now only a sea of glass: a shattered wave of splintered panes, broken frames and ancient artefacts, a landscape of devastation writ small. A few of the display cases were still standing, partially smashed, like buildings towering mournfully over the wreck of a city.

Newbury heard Bainbridge step through the door behind him, his cane clicking noisily on the tiles. There was a pause. "Good God! What a mess."

"Hmmm." Newbury rubbed a hand over his chin, thinking. He stepped further into the room. "This is no bungled robbery, Charles. I'm sure of it. This destruction was systematic. Whoever did this was looking for something specific and they created this chaotic scene to throw us off the scent." He approached the nearest display case, his feet crunching on broken glass. "Look at this." He beckoned Bainbridge over to examine one of the artefacts that was still in situ, a necklace resting on a small black stand. "Ancient gold, inlaid gemstones . . . Charles, this piece is priceless. Why would they leave it here? Anyone—even the most common of thieves—would think to snatch this up on their way out the door." He glanced at the ruination by their feet. "There's more like that, too. A fortune's worth of ancient treasure. Whoever did this left most of the valuables but took the time to smash the displays regardless. What were they looking for? What didn't they want us to see?"

Bainbridge shrugged. "You tell me, Newbury. You were here. You saw the displays intact."

Newbury shook his head. "I didn't have time to look in any real detail. I remember noticing an unusual ushabti, over here. . . ." He stepped over a heap of broken panes towards another partially intact display case. "I only recall seeing it because its inscriptions were so out of the ordinary. Most of these things carry a particular passage from the *Book of the Dead*. This one was inscribed with something different, something I'd never seen before." His voice was subdued, almost a whisper. He studied the remnants of the display, then looked up at Bainbridge. "It's gone."

Bainbridge shrugged. "It could be anywhere in that mess, Newbury. It doesn't mean anything." He shook his head. "And I suppose that was the point of the exercise. It's going to take us days to work out what's missing. We'll have to match the artefacts to Winthrop's inventory, one-by-one, before we'll have any idea what the killer has taken. Assuming Winthrop even *had* an inventory."

Newbury nodded, looking around at the mess. Behind him, he noticed all of the strange, Egyptianlike automatons were still frozen in silent vigil on their pedestals behind the staircase. There was no sign of Winthrop's body. He caught Bainbridge's attention. "Where *is* Winthrop?"

"In the drawing room." Bainbridge sighed. "Come on. Let's get it out of the way. I'm told it's not pretty."

Newbury stepped out from the wreckage of the displays, being careful not to slice his hands on the broken glass. He followed Bainbridge silently across the hallway, towards the double doors that led to the drawing room.

The room was still shrouded in darkness, the heavy curtains pulled across the windows just as they had been the last time Newbury had visited the room. It took a moment for his eyes to adjust to the gloom. Bainbridge coughed. There was a dry, musty odour and Newbury realised immediately that the familiar smell originated from the exposed remains of the mummy, which was still laid out on the long table, just as it had been two nights before. Rolls of unravelled linen bandages surrounded it like a bed of ornamental reeds.

At first, Newbury couldn't see where Winthrop's corpse had been left. There was nothing by the fireplace or by the bookcase on the far wall. He frowned and looked over at Charles, who was staring, dumbfounded, at the mummy's casket, which lay on the floor beside the table. Newbury followed his gaze.

Winthrop's body had been carefully placed inside the casket, his arms folded across his chest in an obscene parody of the mummy's burial pose. His throat had been slit and blood had pooled behind his head, forming an oily, congealing puddle of red. His mouth was set in a terrible rictus grin.

Newbury crouched down beside the wooden coffin. "Someone has a ghastly sense of humour, Charles."

"I'll say. Poor sod. We mustn't let the press get hold of this."

"Quite." Newbury reached down and turned Winthrop's head slightly from side to side. The gash across his throat yawned open like a second mouth with the movement. There was blood everywhere: matted in Winthrop's beard and hair, soaked into his clothes. Gritty arterial spray had spattered the floor around the coffin, too. It had been a quick, effective murder; not the sort of thing Newbury would expect to see from a surprised burglar. "Charles, do you see the precision with which his throat has been cut? This is not the sort of wound one would expect from your average ruffian. It's an execution, very much in the style of one of Her Majesty's agents. And it just so happens I'm looking for one of Her Majesty's agents gone rogue, as we speak."

Bainbridge started. "No, Newbury. I absolutely refuse to believe it. Why would Ashford do such a thing? What possible motivation could he have for murdering Winthrop in such a manner?"

Despite Bainbridge's protests, Newbury's certainty about the case clicked into place like cold steel. He stood, wiping the blood from his fingers with his handkerchief. "I have no idea. But it's clear from what Her Majesty said that Ashford is disturbed. And you've received the same basic training in the combative arts as I have, Charles. You know as well as I do that this is a textbook assassination."

Bainbridge shook his head, distaste evident on his face. "I don't like it, Newbury. Ashford was a good man. And the grotesque way in which this body has been posed . . ."

"It's been a long time, Charles, and a lot of water has passed under the bridge. Ashford has been in Russia for five years, living hand-to-mouth. We have no idea what he's been through, what vile practises he's learned. He isn't the man you once knew. From what I gather, he's barely a man at all. For all we know, someone else could be guiding his hand. He may have defected."

"Still, Newbury, we have to consider all of our options. There remains Blake, and the—"

There was a loud crash from out in the hall, the sound of glass shattering on marble. Both men rushed to the door, Bainbridge hefting his cane, ready to take on the intruder.

A young man was standing amongst the wreckage of the display cabinets, a sheepish expression on his face. His hair was sand-coloured, his eyes a bright, shining blue. He was dressed in a brown suit and tie and he was clutching a notebook in his left hand. Bainbridge started forward, but Newbury put a hand on his arm to hold him back.

"It's alright, Charles. This is Mr. George Purefoy, the young reporter from *The Times* that I mentioned."

"Good afternoon, Sir Maurice." Purefoy grinned. He stepped out from amongst the pile of debris and came towards the two men, his hand extended.

Bainbridge lowered his cane. "What is the meaning of this? This is the scene of a crime, Mr. Purefoy. You have no right to be here. I consider this a case of trespassing."

Purefoy dropped his hand. "Ah, well, I . . ."

Newbury stepped forward. "Mr. Purefoy, how did you happen to find your way onto these premises?"

Purefoy clearly didn't know where to look, but he eventually settled on the floor. "An open window around the back."

Newbury raised an eyebrow. He looked at Charles. "Perhaps that's the entrance our murderer used? We should take a look."

"Murderer? So it is murder, then?"

Newbury smiled. "Do you think, Mr. Purefoy, that the Chief Inspector and I would be here if it were not?"

"I'm not sure what to think, to be truthful, Sir Maurice. Would you care to elaborate on your role in the matter? As I understand it, you're an academic with an office at the British Museum?"

Newbury laughed. "You're bold, Mr. Purefoy, I'll give you that. But if you don't want Sir Charles here to have you charged with trespass, I recommend you be on your way forthwith."

Purefoy nodded. "I think I have enough for the time being."

Bainbridge coughed into his fist. "And I suggest you think carefully before you commit any of it to print, young man. I don't want to hear any of this nonsense about 'the people having a right to know.' This, Mr. Purefoy, is a murder investigation, and I expect you to respect that before you go rattling on about it for the front page. It's difficult enough as it is to catch a villain without having the details splashed all over the morning edition." It was evident that Bainbridge was flustered by the appearance of the young man.

Newbury took that as a cue to put an arm on Purefoy's shoulder and guide him to the door, avoiding fragments of

glass as they walked. He lowered his voice. "Firstly, Mr. Purefoy, if you're going to sneak around the scene of a murder, it's
advisable not to get caught. Secondly, when you write about
this morning's events, you will refrain from printing any details of the murder or any mention of me or Sir Charles." He
looked the young reporter in the eye. "I don't expect to catch
you like this again."

Purefoy took Newbury's hand and shook it firmly. "No, Sir
Maurice. I don't expect you will." He pulled on the door
handle and, without looking back, stepped out into the foyer
and the street beyond.

Newbury turned back to Bainbridge. "One day, Charles,
that boy will make an excellent agent."

Bainbridge shook his head, exasperated. "One day, Newbury, I'll have a notion of what goes on in that mysterious
head of yours." He leaned heavily on his cane. "Now, what
of Winthrop?"

Newbury ran a hand over his chin. "I'm not sure what else
there is to say. Until we have a notion of what has or hasn't
been taken, it's just another despicable murder of a society
gentleman. You need to talk to Blake, of course. And I need
to find out where Ashford is hiding. I can't help thinking he's
at the heart of it, somehow."

"I usually trust your instincts, Newbury, but this time I
think you're on the wrong track."

Newbury sighed. "Time will tell, I suppose, old man.
Time will tell." He turned up the collar of his coat. "Dinner?
There's a new chef at the White Friar's. Excellent *Pigeons a
la Duchesse.* . . ."

"What? You're leaving?"

Newbury looked pained. "There's little more I can do here, Charles, and I promised Miss Hobbes I'd assist her with that damnable situation with the missing women. I need to give some thought to this Ashford situation, too. You have Foulkes. Have him and his men turn the place over. Then meet me at my club at seven and we'll talk it over."

Bainbridge waved his cane at the door. "Very well. Tonight. Seven o'clock. I imagine I'll be needing a brandy."

Newbury laughed. "I imagine we both will." He inclined his head in farewell, then quit the house, relieved to be putting some distance between himself and the horribly brutalised corpse of Lord Henry Winthrop. He had no real notion of what Ashford could be up to, or why he should have executed Winthrop in such a horrendous manner. He needed to uncover the significance of the missing ushabti and the strange engravings he'd noticed during the party. He also needed to find Ashford and work out what his connection to Winthrop might be. Most of all, he needed time to think. And he knew where he could find it.

First, he would call on Veronica at the office to explain why he had been detained and make arrangements to assist her the following day. Then he would pay a visit to Johnny Chang's.

CHAPTER

10

Newbury emerged at the top of the stone staircase to find that the light was already beginning to wane. It was windy and cold—so cold that his breath fogged before his face—but the warm haze of the opium high was enough to dispel the effects of the bracing weather. The street was busy, crisscrossed with people coming and going, shutting up their storefronts and retiring to their homes for the evening. Newbury checked his pocket watch. It was nearly half past five. He'd need to head directly to the White Friar's if he wanted to keep his appointment with Charles.

Newbury blinked as a ground train rolled by, its large iron wheels groaning beneath the considerable weight of the engine. Steam billowed from a wheezing funnel. Carriages clattered along behind the huge machine, filled with passengers making their way home from any number of manufactories and offices, their faces dour after hours spent relentlessly pursuing an inconceivably small wage. The driver looked cold and exhausted in his open-sided cab. Newbury shivered. He hadn't been near one of the vehicles since his encounter with a man posing as a glowing policeman a few months earlier. He'd sustained serious injuries fighting with the man on the roof of one of the trains, and now, any time he found himself in close proximity to one of them, he recalled the fate of the other man, his head cracked open on the cobbles after Newbury had sent him tumbling over the side.

Sighing, he pulled his coat a little tighter around his shoulders and set out, hoping the crisp air would help clear his head before dinner.

He had called for Veronica after leaving Winthrop's house earlier that afternoon but found she had already left for the day. A small terse note printed in her immaculate handwriting had been waiting for him on his desk:

> *Sir Maurice,*
>
> *In your absence, I have taken leave to visit Amelia. I trust I shall see you in the office tomorrow morning so that we may continue with our investigations.*
>
> *Miss Veronica Hobbes*

It pained him to think that he had let her down. He knew in his heart that the missing women were probably already dead, slung into the Thames like broken rag dolls or dumped unceremoniously into hastily dug graves somewhere on the east side of the city. He wished he could help but he had a job to do, and presently Her Majesty considered it necessary for him to curtail the exploits of the rogue agent William Ashford. It didn't sit well with Newbury to consider that the life of a special agent should take precedence over the lives of innumerable working-class women, but he also knew that he wasn't yet in full possession of the facts. He didn't know what Ashford was looking for, nor what he was capable of. He might pose an even greater threat than the kidnapper. And besides, it wasn't just a matter of bringing him in for the death of Winthrop. It was a matter of stopping a traitor—a traitor who knew everything about the innermost workings of Her Majesty's operations—from doing any more damage.

So instead of chasing after his headstrong assistant, Newbury had retreated to the clandestine haven of Johnny Chang's, where he had passed the afternoon in a heady opium dream, cogitating on all of the disparate threads of the case, searching the annals of his mind for a possible solution. A part of him could see that he was deluding himself, but he chose to ignore it. The drug had enabled him to relax, to recede into his own quiet world, where his instincts could come to the fore and he could get a different perspective on the chaotic mess of leads and clues and mysteries that faced him. It wasn't futile, either; the drug had helped him formulate a plan. He knew how he was going to deal with Ashford: he was going to lay a trap. All he needed was a little—

Suddenly, Newbury had the distinct impression that he was being followed. He glanced from side to side, the hairs on the nape of his neck prickling with warning. He turned sharply at the sound of a scuffed heel close behind him, so close that he made a fist in his gloved hand, expecting someone to be upon him at any moment. His breath became shallow, his heart hammering hard in his chest. He spun around on the spot, seeking out his assailant. But there was no one nearby. The street behind him was almost deserted, the earlier bustle gone, as if the shopkeepers and passers-by had simply melted away into the shadows. Now there were just a handful of people on the other side of the road, heading in the opposite direction.

The shadows of the terraced houses loomed large and uninviting, a few gas lamps giving off an amber glow in the wan evening light. The wind whistled ominously through some nearby railings.

Perplexed, Newbury carried on walking. He had the sense of someone lurking in the periphery of his vision, but each time he looked back over his shoulder he saw no evidence that he was being followed. He wondered if it were the opium playing tricks with his mind, causing the shadows to come to bizarre, hallucinatory life. Worse, he knew better than most that the shadows of London *did* contain creeping things that were better avoided; things that lurked in the darkness, preying on the ignorant and unwary; things from children's nightmares, fashioned from both the flesh and the spirit, or more recently, from the steam-powered manufactories of men.

Newbury shuddered, then laughed at himself for allowing his mind to run away with him. It was clear the opium was still influencing his thoughts, much more than he had anticipated.

He was not yet used to partaking of the drug in such a way, to such a degree, and had underestimated its effects. He took a deep breath, trying to cleanse his lungs. The world had a dreamlike quality to it, as if he perceived it through some sort of hazy filter, like the London fog. He relished the feeling, the loss of control, but he also knew how dangerous that could be for a man in his position. Absently, he hoped that Charles would not be able to discern his condition over dinner.

There was another sound from behind him, this time over his right shoulder. Cautiously, he carried on walking so as not to give away the fact that he had noticed. This time he was sure it was no hallucination. He'd heard the sole of a boot scuffing against the road. On his left was the dark frontage of a furrier's shop, the window filled with shop dummies dressed in all manner of animal pelts fashioned into coats, hats, scarves, and more. Slowly, he approached the window, feigning interest. He studied his reflection in the glass. He looked pale and drawn and had dark rings beneath his eyes.

Newbury watched for a moment, looking for signs of the person who had been following him. Sure enough, a moment later he caught a glimpse of something moving in the reflected scene of the street: a large, hulking shape, bigger than the average man, its face hidden in the hood of an ominous black cowl. Newbury spun around, quickly, hoping to catch the creature off guard. Just as before, there was nothing to see, but he heard footsteps padding away, up ahead in the shadows. Whoever had been following him had apparently realised he was aware of them but were not ready to make themselves known.

For a moment Newbury considered giving chase, but he

knew he wasn't up to a fight, and besides, he had to be across town to meet Charles. But this new development altered things, altered the plans he'd been conceiving. Perhaps he wouldn't need to go after William Ashford, after all. Perhaps Ashford was coming after *him*.

He needed to clear his head.

Slowly, Newbury set off, heading in the same direction as the footsteps. He hoped that Ashford—if it was, indeed, Ashford—was not lurking in the darkness up ahead, waiting to pounce on him as he made his unsteady way towards Piccadilly. He kept his hands free as he walked, ready to defend himself if the situation arose.

After a few hundred yards, however, Newbury allowed himself to relax. The mysterious figure had apparently bolted when Newbury had caught sight of it in the shop window. His fingers were growing numb in the biting cold, so although it wasn't far to Piccadilly, he decided that he would hail a cab at the next opportunity. Further ahead, the road opened out into a large set of crossroads and the thoroughfare seemed busy with people and vehicles, even from this distance. He quickened his pace, knowing that he could likely find a hansom at the junction.

A shadow passed overhead, and Newbury looked up to see the dark underbelly of an airship sweeping low over the city, a rope ladder trailing, forgotten, off the port side. He watched it drift lazily across the sky, the growl of its engines a gravelly counterpoint to the sharp, biting howl of the wind. He dropped his eyes to the road ahead and started.

The hooded figure was standing by the corner of the road, about a hundred feet away, regarding him steadily, its face still hidden in the shadows of its cloak. The black fabric trailed in the wind, billowing up around its legs. Beneath the hood, from somewhere within the pool of darkness that hid the person's face, a small, round, bluish light flickered, like a blinking eye. It was a menacing sight that caused Newbury to give an involuntary shudder. There was little else that Newbury could discern from this distance, other than that the man—for, given the figure's size and bulk, it had to be a man—was wearing black leather boots and matching gloves.

Newbury broke into a run, charging towards the solitary figure, his head bowed against the driving wind. The man remained stationary, watching silently as Newbury dashed towards him with no clear strategy. In his present state, Newbury knew he wouldn't be able to put up much resistance if Ashford was angling for a fight, but he couldn't turn down the opportunity to tackle the rogue agent and get the whole matter quickly resolved.

Gasping, he flung himself towards the hooded figure as if to grapple with him, only to see the figure sidestep around the corner at the last moment. Newbury caught hold of the wall, stopping himself from pitching over. He heaved against the brickwork, pulling himself around the corner after Ashford.

Bizarrely, the other man was gone.

Newbury, dumbfounded, glanced from side to side, looking for the means by which Ashford had made his escape. There were no obvious alleyways or doorways he could have dashed into, no ladders or vehicles by which he could have affected his disappearance. Just a series of dreary shopfronts and red-brick walls. He looked up. The sky was a leaden canopy overhead, but there was no sign of Ashford atop the nearby buildings, either. He hadn't somehow managed to scale the wall. The man had simply vanished.

Panting, slowed by the opiate in his veins, Newbury fell back against the wall, attempting to catch his breath. There was a foul stench in the air, a rancid, carrion tang that made him splutter in disgust. Bile rose in his throat. The smell was immediately familiar, and there was no mistaking it. The man in the hooded cloak had most definitely been his quarry. It *had* to be Ashford.

Newbury looked around, frustrated. Was everyone able to disappear at will now? Or was Ashford just fleet of foot and Newbury, in his disoriented, half-delusional state, simply unable to keep up with him? One thing was certain: Ashford was either teasing him or trying to tell him something. Either way, the end result would be the same. Next time they met, Newbury would be ready.

Sighing, he pushed himself away from the wall and checked his pocket watch again. He was late meeting Charles. He looked along the street. A hansom cab was trundling slowly in his direction, and he stepped out in the road and waved his arm to hail it. He needed to get to the White Friar's Club before Charles gave up on him. They had much to discuss.

CHAPTER

11

Y ou're late." Bainbridge's bushy grey
moustache twitched as Newbury approached his table. He had a severe look
on his face. "It's only thanks to Foster—" He
indicated the butler who was standing by the
doorjamb, an implacable look on his face, "that
I managed to get in at all. I'm not a member
here, you know. I wish you'd had the foresight
to—"

"Not now, Charles."

Bainbridge frowned. "What do you mean,
not now? What the devil have you been up to,
man?" He lowered his voice so as not to be
overheard. "Indulging in that blasted vice of
yours, judging by the look of you. It's a despica-

ble business, Newbury. You look terrible." He folded his arms and leaned back in his chair, studying Newbury's face as he awaited a response.

Newbury waved his arm as if to dismiss the point and dropped into a chair opposite his friend. There was resignation in his voice. "You can save the lecture for another day, Charles. I apologise for my tardiness." He looked up and caught the attention of one of the waiters, who stepped forward, smiling, to take an order of drinks. "Usual, please, Williams." He glanced at Bainbridge's empty glass. "And whatever Sir Charles is drinking."

The waiter nodded politely. "As you wish, sir." He retreated to the bar to place their order.

The White Friar's was a gentleman's club on Arundel Street and a second home for Newbury, who often visited the place to conduct meetings, dine with associates or friends, and escape the oppressive pressures of his life as an agent of the Crown. The club itself was a haven for literary types— writers, artists, and intellectuals—and frequently Newbury left the establishment feeling invigorated, as much due to the stimulating conversation as the fine selection of brandy. The dining room, in which he had found Charles, was a smallish room, panelled in dark oak and furnished with a smattering of round tables, each large enough to accommodate five or six people at a time. A fire roared in the grate on the far side of the room, causing shadows to dance haphazardly over every surface like mischievous pixies, and the murmur of conversation from the adjoining lounge was a constant background hum. The room was filled with the pleasant scent of roasting meat wafting from the kitchen. A small army of waiters and servants kept a watchful eye on the patrons, keen to cater to their every whim.

It was quiet that evening, however, and aside from Charles and himself, only two other diners made use of the room. They were huddled over a table in the corner, deep in the midst of some philosophical debate—or so Newbury liked to imagine.

Newbury ran a hand over his face. He was coming down from his opium high. He looked at Bainbridge from beneath hooded eyelids.

Bainbridge leaned across the table towards him, toying with his fork. "Newbury," he said, his voice firm, "you're the only friend I have left in this godforsaken city. I won't lose you, not to something so ridiculous as that dreadful Chinese weed."

Newbury smiled—a sad, knowing smile. He stared at the fire. When, a moment later, he looked back at Bainbridge, he didn't meet the other man's eye. "What are you drinking?"

Bainbridge sighed. "A tolerably good cognac. But my belly is in dire need of sustenance. Let's order some ruddy food."

Newbury grinned. "Yes, in a minute. I need to talk to you first."

Bainbridge looked concerned. "What's happened, Newbury?"

Newbury unfolded his napkin and, placing it on his knee, looked up at his friend. "Don't be alarmed, Charles. I need some more information regarding William Ashford is all. I've been wondering: what became of his family after he died?"

Bainbridge shrugged. "They were moved. To a house near Cheapside. Dreadful place. It was one of the worst things I've ever had to do, Newbury, telling that woman that her husband had been killed, and then, to compound it, that she and her family were being uprooted as a consequence. She broke down on my shoulder. Begged me to let her keep the house. But I had my orders." He fingered the rim of his empty glass. "Now, to learn that it was all a lie . . . Well, it casts things in a different light, doesn't it?"

Newbury furrowed his brow. He'd rarely seen Bainbridge in such a reflective mood. "I'm sure those things were done for the right reasons, Charles. It's been five years." He paused to accept his brandy from the waiter. "Do you think Ashford will go looking for them?"

"Wouldn't you?"

"I suppose that's what I'm getting at. I imagine that's as good a place as any to start my search."

Bainbridge shook his head. "No. You musn't, Newbury. Don't go dragging up the past. Ashford may well be looking for his family—and I feel sorry for the man, I truly do—but the last thing his wife needs is to know that he's been alive all this time, turned into some sort of half-mechanical monster. Besides, he'll never find them. And even if he did, that assumes that the family is still in that Cheapside hovel. As you say, it's been five years. They've probably moved on." He lowered his voice. "God knows, I hope they have."

Newbury took a pull on his brandy. He felt fingers of warmth spreading down through his chest as the alcohol banished his chill. It was clear that something about this case had touched a nerve with his friend. "Very well, Charles. I'll look elsewhere—for now. It may not be necessary to search him out, anyway."

Bainbridge leaned back in his chair. He took up the dinner menu. "How so?"

"I believe I find myself in the midst of a game of cat and mouse, though I'm unsure whether I'm the hunter or the hunted."

Bainbridge looked up from the top of his menu. "Stop speaking in riddles, Newbury."

Newbury laughed, for the first time that evening. "I have reason to believe that Ashford has been following me. I think I encountered him in the street earlier this evening, but he gave me the slip."

"What? Where?" Bainbridge was frowning.

"Not far from here, as I made my way over to meet you. I had the curious notion that I was being followed, but for quite some time I was unable to ascertain by whom. I thought it may have been . . . well, I thought it may have been my mind playing tricks on me."

"But it was Ashford?"

"I believe so."

"Well, why the devil should he be following *you*?"

"A good question, Charles, and one for which I intend to find an answer. With any luck, this may not turn out to be the protracted affair I had initially feared." Newbury regarded the menu on the table before him. "Venison and creamed potatoes, I should say."

"Well, just be careful, Newbury."

Newbury gave his friend a sly look. "Of the venison?"

Bainbridge shook his head, exasperated. "Look, the Ashford I recall was a decent man, but having seen Winthrop today . . . I don't know any more. Just look after yourself. I'll help however I can."

"So, you've changed your mind about the nature of our suspect, have you, Charles? I take that to mean that Wilfred Blake has an alibi?" Newbury offered the Chief Inspector an amused grin.

Bainbridge nodded. "Indeed. And a solid one, at that. He was in the company of a lady, dining out in full public view. He cannot be considered a suspect for the murder." He sighed. "It looks like you may be right about Ashford, unless we have a foreign agent in our midst, someone who knows our ways."

"It's possible. But unlikely, I think. The simplest explanation is often the correct one, Charles. We have a rogue agent loose in London and a corpse with all the hallmarks of a swift, purposeful execution. I do not think it is too much of a stretch to assume that we know the identity of our quarry, if not his motivation."

"Perhaps." Bainbridge drummed his fingers on the table. "Now, however, I believe I must eat, or I shall waste away to nothing and you shall have to find yourself another dining companion."

"Well, that, of course, would never do!" Newbury, laughing, turned and gestured for the waiter. His stomach was growling and his head was finally beginning to clear. Soon, he'd need sleep. But first, he needed food, drink, and the company of a good friend.

CHAPTER

12

THE CURSE OF
THE SCREAMING MUMMY
By Mr. G. Purefoy

Death and despair surround the discovery of the mysterious Screaming Mummy as Lord Henry Winthrop is found dead at Albion House, only two days after receiving society visitors for a grand unrolling party. Whilst Scotland Yard struggles for leads, talk of an ancient curse is rife amongst the other members of the expedition, now fearing for their lives.

Turn to page 3 to read the full story.

Newbury dropped the morning newspaper on the table with a hearty laugh, causing his housekeeper, Mrs. Bradshaw, to jump and nearly miss the teacup she was pouring tea into. A small amount of the pungent brown liquid sloshed into the saucer. She was clearly flustered by the experience, and Newbury eyed her warily as she swept the offending china up into her arms, making a short "tut" under her breath as she stomped out into the hallway. Newbury couldn't help but smile.

Reaching for another slice of toast, he scanned the front of the newspaper again with a chuckle. Purefoy had taken him at his word, anyway. When he'd told the boy to desist from sharing any details of the murder or mentioning him or Charles by name, the reporter had evidently concocted some sort of elaborate story to explain away the lack of facts. Newbury wondered if the young man wouldn't be better off turning his talents to the writing of fiction. He clearly had an eye for it. Still, Newbury supposed it would sell newspapers, and besides, Purefoy had done him a favour. At least this way the public had something trivial and sensational to focus on rather than dwelling on the more disturbing fact that a rogue agent was on the loose somewhere in the city. If the real details of the case had been splashed across the front page that morning, he and Charles would have been hauled up before Her Majesty with any number of her own difficult questions. At least this way most people would dismiss the story as supernatural claptrap, assuming it was just another botched robbery of the type they read about almost daily in the national press. With luck, Purefoy's actions would enable him and Charles to continue unimpeded with their investigations. He made a mental note to thank the young reporter at the next available opportunity.

Newbury had left Charles at the doorway of the White Friar's the previous evening, then retired to the club's drawing room after dinner to enjoy a conversation and a pipe. It hadn't been late, but after the trials of his day, Newbury felt that it would have been a poor choice to make a night of it. Sure enough, upon returning to his Chelsea home, he had slept for a good nine hours. Now he sat at his breakfast table in his red silk dressing robe, picking at the remnants of the morning's feast. He could always rely on Mrs. Bradshaw for a hearty breakfast, no matter what time of the day he actually found himself in need of it.

Pushing the newspaper to one side, Newbury turned his attention to the small silver tray of post that Mrs. Bradshaw had brought up with his tea. Idly, he flicked through the smattering of envelopes, ignoring anything that looked like correspondence from abroad. He was expecting a number of letters from Venezuela that pertained to a private matter involving his deceased father, but he could deal with those later, when the whole Ashford matter had been resolved. Reaching the bottom of the pile, he gave a brief exclamation, pulling out a small white envelope that had been scrawled upon in black ink. The handwriting was scratchy and ill formed. A large, oily thumbprint blighted the otherwise crisp envelope in one corner, and there was no stamp upon it, suggesting the letter had been sent round to the house via courier.

Leaning back in his chair, Newbury used the edge of his

index finger to tear the envelope open and unfold the short note he discovered inside. As anticipated, it was a reply from his old friend Aldous Renwick, barely legible and smudged where Renwick had not waited for the ink to properly dry. Newbury angled it towards the window to see it better.

> *Newbury,*
> *Come to the shop immediately. I have the infor-*
> *mation you require.*
>
> > *AR*

Short, but pointed. Newbury sighed. Another detour, but clearly one he could not avoid. If Renwick had put his finger on the mystery of the screaming mummy, it could make the circumstances surrounding Winthrop's death far clearer. Indeed, it might explain Ashford's motive for enacting such a horrific execution in the first instance.

Newbury looked up to see Mrs. Bradshaw returning with a fresh teacup and saucer. "Ah, Mrs. Bradshaw—perfect timing." He dropped the letter onto the table beside his plate. "I'll take my tea whilst I dress."

"Very good, sir." The housekeeper placed the china on the table and began pouring another cup.

Newbury stood, dabbing the corners of his mouth with his napkin. "Thank you, Mrs. Bradshaw. Another excellent breakfast." He collected his cup and saucer with a smile and began making his way towards the hallway. Then, on second thought, he paused, hovering in the doorway. "Oh, and Mrs. Bradshaw? If I could prevail on you to send for a hansom forthwith, it would be very much appreciated."

The Scotswoman nodded, gave an exasperated sigh, and began noisily collecting up the remaining bowls and plates.

Laughing, Newbury sipped at his Earl Grey and made his way to his room to hastily prepare for the day ahead.

"Miss Hobbes. I daresay I did you a disservice yesterday, and I'm fearful I'm about to do it all over again." Newbury was framed in the doorway that separated his and Miss Hobbes's desks from the rest of the small office, still attired in his hat and coat. It was early, and he'd travelled directly to the museum after finishing his daily ablutions and dressing in his usual black suit. He gave his assistant an earnest look, awaiting her response.

"No need to apologise, Sir Maurice, I saw the morning edition of *The Times*. I gather you're contending with an ancient curse now, amongst other things?" She offered Newbury a wry smile. She was dressed in a smart grey frock with a matching jacket and her hair was tied back from her pretty face.

Newbury laughed. "Well, quite so. You know how these things go: a murder in the night, an ancient curse before breakfast. All in a day's work." Veronica grinned. "In all seriousness, however, I find myself terribly preoccupied by this Winthrop situation. I believe it somehow ties in with that missing agent I was intended to meet at the station the other morning."

"So it's *not* a curse then?" It was clear she was toying with him.

"Not in the supernatural sense of the word, no. But it

feels somewhat like a curse, I assure you." He adjusted his collar ruefully. "I admit I'm finding it difficult to give my attention to anything else. I must attend to a small matter this morning off the Tottenham Court Road. Perhaps you could accompany me there and then together we can go on to Soho and attempt to locate the lodgings of this Mysterious Alfonso character?"

Veronica shook her head. Her expression grew serious. "I'm afraid there has been a further development since we last spoke. Another missing woman. This time there's a clear link between the disappearance and the theatre. The woman was last seen in attendance at the show, volunteering for the disappearing act. She failed to return home that evening and she hasn't been seen since. There's little room for doubt."

Newbury looked thoughtful. "Yes, I see your dilemma. But I must insist, Miss Hobbes, that you do not, under any circumstances, confront this man on your own."

Veronica frowned. "Sir Maurice, I'm quite capable—"

"—yes, yes. It's not a matter of capability, Miss Hobbes, but one of safety. Whilst you are in my employ, you are in my care. I understand how frustrating it must be to have to sit by and wait while I deal with this damnable Ashford thing, but really, I must insist that you will not commit yourself to any dangerous course of action in my absence."

Veronica had fire in her eyes, but she nodded. "I plan to visit the family of the missing woman this afternoon, to obtain a better understanding of the circumstances. I thought it wise to gather some further evidence, no matter how circumstantial, before we try to tackle Alfonso again."

Newbury smiled. "An excellent plan, Miss Hobbes." He

paused. "Then perhaps, this evening, we could make an appointment to meet for dinner . . . ? You could fill me in on your findings and we could plan ahead to our next encounter with the dubious magician."

"Very well." Her lips curled into a smile. "Where shall we meet?"

"I'll call for you, at Kensington, around seven. Does that suit?"

"It does."

"Excellent. Then for now, I'll be on my way." He lifted his hat from his head. "Until this evening, Miss Hobbes."

"Until this evening, Sir Maurice."

He turned as if to make an exit from the office. Then, recalling an errand, he stopped by the door and pulled a slip of cream-coloured paper from his pocket. He crossed to where Miss Coulthard was sitting behind a new, broad, mahogany desk. She looked up from amongst unruly piles of paper. "Sir Maurice?"

"Miss Coulthard, as busy as you are, I wonder if I may trouble you with one additional burden." He held the piece of paper out between two fingers with a smile. Miss Coulthard accepted it, the hesitation evident on her face. She unfolded it and examined the contents. On it was scrawled a woman's name and the word 'Cheapside,' in Newbury's loose hand. "I need you to find an address for this woman, as soon as possible. She may have moved location at any point in the last five years. Can you do it?"

Miss Coulthard nodded. "Of course."

Newbury grinned. "You really are a treasure, Miss

Coulthard. My thanks." And with that, he bid her good morning and took his leave.

Aldous Renwick's bookshop was, upon first appearances, not unlike any of the other small emporiums that could be found amongst the winding side streets that branched off of the Tottenham Court Road. It sat nestled between a small general store and a haberdashery, its windows piled high with gaudy works of modern fiction, bound in leather or bright paper wraps. It was a cold, crisp morning, and Renwick had placed a small table outside of the door displaying a smattering of penny papers and cheap mystery stories, their covers fluttering in the light breeze. The legend above the door read simply BOOKS.

Newbury had discovered the place many years ago, when engaged in the hunt for a rare Venetian treatise on the occult. A mutual acquaintance had tipped him off that Renwick might be able to source such a work, so, after due consideration, he had paid the man a visit. Renwick had found the book, along with many other archaic tomes in the intervening years. Although Newbury had paid dearly for them, he appreciated the discreet manner in which the man carried out his business. Renwick was one of the most learned men that Newbury knew, with a particular knowledge of esoteric literature, and as such Newbury had found numerous occasions to pay him visits over the years.

Stopping momentarily outside to glance at the cover of a tattered copy of the *Union Jack*, Newbury then turned the doorknob with a gloved hand, allowing the door to creak open loudly on its hinges. He stepped over the threshold. Inside, the shop was filled with a cornucopia of books and periodicals piled high in huge stacks or pressed tightly onto bulging shelves of dark, heavy wood. There appeared to be no method in the way the various volumes had been scattered, chaotically, around the room, but Newbury had every suspicion that Renwick would be able to swiftly put his hand on any title that a given customer might request. Newbury, smiling, mused that the interior of the shop was ordered somewhat as erratically as its owner's mind, and that, in all probability, one was a close reflection of the other.

Newbury looked around for the man he had come to see. The shop was devoid of life. There was a musty odour about the place, and he filled his lungs, enjoying the familiarity of it. He called out. "Aldous? Are you there? It's Newbury. I received your note this morning and came forthwith."

There was a dull, repetitive thudding sound from somewhere behind one of the bookcases. Newbury approached it warily. It sounded almost like an engine turning over and it was coming from the other side of the wall. "Aldous?"

The banging ceased, momentarily, and then was followed by a muffled shout from the same direction. "I'll be out in a moment, Newbury. Bear with me." The voice was sharp and high-pitched. Newbury smiled. The banging resumed, so whilst he waited for the other man, Newbury turned his attention to the spines of the nearest stack of books. Many of the titles were old, but distinctive and in excellent condition. There was everything from a monograph on the nature of steam power in the horticultural industry to Dickens novels to bound collections of *Blackwood's Magazine*. It was a bibliophile's dream, but Newbury knew that, in reality, Renwick's real treasures lay in the back room, beyond sight of the casual customer.

A moment later Newbury became aware of the sound of the other man coughing fitfully, and then the door behind the counter—previously concealed behind a collage of gaudy posters—swung open and Aldous Renwick stalked in, his hand outstretched in greeting.

Aldous Renwick was one of the most unusual characters that Newbury had the pleasure of calling a friend. He bore all the hallmarks of a caricature. He was rough around the edges: unshaven, with a wiry, bristly chin, a wisp of chaotic white hair, and yellowed fingers from the excessive smoking of cigarettes. He wore his usual old leather smock over a stained white shirt, open at the collar. His left eye had been replaced by a remarkable mechanical device that whirred and clicked disturbingly when he looked around. It was not as elegant as something designed by Dr. Fabian, but then, Renwick was only a civilian and clearly valued function over aesthetics. Newbury had no idea if the false eye was elective or the result of some earlier, undisclosed adventure. Whatever the case, Newbury had long wondered over the sanity of his friend but was still undecided as to whether the man was actually mad, or simply had a degree too much insight into the darker side of the human psyche.

Newbury stepped forward to meet Renwick, clasping the other man's hand in his own. "Good to see you, Aldous. How the devil are you?"

The bookseller chuckled, his good eye twitching with an

alarming nervous tic. "A darn site better than Lord Henry Winthrop, from what I gather!"

Newbury sighed. "Well, I don't think I can contest that." He met the other's gaze. "I received your note."

Renwick studied him, his strange mechanical eye whirring in its socket. It protruded from the empty cavity with the look of a magnifying glass, not unlike the sort of tool used by jewellers to examine precious stones. But this device, Newbury knew, was wired directly into Renwick's brain. Absently, he wondered if this was the cause of his nervous tic, or worse, his generally neurotic demeanour. A glass plate fixed into the end of the device turned slowly as the mechanical eye drew its focus, and deep inside, down in the dark depths of Renwick's skull, a pinprick of orange light wavered and blinked as information was transmitted to his visual cortex. All of this had been explained to Newbury some time ago, but it never failed to both fascinate and unnerve him when he spent time in Renwick's company.

"The note. Yes. Lots to discuss." Renwick wheezed noisily and raised his fingers to his lips, as if expecting to find a cigarette smouldering there. He looked disappointed when he realised there was not. He looked back at Newbury. "Tea?"

"Yes. . . ." He hesitated. "Well, actually, it depends. What exactly do you mean when you say 'tea'?"

Renwick laughed, a dry, crackling laugh. "Don't worry, old friend. I know you too well by now to offer up any of my usual concoctions. I have a tin of Earl Grey in the back room. Let me finish up in the workshop and I'll set a kettle on the stove."

Newbury grinned. "My thanks, Aldous."

The other man rubbed his hands on the front of his apron. He nodded. "I'll just lock up the shop. You go on, through here. . . ." He turned and pushed on the concealed door, which swung open once again, and ushered Newbury through to the back room.

Newbury stepped over the threshold, taking care not to miss his footing on the step down. The large room on the other side of the door was cast in a dim half-light, the only illumination coming from a flaming Bunsen burner and a strange glass orb in one corner, which flickered with a violent storm of bright electrical currents. On the workbench in the middle of the room, a series of bulbous glass flasks and connecting rods had been set up, and an unusual pink liquid was bubbling over the Bunsen's flame, the vapours being siphoned off into another nearby flask. The dull thudding noise continued, and Newbury realised that the device responsible for the sound—a large iron box on the floor, with two protruding levers, a trail of thick cables, and an unmarked dial—was a generator of some description, powering the electrical orb in the corner. Other bizarre props were heaped in piles upon the floor or stacked haphazardly on the shelves that lined every inch of available wall space: unusual masks, vials filled with unaccountable specimens, strange African idols, and assorted components from any number of mechanical devices. Newbury smiled. It reminded him somewhat of his Chelsea study, although there was a far greater selection here, in far greater disarray. Yet it was the other contents of Renwick's shelves that held the real attraction for Newbury. Here, in the back of this small shop, was perhaps the finest collection of occult and esoteric literature

ever amassed under one roof. The library far outshone Newbury's own, not insignificant, collection. He'd spent hours
here in the past, browsing the shelves, amazed at the rare
editions that Renwick had somehow been able to acquire.
There were copies of ancient hermetic treatises thought lost
in the sacking of the library at Alexandria, rare Venetian
tracts on summoning evil spirits, details of arcane rituals attributed to the lost druidic tribes of Prussia and much more.
It was a delight to behold, and one of the best-kept secrets
in the Empire. Unlike the more sedate tomes that lined the
shelves in the front of the shop, these exquisite volumes
were not for sale. But, as Newbury had learned over the years,
Renwick was a genial fellow, and for the right person asking
the right question, he could be a marvellous repository of
rare and unusual knowledge.

Renwick stepped through into the room and pulled the
door shut behind him. He looked around absently for a moment, then crossed the room, pushing past Newbury unceremoniously and setting to work putting a kettle on the small
stove.

Newbury examined the back of the door, which was carved
with all manner of intricate runes and wards. He recognised a number of them. The six-fingered hand in a circle was
intended to prevent witches from crossing the threshold.
He shook his head. The room, like Renwick, was the embodiment of a contradiction. The juxtaposition of the progressive
science—the generator, the electrical orb, the artificial eye—
seemed to sit ill beside the more supernatural preoccupations
that typically concerned the man. Science and the occult. In

truth, Newbury had no real notion where one stopped and the other began. Clearly Renwick was intent on exploring that boundary, and judging by the protective wards he had chiselled into the doors, walls, and floor, he was taking no risks.

Renwick set the kettle to boil, then turned and waved Newbury in the direction of a chair heaped with papers. "Take a seat, man. You may be here for some time."

Newbury smiled and, bending low, scooped the debris from the seat and placed it in a neat pile by the foot of the chair. He lowered himself into the chair, dropping his coat over the back and resting his hat on the white porcelain phrenology bust that sat on a low table beside him. He watched Renwick cross to his still, use a pair of tongs to remove the flask of bubbling pink liquid from the heat, and pour a measure of the stuff into a blue coffee cup before returning the vessel to the flame. He blew gently on the hot liquid, then took a long draw, swallowing it with a hearty gasp. He placed the empty cup on the workbench beside him, then turned to Newbury. "Right. Your screaming mummy."

Newbury chuckled. He had no idea what the pink concoction contained, but he was sure it had a large measure of alcohol in it, whatever else. He met Renwick's strange glowing gaze. "So tell me, what have you found?"

Renwick's mechanical eye emitted a grinding sound as it refocused on the Crown investigator. His other eye continued to twitch nervously. "I believe I know the identity of your mysterious dead man. A priest who served Pharaoh Thutmose I at Thebes, around fifteen hundred years before Christ."

"Go on."

"His name was Khemosiri, 'the black Osiris.' You do know the story of Osiris, don't you, Newbury?"

Newbury shrugged. "I have a rudimentary understanding of the myth. But go ahead—enlighten me." He sat back in the chair, intrigued, his fingers forming a steeple on his lap.

"Osiris was the king of the Land of the Dead. He stood in judgement over the dead, having supplanted the god Anubis as the overseer of the afterlife. To an ancient Egyptian noble, the afterlife was everything; the chance to live forever beyond the physical world. Osiris was the god who straddled the two realms, who ultimately decided their fate. He enabled their resurrection after mummification." Renwick paused as he collected his tongs and poured himself another measure of the pink liquid. He nursed the coffee cup in his hands as he continued. "Osiris was unique in the Egyptian pantheon, however. The myth tells of how he was murdered by his brother, Set; first drowned and then cut into thirteen pieces and scattered throughout Egypt. Osiris's wife, Isis, was able to find twelve of these parts, however, and was able to affect a resurrection with a singing spell she learned from her father. The lovers then enjoyed congress, in which their son, Horus, was conceived. Shortly after that Osiris died once again and became King of the Land of the Dead."

"Fascinating. A resurrection spell. And so the mummy— Winthrop's mummy—was known as 'the black Osiris'?"

"I believe so, if it is indeed him. Khemosiri has long been considered apocryphal, a footnote in the story of Thutmose I. A cautionary tale, if you will, to ensure adherence to the core belief system of rebirth in the afterlife." Renwick crossed the room to one of his tall bookcases, removed a dusty cat's skull from where it was resting in front of a neat row of books, and pulled down a leather-bound volume. He flicked through it purposefully, and, finding the page he was looking for, crossed the room and handed it to Newbury. "Here. These are the only contemporary references to Khemosiri that survive."

Newbury examined the book. The first page bore a copy of a long document written in hieratic script. The accompanying footnote explained that it was the record of the trial of a priest found in the tomb of an Egyptian noble at the turn of the nineteenth century. The facing page showed a black-and-white photograph of a faded papyrus scroll, which—although stylised—was clearly a diagrammatic drawing of a human skull, perhaps illustrating some sort of mummification technique. Markings indicated where a hole could be made in the forehead and something—presumably brain matter—could be extracted with a long, thin tool. Hieroglyphs accompanied the bizarre illustration. Newbury handed the book back to Renwick. "What does it say?"

"It basically sets out the case against one of Thutmose's priests, who is accused of blasphemous behaviour for attempting to extend his life in the physical world and avoid the judgement of Osiris. It claims he had perfected an 'Osiris Ritual,' a means by which to affect this longevity, but all records of the actual ritual are lost." Renwick shrugged. "It seems this particular priest wasn't a true believer in the eternal resurrection of the spirit. Either that or he didn't want to give up all his earthly possessions."

Newbury smiled. "So what happened? What makes you

think there is any connection between this story and the mummy lying in Winthrop's dining room?"

"Ah . . . well, that's due to the punishments that were enacted upon the priest and the description you gave me of the casket. The document here lists the horrifying sequence of measures that were carried out to make sure that the priest suffered a very full and real death, in both the physical world and the afterlife. He was essentially obliterated from history." Renwick looked up at the sound of the kettle whistling on the stove. He set the book down on the arm of Newbury's chair and crossed over to where he'd laid out a teacup and strainer. He continued talking as he worked. "First of all, the man was stripped of his true name and all records of it were purged from his house, his family, and his temple. They even destroyed a royal stele that mentioned the priest by name. No stone was left unturned. Without a name, you see, an Egyptian soul was not permitted to cross into the afterlife. It was only after his death that others began to refer to the now nameless man as Khemosiri." Renwick coughed loudly, groped around for his pouch of tobacco, which he found amongst the flasks and vials on the workbench, and began rolling himself a cigarette. Then, after allowing the tea sufficient time to brew, he handed Newbury a cup of Earl Grey, his cigarette drooping from the corner of his mouth. "Next he was sentenced to be mummified alive, his body preserved as a warning to those who may have been harbouring similar notions or persuasions."

Newbury shook his head. "You should see the expression on his face, Aldous. It's like nothing I've ever seen before. He must have suffered terribly."

"I don't doubt it." Renwick's face was grim. "Do you know what they did to people during the mummification process?"

"Yes, I'm well aware of the procedure." Newbury frowned. "I can imagine what they did to him. It's barbaric."

"Hmmm. Well, that wasn't the end of it. The list goes on. It was decreed that once the priest's name had been erased and the mummification process complete, a curse was to be written upon the linen bandages that covered his body and he was to be interred in a black-and-gold casket, which itself would be painted with wards and warnings. His tomb would then be hidden at an undisclosed location so that thieves would not accidentally stumble upon the cursed remains."

Newbury sat forward in his chair. "That matches the description of the mummy almost perfectly. I think you have our man. How the devil did you put your finger on it?"

Renwick grinned. His glass-fronted eye shimmered in the harsh electrical light of the orb. "A half-remembered tale is all. Your letter provoked a memory. I found the book, and upon rereading the hieratic script, realised Khemosiri was your man."

. "I wonder why Peterson didn't see it."

"What, at the *British Museum*? Newbury—as I mentioned, Khemosiri is a footnote, a reference in a long-forgotten document that most professionals would dismiss as naught but fiction. Only specialists with a deep interest in the occult such as you or I would place any value in such a story, and not for its historic significance, either."

Newbury looked doubtful. "What? You believe that Khemosiri really did find a means of extending life beyond the natural span of a man?"

Renwick laughed. "Of course not. I believe that *he* believed he had. And others believed him, too. The Pharaoh,
of course, and the priests that committed him to such a terrible fate. But more than that. He was said to have a coterie
of followers, others who subscribed to his beliefs, who aided
him in his bizarre practices. When the military men purged his
home, they found no records, no trace of the so-called Osiris
Ritual. Just a pile of corpses, young women with holes drilled
into their skulls, victims of his bizarre ritualistic experiments.
No one knows for certain, but it's thought that his followers
had secured his secrets and that they were buried with him—
hidden, somehow—inside his tomb. His followers planned to
resurrect him, to give Khemosiri new life, just as the original
Osiris had been brought back from the dead by his beloved
Isis. But most of that is nothing but speculation and myth.
We have no proof either way."

"Other than a corpse that proves that they did not achieve
their goal."

Renwick laughed. "Quite so." He took a long draw on his
cigarette, watching the smoke form lazy rings around him as
he exhaled. "That wasn't the point I was getting at, though."

Newbury nodded. "Indeed. I understood your reasoning.
If there were others who believed in the ritual *then*, there
may be others who believe in the ritual *now*."

Renwick's lips curled in a satisfied smile. "Exactly so. The
man who killed Lord Winthrop may have been looking for
the secrets of the ritual. I doubt very much that Winthrop
himself had an understanding of what he'd found."

"No, he didn't." Newbury leaned back in the chair, resting
his chin on his fist. It was impossible to second-guess Ash-

ford's motives. He'd spent five years hiding in St. Petersburg, kept alive by the machines that Dr. Fabian had installed
inside his broken body. Had he turned? Was he working for
the Russian government? Or had he spent the time looking
for ways to regain the life he'd once had, turning to the occult
in desperation? Perhaps he thought this Osiris Ritual would
somehow restore his body to its former state. Only finding
him and bringing him in would provide Newbury with the
answers.

Newbury looked at Renwick. "Do you know of anyone else
who might have a notion of the link between Winthrop's
mummy and the tale of Khemosiri?"

Renwick looked thoughtful, considering his answer for a
moment. "No. I might have named you, if the circumstances
had been different. But I can think of no other, in London at
least, who would have access to the necessary texts. It's not
the sort of thing one would happen across in an academic
journal." He paused, rapping his knuckles on the workbench.
"You might consider discussing the matter with Wilfred
Blake, one of the men who aided Lord Winthrop during the
expedition. I doubt he'll give you anything new, but I understand he has an appetite for all things mystical."

Newbury raised an eyebrow. "Indeed?" That certainly
shed a different light on the man he'd seen arguing with
Winthrop during the unrolling of the mummy. Perhaps his
ironclad alibi wasn't as secure as it had at first appeared to
the Yard? He'd taken the liberty of obtaining the addresses
of all the members of the expedition from Charles the previous evening. He'd been considering paying Blake a visit
that afternoon and it now appeared he had another good

reason to do so. He downed the remains of his tea and leaned forward, placing the empty cup and saucer on the workbench. "Thank you, Aldous. I believe you've been of great service to me today."

The other man chuckled, sprinkling the ash from the end of his cigarette carelessly onto the floor. "Never any trouble, old man." He sighed. "There is one thing you could do for me, though."

"Name it."

"Can I see it?"

Newbury grinned. "I'm sure it can be arranged. Just as soon as Winthrop's funerary arrangements are finalised."

Renwick nodded appreciatively.

Newbury stood, collecting his coat and hat. He grinned at Renwick. "Thank you once again, Aldous. I can find my own way out."

Renwick was already fumbling with his tobacco pouch, intent on rolling himself another cigarette. He didn't look up again as Newbury, bracing himself for the cold, pulled the inner door shut behind him and took his leave.

CHAPTER

13

Arbury House in Regent's Park was exactly the kind of respectable, middle-class address that Newbury expected a successful bachelor such as Wilfred Blake to keep. It was a large, austere building with a Georgian edifice: square, with tall sash windows and a grand entrance. It was, Newbury considered, a fine example of the less ostentatious architecture of a time that had now passed. These days, it was difficult to avoid the horrors of the neo-Gothic and one risked facing gargoyles and other grotesques at every turn.

To the casual passer-by, Arbury House had the air of a large townhouse about it, but on closer inspection it became apparent that the house was in fact divided into a number of smaller apartments. Wilfred Blake, Newbury gleaned from the address plaques, had taken up residence in apartment number six. Newbury rapped the appropriate knocker with three sharp bursts, then stepped back onto the street, awaiting the attention of the doorman.

After a moment he stepped forward and rapped the knocker again. This time he also called out, "Hello?," but there was no response. "Hello?" Shrugging, Newbury tried the handle. It turned. He pushed the door open, surprised by the weight of it, and stepped inside, closing it carefully behind him.

If the exterior of the house had been impressive, the hallway proved even more so. The foyer was expansive and had a a series of large sash windows in the south wall. The afternoon light spilled through these in long, lazy shafts, picking out the dust motes that swirled chaotically in the air. The floor was tiled in black and white Minton, and a huge staircase wound up to the next floor and beyond. It was startlingly quiet, save for the barely audible strains of someone playing a violin elsewhere in the building. There was no sign of any doorman.

Newbury looked around. He could see the stairway to the basement levels and doors to apartments one to five. Blake's residence was obviously on the first floor. He took to the stairs, admiring the portraits that lined the wall as he climbed. The people represented were obviously members of the owner's family, going back, he guessed, over a hundred years. Their baleful faces watched him as his footsteps scuffed on the marble steps.

The first floor landing was a mirror image of the hallway

below. The staircase continued up to a second floor, and a series of doors, all painted royal blue, suggested that the floor
plan of the apartments on this level precisely matched those
of the apartments beneath. Newbury crossed the landing towards the door marked with a brass number six. A few feet
from the door, however, he stopped short. From the angle of
his approach he could see that the door had been left slightly
ajar. Walking carefully across the landing on the balls of his
feet to be sure that his footsteps were not heard, Newbury
crept closer to the door. He stopped just before the threshold
and hovered in the hallway. The door stood open by just a
couple of inches, but it was enough to cause Newbury to hesitate. Why would Blake have left the door open in such a
manner? Newbury put his head close to the opening and listened. There were sounds of someone moving around inside:
papers being shuffled, drawers being opened.

What if someone had broken into Blake's apartment?
Newbury realised he would have to tread carefully. He was
unarmed and alone and he hadn't told anyone where he
was going that afternoon. If he found himself in a difficult
spot, he'd only have his wits to get him out of it.

There was a gust of sharp, cold air from along the hallway,
and Newbury stepped back from the door, glancing to his
left. Along the landing, past the row of doors that led to the
other apartments on this floor, was a large window. This window, he assumed, looked out from back of the house to the
streets below. The netting that covered the window was billowing luxuriously in the breeze. Someone had lifted the
sash.

Taking care not to make any sounds, Newbury walked to

the end of the landing and examined the window frame and ledge, holding the netting back from the frame with his right hand. It was far too cold for someone to have opened the window for air. He ran his other hand around the frame, looking for signs that it may have been forced from the outside, but the catch was perfectly intact.

Holding on to his hat so as not to lose it to a sudden gust, Newbury leaned out over the window ledge. To his surprise, the drop on the other side was only a few feet, terminating on a small roof terrace that must have been accessible from one or more of the apartments below. Beyond that, the building was buttressed by a number of other single-storey buildings, with only a network of thin alleyways between them. If someone planned to use this window as an escape route—or, indeed, a makeshift entrance—it would not have been difficult to get away over the rooftops and from there, down into the relative anonymity of the backstreets of Regent's Park. He considered climbing down to take a better look, but he was conscious of the fact that there was still someone poking around inside the apartment and it wouldn't do to let them get away unchallenged. The window could wait. The likelihood was that whoever was in the apartment—assuming it wasn't Blake himself—was responsible for opening it anyway.

Newbury crept back to the door to apartment number six. Steeling himself, he gently pushed on the open door, hoping that the creak of the hinges wouldn't betray his presence to the person inside. He realised that he was holding his breath, trying not to make a sound. The door caught a little on the deep pile of the wine-coloured carpet on the other side, but Newbury was able to squeeze into the hallway beyond.

The apartment appeared to be well-furnished and clean. The hallway had three doors opening off of it and a small table just behind the door, its surface covered with a scattering of unopened letters. The first thing that struck Newbury, however, was the rank stench. An odour of rotten meat and decay filled the hallway, assaulting his nostrils and causing bile to rise in his throat. He immediately knew the source: Ashford. He must be the one in the other room.

Newbury inched along the hallway, staying close to the wall. He could see into the room at the far end of the corridor, which appeared to be a kitchen. He paused, listening for sounds of movement. It was clear that someone was rifling through Blake's belongings in the room just behind where Newbury was standing, which must have been the drawing room.

Newbury moved across the hall, switching sides so that he was facing the door to the drawing room, his back protectively against the wall. He shuffled a little closer until he could see through the open doorway into the room beyond. From the angle he'd achieved, he had a fairly good view of the back half of the room. He noted a cold fireplace, stark in its simplicity; a large mirror in a gilt frame over the hearth; a busy mantel covered in photographs and statuettes; and the corpse of Wilfred Blake, sprawled messily on the floor.

Newbury almost gasped aloud. Blake was still dressed in his evening wear, a black suit and white shirt. But the white shirt was spattered with a spray of dark, arterial blood, turning it a dirty crimson. More blood had pooled on the floor beneath his head: His face was turned so that Newbury could see his gaping, silent mouth and milky eyes which had rolled back in their sockets. His throat had been cut, roughly, with a blunt blade. His body was surrounded by scattered papers and ancient Egyptian artefacts which had been cast unceremoniously to the floor during the killer's frantic search. This time, Newbury mused, there hadn't been time for ceremony like Winthrop's casket.

Newbury felt his ire rising. The person on the other side of the wall—Ashford, he was sure—was pacing back and forth. Newbury knew from his brief encounter with Ashford that he was a powerhouse of a man, but Newbury had the element of surprise. He hoped that would be enough. He had no idea what Dr. Fabian had done to upgrade Ashford's rebuilt body, but he was certain he was about to find out.

Quietly, Newbury removed his hat, placing it on the floor beside him. He flexed his neck and shoulder muscles. Then, before he could reconsider, he pushed away from the wall, propelling himself forward into the drawing room to face Ashford and, quite possibly, the fight of his life.

CHAPTER

14

As was typical for this time of the afternoon, the streets of Soho were bustling with people. Veronica made her way from the bus stop towards the Archibald Theatre dressed in a smart mauve jacket with matching culottes and a white blouse. Her hair was pinned back beneath a small mauve hat that completed her professional ensemble. She'd come directly from the home of Miss Rebecca Irlam, the most recent of the missing women, where she'd spent two hours consoling the woman's mother and digging around for any information that could put her on the trail of the woman's abductor. As anticipated, the details were sketchy, but everything the woman's mother had told her matched what was written in the police report, which

Veronica had managed to obtain a copy of from one of Sir Charles's young protégés. Sometimes, being an attractive young woman had its advantages.

The woman had attended the previous evening's performance of The Mysterious Alfonso, where she had taken a seat in the stalls with her fiancé and enjoyed the ensuing show. The last anyone had seen of her was when she had volunteered for the disappearing act at the end of the show, made her way up onto the stage, and been vanished by the illusionist. The pattern was exactly the same as that witnessed by Veronica and Newbury earlier in the week, yet something was fundamentally different. This time the young woman had not made it home at the end of the performance. Her family and fiancé had searched frantically for her in the hours that followed, but there was no sign of her whatsoever. The police had been called and Alfonso had been taken away for questioning, but a cursory search of the theatre had yielded no leads. Alfonso himself had assured the men at the Yard that he had given the woman the fare for a hansom cab—much as he had assured Veronica and Newbury earlier in the week—and could not be held accountable without evidence to the contrary.

Veronica, however, felt differently about the matter. For some time now she had suspected that there was a connection between the events at the theatre and not only the disappearance of Miss Rebecca Irlam, but a string of young women throughout the whole of the home counties where Alfonso had toured with his illusionist show.

Veronica had come to Soho alone, expressly against the wishes of Sir Maurice. She knew she was playing a dangerous game, that she risked exposing the truth about her situation. She found herself wishing—as she did most days—that she were able to reveal the truth to Sir Maurice: that she, herself, was also an agent of Her Majesty Queen Victoria, and that she was quite capable of managing a case of her own. She was fully aware of the risks and saw nothing unduly dangerous about choosing to tackle Alfonso on her own. If he proved difficult, she at least had the wherewithall to incapacitate him and call for the police.

Telling all of this to Sir Maurice, of course, was out of the question. Her Majesty had specifically forbidden it, and besides, she was already abusing her duty to the Crown. She could hardly claim that she had been fulfilling her primary mission, which was to keep a watchful eye on Sir Maurice. She had been entirely absorbed in the case of the missing women. Something about the case, something about the manner in which the women had been plucked from their daily lives, struck a chord with her. Not only that, but she felt a fierce need to find justice for these young victims. The police seemed to care little about the plight of a few missing girls from the slums, and despite making her feelings clear to Sir Charles, Veronica had faced a dismissive attitude from many of the policemen she had tried to engage to assist her. The thought of it made her blood boil.

Perhaps, in some way, the situation faced by these missing women reminded her of her sister, Amelia, who had been wrenched away from the family home at a tender age, only to be deposited in a series of increasingly bleak sanatoriums, where she had been left to suffer in isolation. Perhaps that was the root of her obsession with the case. Nevertheless,

Veronica knew that the police were getting nowhere, and whilst Sir Charles was tied up with the Winthrop situation and Sir Maurice aided him, all she could do was press on. She hoped to bring the matter to a conclusion before any more women found themselves "disappeared away" by the errant magician. It pained her to lie to Newbury, of course, and she recognised that it drove a wedge between them—a barrier that prevented them from being truly honest with one another—but she could see no other satisfactory recourse. One day, she knew, the truth would come out. She only hoped that it would not result in Sir Maurice losing all trust in her or pushing her away. She couldn't bear that, she cared for him too much. She was, she reminded herself, only acting in his best interests—in the best interests of the Empire, no less—but in the back of her mind she knew that Sir Maurice would not see it that way. It was a betrayal. A betrayal of the most gentle kind, but a betrayal nonetheless.

She tried to put this out of mind as she arrived at the theatre. It was clear immediately that the place was closed. A number of bills had been pasted on the windows, informing any potential theatregoers that the evening performance had been cancelled. Inside, the lights in the lobby appeared to have been extinguished. Frowning, Veronica tested the door. To her surprise, it was open. Glancing from side to side, Veronica crossed into the dim foyer. There was no sign of the commissionaire. No sign, either, of anyone manning the kiosks or ticket booths that ran around the edges of the lobby. Like the rest of the dilapidated theatre, the lobby had once been a grand reception hall worthy of even the most prominent of visitors. The floor was a stunning white marble, although it

was now covered in a patina of dust and dirt from the tread
of innumerable boots. Tall Corinthian columns stood proudly
on either side of the archways that led through to the theatre
proper. The ticket booths on Veronica's left were now cast in
darkness, with shutters pulled low to obscure the glass parti-
tions. To her right, a number of small kiosks had been set up
to sell food and drinks, but they were presently silent, like
small abandoned islands in the murky light.

Veronica drew a deep breath. She almost turned on her heel
and left, assuming the theatre to be empty, but then, from
somewhere inside the auditorium, she heard faint clanging
sounds. She still hoped to find and confront Alfonso before the
day was out, for if he too had somehow disappeared, the trail
would grow cold.

Quietly, so as not to disturb whoever was at work in the
main theatre, Veronica approached the entrance to the
stalls, sweeping aside the heavy velvet drape and peering into
the dimly lit arena on the other side. The darkness, Veronica
thought, had a kind of texture to it, an oppressive air. The
empty stalls and seats were like a sea that stretched out before
her, unmoving. She gave an involuntary shiver. The only sign
of life in the entire auditorium was a man, Alfonso, who stood
on the stage spotlit by the harsh glow of an electric lamp. He
had a frustrated look on his face as he tried, over and over, to
insert a sword blade into his upturned hat. Clearly, he was
practising a new illusion for his act.

Veronica stood in the shadows at the back of the hall, ob-
serving what was happening on the stage. She realised she
was holding her breath. She studied Alfonso as he made another attempt. His top hat had been upended on a small

round table that rested on the stage. She could see clearly between the three wooden legs. There appeared to be nothing underneath it, although Veronica fully expected the table to be rigged in some way. Alfonso raised a sword, placed the point of it inside the upturned hat, and gave a sharp thrust downwards. This time it appeared to work. The blade slipped down inside the hat until only the hilt was standing proud, still held firmly in Alfonso's right hand. The blade itself, however, was nowhere to be seen. As far as Veronica could see, it had not pierced the tabletop. She could see nothing between the legs of the small table. It was rather a marvellous illusion, Veronica considered, and whether it was affected with a collapsible blade or, as she first suspected, a simple trick of the light, she could not say. Most likely, the blade had passed through a notch in the table and was simply not visible from the angle at which the audience viewed the stage.

Alfonso stepped back and rubbed his hand across his chin, thoughtfully regarding his handiwork. He smiled. Veronica took this as her cue to approach. Making no attempt to hide her presence, she descended the stairs at the back of the hall and walked up one of the aisles, her boots echoing loudly on the wooden floor. Alfonso turned to watch her approach, a surprised look on his face. He clearly wasn't expecting any visitors. Veronica was a picture of professionalism. "Good afternoon, Mr. Alfonso. My name is Miss Veronica Hobbes. You may recall we met earlier in the week?"

Alfonso narrowed his eyes and gave her a disdainful look. "Indeed, I recall your visit. But Miss Hobbes, it unfortunately seems that you've wasted a trip this evening. The theatre is closed. I fear I must ask you to leave."

Veronica smiled. "Ah, well, I'm afraid it's not quite as simple as all that. I have some further questions for you regarding Miss Rebecca Irlam."

"Who?" Alfonso furrowed his brow. Then, as if realisation had suddenly dawned on him, he nodded in acknowledgement. "Ah, yes, the girl who went missing from the theatre on her way home last night. A sad affair. I've already given all the information I have to the police." He waved his hand dismissively. "Now, I'm sure you'll understand that I'm a busy man. If I can ask you to be on your way . . ." He turned away from her, examining the hilt of the sword, which was still protruding from the brim of the hat on the table.

Veronica stepped closer to the stage. Her eyes were hard and they gleamed in the harsh electric light as she mounted the small set of steps that led to where Alfonso was standing. She hadn't noticed on her previous visit how high the stage itself was raised from the floor. She regarded the magician. The set of her jaw was firm and unyielding. Her blood was up. "Mr. Alfonso, for what reason has the show been cancelled this evening? I should imagine that means a great deal of lost revenue. Surely you are not ending your run at the Archibald prematurely? It appears to have been a magnificent success."

Alfonso looked sheepish. "Something like that," he muttered under his breath. Veronica stepped forward, closer to him now. "Look, Miss Hobbes, I assure you that the disappearance of this woman has nothing to do with me!" He was flustered now.

"Ah, so you *didn't* make her vanish on stage last night, then?"

He was growing increasingly agitated. "Not *that* disappearance. The one that happened later, after she had already left the theatre."

"It sounds like you're splitting hairs to me." Veronica put her hand on her hip. "Mr. Alfonso—or whatever your real name is—I suggest that quite the opposite is true. That you had everything to do with the disappearance of Miss Rebecca Irlam, as well as any number of other young women, such as Miss Cordelia Fletcher, Miss Jane Eyles, or, indeed, Miss Sophia Caithness. Women you spirited away from towns all over the home counties before bringing your illusionist show to the capital. Can we forgo the pretence now, Mr. Alfonso?"

Alfonso looked shaken. He stepped back, edging away from Veronica. "Look, I really must ask you to leave now. I'm afraid I cannot help you with your enquiries." It was clear to Veronica that she had him cornered. The guilt was evident in his eyes, written in the signs of panic that had suddenly gripped him. "You were here just the other evening, Miss Hobbes. You saw a young lady disappear on stage and enquired of her well-being after the performance. Did she not make it home safe and well?"

Veronica smiled. "Yes, and that's the clever part, isn't it? They don't all disappear. That would be far too obvious and you are much cleverer than that. Any number of young women have taken part in your disappearing act, been whisked away before a large audience. And many of them you set free, to minimise suspicion." She paused. "What is it that you are looking for? What makes you choose one woman as a victim over another?"

Alfonso glanced nervously from side to side, unsure how to respond. He stepped backwards, stumbling as the back of his knee encountered the large wooden rack of swords that had been placed on the stage for his act. He jumped as the rack clattered noisily to the floor. He glanced down at the mess around his feet. Then, realising that his options were swiftly diminishing, he reached down for one of the swords and came up again in a crouching position. Without hesitation, he swung the sword deftly in Veronica's direction.

Veronica moved quickly. She'd been trained for this sort of situation. She leapt backwards, away from the tip of the blade, as it swept past her in a wide arc, narrowly missing her breast. Alfonso grinned. He stabbed forward and Veronica twisted away, causing his thrust to fall short. It was immediately clear to her that Alfonso was no brawler. He was lacking the finesse, the confidence. She stepped forward, grabbed Alfonso's outstretched wrist with her right hand, twisted it hard, and caused him to yelp and release the sword, which clattered loudly to the floor. With her left hand, she jabbed out, striking him sharply on the chin. He staggered backwards but Veronica, still retaining a grip on his sword arm, did not allow him to get away and returned for another quick jab to his face. By now, panic had entirely gripped the magician and he realised he was fighting for his life. If Veronica was able to prove his connection to the missing women—of which she had no doubt—Alfonso would surely swing from a taut noose.

Alfonso kicked out hard at Veronica's ankles, attempting

to unbalance her. The blow connected, but Veronica was too deft on her feet to tumble. She danced away, releasing her grip on his arm and wincing at the stinging pain of the blow. She kept her eye on Alfonso, trying to judge his next move. A change had come over him. He looked desperate, animalistic, even. His mouth was set in a grim sneer, his dark eyes seemed to bore holes through her to the back of her skull as they met each other's glare. Shuddering, Veronica skipped forward and aimed a blow at the man's chin. She was fast and she struck home, not giving him any chance to react. His head twisted awkwardly to one side with the force of the impact. Blood trickled down his chin from a split lip.

Veronica stepped back. She knew she needed to bring him down quickly, incapacitate him so that she could call for the police. Alfonso, however, was not giving up easily. He was like a cornered bear and he lashed out, his bony fingers clawing at her face. She felt his nails biting painfully into her cheek and she gasped as he raked them across her face, drawing bloody welts. She battered his arms away and kicked out at him in an attempt to maintain some distance. If she let him in too close, she feared he may manage to overcome her. She caught him forcefully in the upper thigh and he fell back, stooping low and cursing loudly. "You filthy whore!"

Veronica rushed him as he was still bent low from the blow to his leg. She drove her fist hard into his gut. He creased, choking as the wind was driven out of him, doubling over at the waist. He clutched at his belly. Veronica saw her chance. She grabbed the straggly hair at the back of his head and brought her knee up, connecting resoundingly with his face. His nose burst with a sickening crunch, spreading a fountain of dark red blood and staining her culottes. Alfonso gave a pitiful wail and sank to the floor. He was panting, spitting blood, pawing at his broken face. Veronica stepped back, looking down at the sorrowful wretch. Alfonso looked up at her. He was giggling like a lunatic.

"What? What is it?" Veronica was disconcerted by the sudden outburst. There was no reply, other than more of the insane laughter. She could only conclude that his mind had finally broken under the strain. She cast around, looking for a length of rope or fabric she could use to bind him whilst she fetched the police. She stepped towards the round table at the centre of the stage, where Alfonso's upturned hat and sword were still in situ. The pitch of the man's bizarre giggling increased. The noise was like insects crawling up and down her spine, like nails being dragged across a dry blackboard. She gave an involuntary shudder. Still, she had him, finally, and as soon as she had bound him and arranged for the police to detain him, it would be over. No more missing women.

She examined the hat, glancing back at Alfonso to ensure that he hadn't decided to risk trying to escape whilst her back was turned. He was still clutching at his bleeding face but he glowered back at her, almost expectantly. She had a feeling she was somehow missing something. Then, with one sudden, unexpected movement, he flung himself to the right, slamming the heel of his hand down hard against the wooden stage. He must have hit a pressure paddle for, to Veronica's astonishment, the ground beneath her feet suddenly gave way and before she could react—before she could even fling her arms out to brace herself—she was falling.

She landed, hard, feeling her legs buckle beneath her. The trapdoor through which she had fallen slammed shut above her, throwing her into impenetrable darkness. She could still hear Alfonso's mad laughter echoing in the auditorium above. Veronica tested the space around her. She was encased within some kind of coffin-shaped box. It was made of rough, untreated wood and it splintered against her palms as she slapped at the sides of it, frustrated and scared. She thrashed out in every direction, trying to find some means of escape or to knock the box over, but it would not give. Above her, the trap mechanism had locked into place, and try as she might, she could not prise the panel open again from the inside. She was trapped.

She kicked, testing the floor, and she noticed that there was something at her feet. She reached down as best she could in the confined space. Cloth. Bundles of heavy cloth. She frowned in the darkness. And then, with rising panic, she realised what they were: the rags had been soaked with chloroform. There was no mistaking the sickly sweet perfume of the drug. She didn't have long before the fumes would overwhelm her.

Something creaked beneath the box and Veronica felt it shake. She fell awkwardly to one side as the box began to move. She could feel it rolling downwards, further underground. It must have been on casters triggered by the introduction of her weight. This was clearly the mechanism that Alfonso had used to cause the women to disappear during his act. The chloroform explained why the women who were later freed were left dazed and disoriented. And the women who weren't freed . . . Veronica tried not to think of that.

She had no idea what to do. She was trapped beneath the stage in a narrow wooden box that was creeping inexorably towards an unknown destination where Alfonso was likely waiting for her, his motives still unclear. This time, there was no one to save her. She cursed herself for not listening to Sir Maurice. Nobody knew she was there. She had to face facts: her time was running out. If she didn't find a way out soon, she'd likely die in the casket, or worse. She called out, knowing it was a useless endeavour. The only person there to hear her was her captor.

The floral scent of the chloroform became overbearing. Veronica felt her senses fogging. She knew she had to fight it, knew that whatever happened, she couldn't allow herself to be overcome. She had no idea what Alfonso had in store for her if she did. She gasped for breath. But her fate, under the circumstances, was inevitable. The casket continued its slow descent.

Soon darkness overcame her.

CHAPTER

15

Newbury barrelled around the corner of Blake's drawing room, fully expecting to confront a large man clad in a thick black cloak. What he actually found was a younger, more diminutive fellow, dressed in a brown corduroy jacket and slacks. The other man turned, startled, when he heard Newbury burst into the room.

"Ah! Sir Maurice! Thank goodness you're here. I was about to send for the police."

"Purefoy! What the devil . . ." Newbury lowered his guard, but only fractionally. He glanced at the corpse on the floor, spattered in blood, and then back at the young reporter.

Purefoy looked sheepish. "I can explain!"

Newbury regarded him. Could it really be

that this young man was mixed up in these murders? He thought it unlikely. But Newbury had now found Purefoy hovering at the scene of two of the crimes. What was his connection to the dead men? Newbury couldn't, at this stage, discount his involvement. He hoped it was only a journalist's instinct that had led the reporter to the murder scenes.

There were questions that needed answers. "Mr. Purefoy, this is the second time I've encountered you in less-than-savory situations. I think it is time we had another of our little discussions." Purefoy nodded, a serious expression on his face. "So, tell me: how did you come to be in the apartment of a murdered man, searching through his belongings in such a manner?"

Purefoy dropped the sheaf of papers he was holding onto the rosewood writing desk that stood against the far wall and crossed the room to stand before Newbury. Blake's belongings were scattered everywhere, everything from fine antiquities to old editions of *The Times*.

"Did you make this mess?"

"No! Not at all. It was like this when I entered the apartment. The killer was evidently searching for something, just like he had been at Lord Winthrop's place."

Newbury sighed. "Hmmm. Let's just slow down a little, before you jump to that kind of conclusion."

"What conclusion?" Purefoy looked a little bemused.

"That the person who murdered Lord Winthrop is the same person responsible for . . . this." Newbury grimaced as he glanced down at Blake's body just a few feet from where he was standing. He cleared his throat, a thoughtful look in his eyes. "So, tell me, what was the purpose of your visit?"

"I came to interview Wilfred Blake—about the expedition, you understand. And Winthrop's murder. I wanted to see if he had any comments. If he felt his own life might have been in danger. . . ." Purefoy trailed off as he realised the weight of his own words. He met Newbury's unwavering gaze. He sighed. "To be truthful, Sir Maurice, I hoped to discover whether Mr. Blake had any real notion of what had happened to Lord Winthrop."

Newbury couldn't help but smile. Perhaps he had been right about the boy, perhaps he did have the necessary instincts to make it as an agent of the Crown. He resolved to find out. "Carry on."

"Well, I arrived about ten minutes ago. I had Blake's address from the offices of *The Times*. We'd interviewed him before, in relation to the Theban expedition. I made my way here by ground train from Westminster and approached the building in plain view. Finding there was no commissionaire on the door, and that the door was open, I entered and made my way to Blake's apartment. Until that point I had no reason to suspect that anything was wrong." He paused for breath. The story was spilling out of him at a remarkable rate, and Newbury had to pay close attention to decipher the stream of gabbled words. "When I got here the door was slightly ajar. I knocked, but received no reply. I hesitated on the threshold, trying to discern the best course of action. It was then that I became aware of a banging sound from somewhere inside. I pushed on the door and, to my surprise, a large chap, whose face was obscured by a thick black cloak, came charging out of the apartment, slammed into me, knocked me to the floor, and hurtled away down the landing. I called out, but he didn't stop. A moment later he slipped out through that open window and onto the rooftop beyond."

Newbury noticed that Purefoy was holding his right arm awkwardly by his side. If his story was to be trusted then he must have been hurt in the fall, when Ashford had pushed him to the ground. "So you didn't think of following him or calling for the neighbours?"

Purefoy didn't know where to look. "I . . ." Newbury could tell he was embarrassed to speak the truth. "I fear my reporter's instinct overtook me. That and the fact that I was concerned for Mr. Blake's well-being. I pushed my way into the apartment and found him like this." He indicated Blake's corpse. "It was a shock, I'll admit that much."

Newbury nodded thoughtfully. "Did you touch the body?"

Purefoy shook his head resolutely. "No. Not at all. I even thought about calling the police. But then I got to thinking, who was the chap in the black cloak and what was it exactly that he'd been looking for? I was taking a look through the items he'd strewn around the place when you burst in a few moments ago."

Newbury sighed. It sounded like a believable tale, and his instinct was to trust the young reporter. Nevertheless, he couldn't discount the potential that Purefoy was somehow involved.

Purefoy filled the silence that had grown between them. "So, Sir Maurice, do you have any knowledge of who that man could have been? The man in the cloak, I mean?"

Newbury nodded. "I do. I do indeed." Purefoy looked at him expectantly. "He's a very dangerous man."

"A foreign agent?"

Newbury frowned. "You could say that." His voice was grim.

"And what of the stench? He carries a rank odour if ever I encountered one."

"He is . . . not the man he once was," is all Newbury offered in reply. In truth, he still had no real notion of the origin of the foul smell. He presumed it must have something to do with the dubious work that Dr. Fabian had carried out on the man.

Purefoy looked curious. "What did he want with Winthrop and Blake? What is he looking for?"

Newbury was unsure how much to tell him. He hadn't yet decided if the reporter was involved in the murders, and besides, for all Newbury's theorising, much of his information was nothing but supposition. "Something to do with the expedition. Something they found. It's all connected with that screaming mummy we saw back at Winthrop's party. There were secrets buried with that ancient priest. Secrets that our killer appears anxious to get his hands on."

Purefoy nodded. "So what next?"

Newbury glanced down at the contorted cadaver on the floor. "Next we examine the body."

"Turn up that gas jet over there, Purefoy. It's too dark in here. Oh, and see if you can find some brandy."

Purefoy looked perplexed. "Do you intend to use it to clean the wound?"

Newbury looked up from the body. His face was serious.

"No. I intend to drink it." Purefoy chuckled and set about his tasks.

Newbury was kneeling by the corpse. It was a bloody mess. The man's throat had been entirely gouged out, ripped open with a blunt instrument such as an old penknife or letter opener. It was different from Winthrop's murder, executed with less finesse, but just as effective. Newbury was convinced that whoever had committed the murder had a hand in both deaths. The motivation was clearly the same: the victims had something the killer wanted.

He walked through what he supposed had happened in his mind's eye. Blake had been grabbed from behind, his throat slashed rudely from right to left. His body had been dumped unceremoniously on the floor and left there to bleed out on the oilcloth. His formerly white dress shirt was now stained a deep crimson and his eyes stared blankly at the ceiling, as if searching for an absent God. They were developing a milky, glazed appearance. Newbury, shuddering, reached over and closed the lids with his fingertips. It was a dubious kind of rest, but Newbury could not stand the cold, accusing glare any longer. He couldn't help thinking that he should have somehow warned the man earlier. He resolved to take it up with Charles. The other members of the expedition had to be protected.

Newbury rocked back on his haunches. The problem, he mused, was not in identifying the nature of the killer, for he was already convinced that Ashford was the culprit, but in tracking the man. Ashford knew how to disappear. That much was clear to Newbury. His quarry had spent years living undercover in one of the most dangerous cities in the world. An agent could not live through an experience like that without gleaning at least a handful of new tricks. Even putting that aside, Ashford had once been an agent for the British Crown, and as such, he had received at least the same measure of training as Newbury himself. If Ashford remained hidden, Newbury could be in for a very long game of cat and mouse, indeed.

He glanced over his shoulder, looking to the door. He hoped that brandy would come soon. His skin was starting to crawl and he was beginning to sweat—symptoms, he knew, of his addiction. Hopefully, the alcohol would help to take the edge off, for a short while, at least. He listened for Purefoy. He couldn't hear the boy. For a moment he almost panicked, thinking that he may have allowed Purefoy the perfect opportunity to slip away, but a moment later the reporter reappeared from the hallway, bearing a large tumbler and a wide grin. "Here you are, sir. I hope that helps." Newbury looked at him suspiciously. He couldn't possibly know . . . could he? Newbury accepted the glass, regardless. He didn't have time to concern himself with the matter.

Purefoy leaned forward, resting his hands on his knees and examining the corpse with inexpert eyes. "So, what of the body?"

Newbury followed his gaze. He could see no real harm in making Purefoy aware of the details. He'd given the young man plenty of opportunities to trip himself up, and so far Purefoy had only managed to reward Newbury's faith in him. He was perceptive and inquisitive and could prove to be a great asset in helping to bring Ashford to justice. Newbury continued to stare at the body whilst he talked. "Assuming that none of this is going to end up in the morning edition . . ." He paused, waiting for Purefoy to nod his agreement before continuing. He indicated Blake's devastated throat. "His throat has been cut from behind, the perpetrator using his left hand to slash from right to left. It was a brutal murder and the killer showed no respect for his victim. Nevertheless, it was an efficient execution. Whoever it was wanted Blake dead and he achieved that goal swiftly and without emotion. It's not unlike Lord Winthrop's death, in many respects, aside from the ceremony. The killer had time to place Winthrop's body where it would have maximum effect—a calling card, if you will. Here, he had no such luxury and was forced to leave Blake's body where it fell." He took a long draw of his brandy, feeling the warmth of it spreading, most welcome, throughout his body. "I don't believe the killer came here specifically to murder Blake. I think Blake is almost irrelevant to the equation. The killer wanted something that Blake had, and Blake, unfortunately, just found himself in the way."

Purefoy looked taken aback. "My God. . . ."

Newbury empathised with the sentiment. "Quite. Quite so."

Newbury downed another measure of his brandy, then placed the empty glass on the mantelpiece. He glanced around. Items were strewn all over the place. He didn't know where to start. If Purefoy's testimony was to be believed, the reporter had disturbed Ashford midsearch. Whatever he was trying to find could still be there, buried somewhere under the mess.

He leaned on the mantel, considering his next move. The grate beneath was cold, well stocked with coal. But something about it struck a sharp note of discord. There! Buried in the coals to the far right of the grate was something small and metallic. He stooped closer to see. It was long and thin, the pommel and guard of a small silver blade. Purefoy moved round to stand beside him. "What is it?"

Newbury smiled. "The murder weapon." He reached into his breast pocket and produced a white monogrammed handkerchief. "The killer has abandoned the knife in the fireplace."

Purefoy crouched down to take a closer look. "Yes. Yes, you're right!"

Newbury pinched the handkerchief between his fingers and reached down, withdrawing the blade from where it jutted inconspicuously between the coals. It was covered in blood and gritty black dust. It was about five inches long from its tip to its hilt and fashioned from fine silver. Newbury turned it over in his hand and regarded it carefully. "It's an antique. A letter opener." He glanced over at Blake's desk, but the leather writing surface was so buried in Ashford's mess that he was unable to tell if that was where it had come from. "I think our killer must have simply grabbed the first thing to hand. It shows incredible resourcefulness. Not that that's any consolation for poor old Blake here."

"Do you think the police will find fingerprints? Something to help us confirm the identity of the killer?"

Newbury shrugged. "I don't suppose we will, no. The killer's too clever for that. And besides, he knows we're on to him. He'll have to try a different tactic now." Newbury looked thoughtful. "I wonder where he was going when he bolted through that window. Those rooftops could lead him anywhere."

"Assuming he found what he wanted, of course."

Newbury turned towards Purefoy. "How so?"

Purefoy gestured around the room, both of his arms out-stretched. "Look at this place. He's turned the apartment upside down looking for . . . whatever it is that you think he's looking for. It could be that I disturbed him before he found what he wanted." He shrugged. "I don't know. Perhaps he'll return when he thinks it's safe. It depends very much on how much he needs what was here. And judging by the state of Blake, I'd say he needed it very much."

Newbury was impressed. "Good thinking, Purefoy. It's certainly a possibility." Newbury bent low and placed the letter opener neatly on the floor beside the body. He folded his handkerchief, which was now filthy with blood and coal, away into his trouser pocket. It wouldn't do to leave the mur-der weapon at the scene, wrapped in one of his personal, monogrammed items. Not that he feared the police would in any way consider him a suspect, but he didn't want to acci-dentally set them down the wrong path. He brushed himself down. "Come on, Purefoy. There's little else we can do here. We need to inform the police. Sir Charles and his men will be here like a shot." He turned and left the room, Purefoy following closely behind.

On the landing, Newbury stopped and looked back over his shoulder to be sure the reporter was following. "Before we take our leave I want to have a look at that rooftop, to see if the killer left any traces behind in his haste." He ushered Purefoy out of the apartment and then pulled the door shut behind him, testing it to ensure it was secure. He didn't want any of the neighbours accidentally stumbling across such a terrible scene.

At the end of the landing, the window was open, just as Newbury had left it. A cold breeze was gusting in from outside. He could hear the sounds of distant traffic: horses, ground trains and carriages, all clattering along the busy thoroughfares of the city. Newbury brushed the netting aside and leaned out, taking another measure of the drop to the rooftop below.

"Here, hold this." Newbury slipped out of his topcoat and handed it to the reporter. Then, grasping hold of the edges of the wooden frame, he placed his foot on the windowsill and hauled himself up, propelling himself through the opening and down to the roof below. He landed in a squat. Rising to his full height, he looked back to see Purefoy following suit, leaving his topcoat draped over the window frame. Newbury chuckled to himself. The young man was incorrigible. The coat would be lost now and he'd have to explain to Charles why it had been left at the scene. Thankfully, Newbury knew many of the inspectors at the Yard, and they in turn were aware of the services he had provided over the years in helping to bring a variety of criminals to justice. Newbury regularly left traces of his presence behind at crime scenes, but a mixture of police incompetence and Newbury's reputation meant that he was seen as being above suspicion and such matters were disregarded.

The light was fading now, and a wispy mist was beginning to settle on the rooftops. The moon was peeking out behind grey clouds; the bright, shimmering orb hung low in the sky like a curious Chinese lantern. In the distance, airships soared lazily over the city. Soon the night would draw in. Newbury, feeling the bite of the cold, looked around, trying to spot any trace of the rogue agent. The roof terrace stretched away in both directions. It had once been grand, affording an admirable view of the urban spread of the capital, but it was clearly now in disuse. A row of large plant pots abutted the wall, the flowers in them now choked by weeds and fumes from the steam engines that traversed the streets below. A small rail ran around the outer edges of the terrace, there, Newbury presumed, to prevent people from accidentally tumbling to their deaths. Two old wooden chairs, rotten through, had been abandoned in one corner, surrounded by the spent ends of expensive cigarettes that had been cast haphazardly from the window above. They were scattered, too, across the paving stones upon which Newbury now stood. There were no signs that the terrace was ever used by the current inhabitants of the house.

Newbury, stooping low, examined the ground beneath the window, near where he had landed. In the dusty mulch was a clear footprint: a large, booted foot had made an impression as its owner had dropped heavily from above.

Newbury moved to one side to allow Purefoy to see. He pointed to the boot print. "There, look. It's a fresh print. Someone definitely jumped down from this window earlier this afternoon." He glanced surreptitiously at the reporter's shoes, just to be sure of his earlier judgement. Purefoy was wearing smart brogues and his feet were at least two sizes smaller than those of the man who had left the print. Newbury smiled. Ashford, then. He could now, without doubt, place the rogue agent at the scene of Blake's murder. Not only that, but he was close to ruling out Purefoy's involvement in the matter. His instinct told him to trust the young man. He decided to follow it.

Newbury scanned the surrounding rooftops. In the hazy light it was like a rich landscape punctuated by innumerable chimneys belching dark foggy clouds into the sky. The horizon was like a microcosm of all of London: industrial buildings, terraces, slums, and large mansions, all clustered together in an unlikely arrangement. Then, about two hundred yards away on another, lower rooftop, Newbury saw his prey. Or rather, he saw two glowing pinpricks of light emanating from where Ashford's eyes had once been. They were staring out—unwavering—from behind a large terracotta chimney pot. The rest of the man was obscured by the shadows.

"There he is!" Newbury exclaimed, pointing across to where the rogue agent was lurking.

Purefoy couldn't see. "What! Where?"

But Newbury wasn't waiting. He rushed to the edge of the terrace, looking across at the intervening gap between Arbury House and the building behind it. The gap was around six feet wide and ran between the two rooftops. There was no clear run up to it and only a small ledge on the other side of the iron railings from which to make the jump. Below was only darkness and swirling fog. If he missed his footing and pitched into the gap, all that awaited him below was death; he would be dashed on the uneven cobbles and lost amongst scattered piles of refuse and human waste.

He glanced back at the bizarre eyes of his enemy. They seemed to bore into him, urging him on. He had no time to consider. Grasping hold of the top of the railing, he swung one leg over, trying to avoid impaling himself on the rusty fleur-de-lys that topped the ironwork. He climbed cautiously onto the ledge on the other side. There was little room to move, and his left foot slipped, causing him to grasp hold of the railing once again to maintain his balance. Crumbling brickwork scattered down into the grey darkness. He didn't hear it strike the ground. His heart was hammering hard in his chest. He was sweating, too, feeling an intense, burning desire for the narcotic that sustained him. He gripped the railing, fighting the urge to climb back onto the relative safety of the roof behind him.

He heard Purefoy run over to stand beside him, on the other side of the railing. "Sir Maurice! You're not going to . . . ?"

Newbury paid him no heed. If he thought too long about what he was about to do, he simply wouldn't do it. Keeping his head up to avoid looking down at the sheer drop beneath him, Newbury examined the other rooftop. There was a small decorative stone lip that ran around the edge of the roof. At least, he mused, if he misjudged the jump, he'd have something to attempt to catch hold of. He had no idea how Ashford had got across the gap or, indeed, why the man was still lurking in the shadows when it was clear that he had been spotted. Perhaps he didn't expect Newbury to successfully leap across the two rooftops to confront him. Whatever the case, this was the best opportunity Newbury had yet encountered to bring the man to justice, and he planned to do it before any more people died. Assuming, of course, that he wasn't about to kill *himself*.

Coiling like a spring to get as much power into his legs as possible, Newbury pounced. He flung his arms out as he sailed across the alleyway, keeping his eyes fixed on the point where he intended to land. He almost made it, but a trailing foot caught the stone lip and sent him sprawling. He slammed down hard onto the other roof, only just managing to get his arms up in time to protect his head. His elbows smarted from the blow and he'd knocked his wind out. He lay on his front for a moment, breathless, before rolling onto his back and sitting up. He took a moment to regain his composure. Then, not wanting to provide Ashford with a chance of escape, he clambered to his hands and knees and then to his feet, gasping as he finally managed to pull the cold damp air down into his lungs. He turned, fully expecting Ashford to be rushing him across the terrace. But he was still there in the shadows, still watching. Newbury could make no sense of the man's motivations.

He heard a crash beside him. Surprised, he turned to see Purefoy landing neatly on his haunches and breaking into a forward roll to cushion his landing. He came up standing beside Newbury, a wide grin on his face. They looked at each other, something wordless passing between them. An understanding. And then Newbury set off, bolting across the rooftop towards the glowing lights that represented his murderous prey. Purefoy's footsteps fell in behind him.

As they drew closer, Newbury watched the shape of Ashford resolve in the dim, foggy light. He made no attempt to conceal himself. He was dressed as Purefoy had claimed—as he had been when Newbury had last encountered him—in his flowing black cloak, hulking beside the towering chimney stack. His eyes seemed to track Newbury's progress across the rooftop. Newbury skidded around a skylight and then realised, with shock, the reason why Ashford had not yet taken flight. He was rushing headlong towards the lip of another building. Newbury had misjudged the distance in the fog. Ashford was on the *next* rooftop, and it was too late to stop. Newbury was already careening towards the drop, which yawned open before him like an ominous chasm. There was no railing this time, only the same decorative lip that had caused him to trip on his first jump.

Faced with his inability to stop in time, he *didn't* stop. Reaching the edge of the building, he leapt up onto the lip and propelled himself forward, flinging himself through the air so that he hurtled across the gap and landed at a run, stumbling slightly but managing to maintain his momentum. His arms wheeled as he tried to regain his balance. He didn't have time to congratulate himself for the manoeuvre, however, as Ashford turned and began to flee.

Ashford's legs drove him forward at a phenomenal speed. He was a blur as he shot towards the other end of the building. Newbury's legs pumped hard as he tried, ineffectually, to keep up, darting between the chimney stacks that peppered the roof.

Then there was a terrified cry from somewhere behind him. Newbury skidded to a halt, glancing back over his shoulder. He realised almost immediately what had happened. Purefoy hadn't seen the gap between the two rooftops until it was too late and had failed to clear the opening. A lump rose in Newbury's throat. He was labouring for breath, not used to the exertion. Turning, he rushed back towards the alleyway. He knew he was allowing Ashford to get away, but if there was any chance he could help . . .

Newbury scanned the line of the building as he ran, but everything was shrouded in cloying yellow fog. He called out. "Purefoy?"

There was no reply.

Newbury came to a halt a few feet from the drop. He searched the terrace around him. Empty. There was no sign of the young man. The roofline opposite him was also clear.

Purefoy was nowhere to be seen. Newbury, drawing ragged breaths, could only fear the worst.

CHAPTER

16

Hesitantly, Newbury approached the lip of the building. He couldn't see any sign of the other man. He called out. "Purefoy? Purefoy! Are you there?" He was panicking now. He didn't know how he could live with the responsibility if the reporter had fallen to his death.

There was a grunt from down below, somewhere in the fog. Newbury knelt on the edge of the building and leaned over, searching, urgently, for the source of the sound. "Purefoy? Is that you?"

"Here . . ." The voice trailed off, and Newbury heard the sounds of something soft and heavy banging against metal. There! He leaned over as far as he dared. An iron staircase resolved in the fog. It was an emergency stairwell, attached to the side of the building. And dangling from the side, twisting and turning, holding on with only one hand, was Purefoy. He seemed dazed, as if he may have caught a blow to the head in the fall. Blood was smeared in a line across his cheek. Newbury knew the situation was precarious. One slip and the reporter would be dead. He called out to him.

"Purefoy! Focus. Use your other hand. Hold on!" Purefoy responded to this. He eased himself around so that he was facing the building and swung his left arm up, trying to catch hold of the ironwork. His hand, however, did not seem able to find purchase and he slipped, dangerously, crying out as he lurched awkwardly from side to side. Newbury feared the motion would cause him to lose his grip altogether. "Stay there. I'm coming for you."

Newbury stood, surveying the scene beneath him. The fog was thick here and obscured his view. Typically these iron stairwells would have a small platform, just to the right of where Purefoy was hanging, and he guessed that it couldn't be far below the lip of the building itself. But it was difficult to see. Past Purefoy he could make out the indistinct shape of a railing, but little else. He'd have to take it on faith. Edging along the lip of the building, he drew a deep breath. If he missed, they would likely both wind up dead on the cobbles below. He hadn't planned on *this* when he'd decided to visit Wilfred Blake that morning and he wondered, absently, what Veronica would say if she could see him now.

Purefoy had once again disappeared into the syrupy miasma. Below, all Newbury could see was a swirl of grey, but he judged that he was standing above the metal platform.

He took a deep breath. He couldn't put it off any longer and he couldn't let Purefoy fall to his death. He closed his eyes, flexed his shoulders, and jumped into nothing.

His feet clattered against the metal rungs, but the platform was higher than he'd imagined and it was this that nearly toppled him over the side of the railing. Frantically, he scrabbled to get a grip, grasping the iron bars as he slipped and slid on the slick metal. Finding his feet, he heaved a brief sigh of relief then rushed immediately to the left-hand side of the platform and sank to his knees, searching for Purefoy between the metal bars. The reporter was still there, hanging on for his life. Newbury thrust his arm through the grate and reached down to grasp Purefoy by the wrist. The reporter's other arm was still dangling uselessly by his side, and he was unable to gain enough leverage to swing it up to try for a better hold.

"Here! Use my arm. Pull yourself up."

Purefoy stared back at him with panicked eyes. He was breathing quickly and the strain was starting to show. Newbury tried to keep him focused on the task at hand. "Don't look down. No! Purefoy! Keep your eyes on me." Newbury heaved, trying to give the boy a better chance of grabbing hold of the stairwell with his other hand. Purefoy struggled, his feet kicking frantically as they sought something solid upon which to gain purchase. Instead, the result was to pull alarmingly on Newbury's arm as Purefoy swung out wildly. Newbury felt his shoulder burning as he took the other's weight, his arm fully extended, his face pressed uncomfortably against the hard metal bars.

"Oh, God!" Purefoy exclaimed in terror as Newbury's grip

slipped and loosened and he slid a little further towards the alleyway below.

"I have you." Newbury fixed his gaze on the other man. "I *have* you. Now pay attention. You need to get your other arm up here, right now!" Newbury was gasping for breath and struggling to gain leverage. The instructions registered with the young man, however, and with Newbury still hanging on to him by his left wrist, he managed to get a grip on the iron frame with his right hand. "Good. Good! Now, I'm going to let go and reach over to grasp hold of your collar. Then we'll heave you over the top. Hold on!"

Newbury waited a moment to be sure that Purefoy was not going to fall, then scrambled to his feet, leaned over the rail, and used both hands to grab fistfuls of the boy's jacket. "On my mark. One, two, three . . ." He grunted as he lifted the reporter up by his clothes. Purefoy was quick to get his feet into position, jamming them through the bars of the rail to support himself. A moment later, he swung over the top of the railing and collapsed beside Newbury on the cold platform, both of them struggling for breath. He stared with wide eyes at the drop beneath him and gave wordless thanks to the Crown investigator.

Newbury patted him on the shoulder. "You need to thank your tailor, dear boy." He wheezed as he tried to regain his breath. "That's an excellent jacket you have there."

They both laughed out loud, relieved, as they rubbed their aching joints. After a few moments, still gasping, Purefoy turned to Newbury. "Did you catch him?"

Newbury shrugged. "I'm in no doubt that he got away. Once I've regained my strength I'll head up there to take a

look, see if there are any other clues that may help us pick
up his trail."

Purefoy looked sheepish. "I . . ."

Newbury interjected. "Best left unsaid. It's not necessary.
Not at all."

Purefoy nodded gratefully.

After a moment, Newbury, who had been slumped on
the platform, his back to the railing, climbed to his feet and
regarded the building before him. Here, the metal stairs became a short ladder that terminated just below the lip of
the roof. He shook his head, cursing that he hadn't noticed the
ladder from above. Taking hold of the rungs, he levered himself up, leaving Purefoy where he was, still panting and nursing his sore arms on the platform below. It was a short climb
to the roof, and Newbury was soon able to pull himself over
again. He made a mental note of where the ladder was, scuffing the gravel with the edge of his shoe in case he needed to
find it again in the fog.

Newbury looked around for signs of Ashford. The fog was
thickening, but even so, he was shocked to see the familiar
red eyes of the augmented man staring back at him from a
little further along the rooftop. Newbury could barely believe it. Why had he waited? Perhaps he wanted to be sure
that Newbury and Purefoy were gone? Perhaps Purefoy had
been right, and he intended to head back to Blake's apartment before Newbury was able to alert the police? Regardless, he couldn't waste the opportunity.

"Ashford!" The other man's head turned, and Newbury
could no longer see his face beneath the darkness of his cowl.
"Ashford, we must talk." Newbury rushed forward and as he

drew closer, the situation became quickly apparent. Ashford was perched on the corner of the building, his heavy cloak draped over his shoulders, giving him an ethereal, formless appearance in the foggy darkness. The buildings across the alleys to the side and rear were both taller—at least a storey higher than the building on which they were standing—so the leap across to either would be impossible, even for an augmented giant such as Ashford. Newbury smiled. He had him this time. Digging deep for every last reserve of his strength, he thundered forward towards his quarry.

Ashford responded to this with calm acceptance. He turned away, stepping up carefully onto the raised lip of the roof. He seemed to be judging the distance to the bottom of the alleyway, but Newbury knew there would be nothing to see but a thick river of fog. Ashford inched closer to the edge.

Suddenly, Newbury got a measure of the man's intention. Ashford meant to jump. He bellowed across the roof. "No! Don't do it, man! You'll fall to your death!"

Ashford seemed not to hear him. With one last glance over his shoulder, the rogue agent leapt into the air.

Newbury darted towards the edge of the building in time to see Ashford's black, fluttering cloak billow out like an enormous wing as the man soared out into the gap between the two buildings, plummeting into the milky abyss. Surely the drop would kill him?

Newbury gave an involuntary wince at the sound of Ashford hitting the cobbles below. There was a sickening *crunch*—as of metal striking stone—a cry of pain, and then silence. Newbury sighed. It was over.

Newbury turned back towards Purefoy and the metal stairwell. He'd have to recover Ashford's body; first to verify his death, then to keep the matter out of the papers and the police reports. He kicked at the gravel, frustrated. He wanted to know *why*. What had driven this man—this former agent—to such murderous lengths? Had he really believed the secrets of Khemosiri would have granted him a new life? Newbury doubted that very much. But desperate men are often driven to desperate measures. He hopped down from the lip at the corner of the roof.

Then, to his amazement, he heard the sounds of someone shifting around in the alleyway below. There was a groan, followed by the ringing of tentative footsteps as Ashford, invisible in the thick shroud of vapour, evidently climbed to his feet and continued on his way.

"Oh no you don't!" Newbury rushed along the edge of the building, looking for some means by which he could quickly descend to ground level and continue his pursuit. If he lost Ashford now, he knew he risked losing him forever.

Newbury spotted the top of an iron ladder, similar to the one he had ascended a few minutes earlier, bolted to the side of the building below. He smiled with grim satisfaction. Another stairwell. The platform would be fixed to the wall, a storey below. He glanced behind him. Purefoy was watching him from across the rooftop, nursing bloodied hands that had been torn clinging to the iron railing. Newbury weighed his options. Did he risk the jump? Or did he waste valuable time on the ladder? He knew, with steady resolve, that there was only one answer to that question. He didn't look back to see if Purefoy would follow. Hopping up onto the stone lip,

Newbury casually stepped off the side of the building, his body tightening as he prepared for the drop to the platform below.

This time Newbury was ready for the impact and did not lose his footing, instead using his shoulder to take the brunt of his fall. It smarted painfully where it smashed against the hard railing, but he used the momentum to fling himself forward, tumbling down the first flight of stairs. He knew he would be black and blue by the morning, but he barely registered the knocks and scrapes as he dived headlong down flight after flight of metal steps towards the ground. His hands rasped on the worn metal as he slid from one storey to the other, his lungs burning with the exertion.

All the while, the prickly need for opium was a constant pull. He could feel his body craving the stuff. Once this was over, he promised himself, once he'd brought Ashford to justice, then he would attend to his own needs. For now, the needs of the Empire were far greater than his own.

In a matter of moments Newbury hit the ground, breaking into a roll to cushion his fall. Climbing to his feet, he glanced up at the side of the building to see if Purefoy had followed, but everything above was veiled in dense mist. Here, at ground level, the fog was beginning to pool, pulling a thick yellow curtain across the city, but it was still wispy enough to allow Newbury to get his bearings. He took in his surroundings. The alleyway stank of raw sewerage and rotting food. It was filthy, strewn with detritus, and outlet pipes gushed steam and dirty water onto the cobbles, drawn from the innards of the surrounding buildings. A feral cat was mewling loudly somewhere out of sight. Newbury attempted to dust himself down, to little avail. His suit was covered in a layer of grime from the chase across the rooftops and his roll across the greasy cobbles. Mrs. Bradshaw would be delighted.

Newbury glanced from side to side, searching for signs of Ashford. The rogue agent had reached the other end of the alley now, his back to Newbury. He was clearly in no hurry to get away. Newbury grinned. Ashford hadn't heard him on the stairwell and had incorrectly assumed that Newbury would be unable to continue his pursuit, following his leap from the top of the factory. It was an advantage that Newbury desperately needed. If the man could drop four storeys onto cobbles and survive, then Newbury needed all the help he could get. He didn't fancy his chances against such a monster in a fight.

Newbury set off after the hulking form of the former agent, keeping pace. He needed to ensure that he didn't inadvertently give Ashford a chance to lose himself in the warren of backstreets that crisscrossed this district of Regent's Park. The light was almost gone now and without his topcoat, Newbury could feel the damp air penetrating his clothes, filling his lungs like a cold compress. Nevertheless, he crept along the alley, clinging to the shadows, keeping Ashford locked in his sights.

They came to the mouth of the alleyway. Here the street opened up in both directions and directly ahead, across the main thoroughfare, the alley appeared to continue in a straight line for miles, disappearing into the dense fog. The street lamps had been diminished to nothing but diffuse, radial orbs that hung in the sky like a bizarre constellation. Newbury shivered. His face felt slick with moisture from the cold, damp air. The thoroughfare was busy; Newbury could hear the brisk chatter of people, the clatter of horses' hooves and the rude firing of numerous steam engines to his left. To his right, a street vendor was expounding the virtues of the latest edition of *The Evening Standard*.

Newbury lurked for a moment by the corner of a butcher's shop, watching Ashford as he stumbled along in the darkness. Perhaps the fall had caused more damage to Ashford's rebuilt frame than Newbury had first imagined. If he could surprise the man from behind, he might have a chance of taking him down. He needed to act.

Newbury broke cover, dashing forward to make a leap for the other man. Too late he realised there was a broken wooden pallet in the road, abandoned by a market trader and hidden by the low-lying vapour. He lurched to one side to avoid colliding with it, but his foot scuffed noisily on the paving slabs as he righted himself.

Ashford came to life. He spun round to catch sight of the Crown investigator charging him from the rear. Newbury could see no measure of emotion in Ashford's cold, red eyes; indeed, he had yet to properly catch sight of the man's face, concealed as it was beneath his dark cowl. But he knew there was steel and darkness behind them.

As he ran, he considered the fact that he was potentially rushing headlong towards his own death. He was surprised, therefore, when Ashford turned on his heel and fled, somehow managing to spring at least two feet into the air with each stride, his legs pumping furiously as he bounded along the thoroughfare at an incredible speed. He clearly wasn't spoiling for a fight.

For the briefest moment, Newbury stood, rooted to the spot, mouth agape in amazement. Whatever Dr. Fabian had done to Ashford, he was now more machine than man. No human being could ever propel himself along at such a pace.

Newbury, realising that he'd soon lose Ashford in the fog if he failed to act, took after the man, careening along the street behind him, dodging out of the way of confused pedestrians as he ran. He left a young man sprawling in his wake but had no time to stop to help him to his feet. Newbury's lungs burned, his muscles ached, and, with mounting frustration, he watched as Ashford gained more and more distance with every stride.

Realistically, Newbury knew that he could not keep up. He considered his options. If he continued to run, he would surely lose sight of Ashford. The man was tireless, and Newbury was already feeling the strain of the exertion. Ahead of him, a hansom cab clattered along the road and Newbury almost decided to leap aboard. But he knew that even a horse and driver would be no match for the reconstructed man.

He glanced over his left shoulder. There, by the side of the road, a young man was attending to one of the new steam-powered automobiles that had so taken London by storm during the past few months. Despite the risk involved, Newbury needed a means by which to keep pace with Ashford and, as far as he could see, there were no better options available to him at that juncture.

The furnace of this particular vehicle must have been well stoked, for it was belching black smoke from its twin exhaust pipes. The man, who Newbury presumed to be the owner, was dressed in a smart black suit with matching leather gloves and had pushed his flying goggles up on his forehead whilst he regarded his machine. Newbury skidded to a halt beside him. The man looked up, startled at the appearance of the detective.

"In the name of the Crown, hand over that vehicle!" Newbury thought about trying to show some identification, but knew he didn't have time.

"What? I . . . er . . ." The man looked flabbergasted. "Certainly not!" He looked Newbury up and down, unsure how to react to this sweaty, dishevelled man in front of him who, thickly covered with the detritus of his rooftop chase, was claiming to represent Her Majesty Queen Victoria. Newbury stepped forward and pushed the man to one side. He swung his legs up and over into the control pit of the vehicle and began fiddling with the controls, searching for the lever that would propel it forward. He could see Ashford gaining ground in the distance and he wasn't about to let him get away. Wiping his brow on his sleeve, he fiddled with a pair of matching brass handles and felt the front wheel turning from side to side beneath him. That was the steering mechanism then. Next, cranking a lever, he set the vehicle into motion with a jolt. It lurched forward, nearly knocking its owner to the ground. The man was shaking his fist and bellowing for the police, but Newbury chose to ignore the outburst. He didn't have time to engage in an argument with the man, nor to prove his credentials. The man would be suitably reimbursed for his trouble. Probably.

The engine roared and smoke billowed like a black stain from its rear end. The vehicle stuttered forward again, then hopped fifty yards along the road in short, jolting bursts.

Frustrated, Newbury glared after Ashford. He knew that
time was running out.

By this time the owner's cries had attracted a fair crowd
of onlookers and a brief glance over his shoulder warned
Newbury that a uniformed bobby had joined the fray. More
distractions he could do without. He concentrated on deci-
phering the controls. Tentatively, Newbury eased onto the
accelerator lever—which he assumed opened some sort of
pressurised steam valve—and the vehicle kicked into a forward roll. The wheels clattered bumpily against the cobbled
road, and he was jarred awkwardly as he continued to slowly
adjust the lever, introducing more speed. At the last minute,
he grasped for the brass steering knobs and swung the contraption out of the path of a middle-aged woman who was
crossing the road before him, apparently oblivious to the on-
rushing vehicle. He careened wildly to the right and then,
jamming the controls sharply to the left, was able to bring
the contraption back under some semblance of control. Other
pedestrians dived out of his way as he called out to them,
hurtling headlong after the rogue agent.

It was difficult to see anything in the soupy fog, but even
with his remarkable mechanical enhancements Ashford was
no match for the speed of the steam-powered tricycle. Ashford had managed to gain considerable ground, but if he was
intent on losing Newbury, he showed no signs of it. He remained in plain sight, hurtling along the main thoroughfare.
At any point he could have ducked down one of the other
alleyways or side passages and lost himself in the confusing
patchwork of backstreets that Newbury had seen from the
rooftops above. But he appeared to be heading somewhere

with intent, and Newbury wondered whether his pursuit had even registered as anything more than an annoyance. Regardless, he swung the vehicle in behind the man, undeterred. All of these questions could be answered later, once Ashford was safely contained in a cell.

The vehicle weaved wildly from side to side as Newbury tried to maintain control of the steering mechanism. It was an awkward, unwieldy device. The two brass knobs on the dashboard appeared to be rigged to a complex pulley system that changed the direction of the front wheel. The driver was supposed to manipulate the knobs, twisting one to turn right and the other to turn left. If he let them go, the vehicle would right itself, travelling directly forward in whichever direction the contraption was pointed. It was hardly elegant but it was relatively effective and Newbury soon had a measure of how to keep the vehicle from turning over. He continued to barrel along after Ashford, gaining on him with every passing moment. The back wheels of the tricycle were spinning at an incredible speed, bouncing on the uneven road and lifting the vehicle physically into the air, so that Newbury had to maintain a tight grip on the controls and jam his feet under the dashboard to prevent himself being thrown from the driver's pit with every movement.

Ashford had gathered a powerful momentum and was now knocking people bodily out of the way as he charged through the crowds, trying his best to outpace Newbury's borrowed transportation. Newbury had to swerve to avoid hitting the innocent bystanders that Ashford sent sprawling to the ground. It slowed him down, causing him to concen-

trate more on the road than his quarry. He supposed that
was Ashford's intention.

He considered his next move. He could try to mow Ashford down, but after seeing the man leap from the roof of a
four-storey building only to climb to his feet and walk away
unharmed, he doubted that the tricycle would be strong
enough to even knock Ashford over, let alone incapacitate
him whilst Newbury sent for help. Instead, as he drew closer,
Newbury released both steering knobs on the vehicle, wedged
the acceleration lever into its fully open position, and scrambled up into a standing position inside the driver's pit. Then,
taking the steering knobs again, he fought to manoeuvre the
vehicle alongside the sprinting Ashford.

Surprised, Ashford turned to glare at Newbury as he ran,
and Newbury caught his first real glimpse of the man's face. It
was an appalling sight. Ashford's flesh was grey and necrotic,
peeling away around the dark pits of his eye sockets, into
which two bizarre mechanical devices had been inserted to
replace his eyes. These were not makeshift instruments like
Aldous Renwick's, but smaller, more precision-made devices.
They bore the hallmark of Dr. Fabian.

Ashford's jawbone was exposed at the base of his right
cheek where a hunk of skin had been ripped away, either
during a ferocious encounter or simply because it had rotted
and sloughed away. The rest of his skin was pitted and raw,
and pink fluid seeped from open sores around his nose. Newbury was aghast. The sight of Ashford's face reminded him of
the revenant creatures that still prowled the dark corners
of the city. Ashford's rotting, cadaverous face was the mirror

image of these horrifying monsters—half alive, half dead—
yet his steely grimace betrayed a sense of purpose that was
lacking in the revenants. Behind those cold, glowing eyes, a
cool intelligence still lurked, and the thought of it made Newbury shudder. Then there was the smell; even here, standing
shakily in the driver's pit of a moving tricycle, he found the
stench of the man near unbearable.

Newbury was almost caught unawares when Ashford
made a lunge for him, swinging out with a powerful right
hook as he ran. Newbury attempted to duck the blow, causing the vehicle to swerve wildly. Luckily, the other man's fist
landed squarely on his shoulder, missing its target: his chin.
The power behind the punch was phenomenal, intended to
finish the matter, and Newbury wondered, as his shoulder
alighted with pain, what devices buried within the once-
human form of William Ashford had manufactured such a
blow.

Releasing his grip on the steering knobs of the tricycle
once again, Newbury brought his left arm up to protect his
face and jabbed out with his right, raining a series of blows
into the side of Ashford's head. Ashford seemed barely to
notice. He was still running, still keeping pace with the vehicle, and Newbury, bouncing along the uneven road, had to
stoop to regain control of the steering mechanism before
the tricycle swerved from its course and he lost control altogether. His options were running out. He could pounce on
the running man and try to bring him down, but the risks
were far too great: if he missed, not only would he lose Ashford, probably for good, but he would risk his own life. The
speed at which he was now travelling was such that he would

be dashed against the cobbles unless he aimed with the ut-
most precision. Given the circumstances, that seemed unlikely. Instead he grabbed for the left-hand steering knob,
twisting it sharply and causing the vehicle to veer dramatically to the left. He pitched forward as the tricycle slammed
into Ashford's legs.

Remarkably, Ashford did not topple over as anticipated.
The tricycle rebounded, tipping to one side and almost spilling
Newbury out into the street. He clutched desperately for the
steering knobs and tried to right the contraption as it skittered
off to one side. He fought with the mechanism, balancing
the front wheel as best he could. The tricycle glanced off a
newspaper salesman's wooden table and the salesman threw
himself to the ground as his stand collapsed and plumes of
paper flew into the air. It was all the opportunity that Ashford
needed. He veered off sharply to the left, mounting the pavement and darting towards the entrance to Portland Road
Underground Station. He hurtled down the steps towards the
platforms below.

"Damn it!" Newbury gave a howl of frustration, swinging
the tricycle around in pursuit. He jammed the acceleration
lever down, opening the valve to its limit and building up a
head of steam. The vehicle shot forward, bouncing crazily
over the kerb and up onto the footpath. He made a beeline
towards the entrance to the Underground. He couldn't let
Ashford get away. He'd come too far.

Newbury closed his eyes and pointed the tricycle at the
stairwell. He shot forward. The vehicle breezed over the top
of the stairs, soaring into the air as its momentum carried it
forward in a long arc down towards the darkness of the

station below. Newbury realised he was holding his breath, waiting for the impact that seemed to take forever to arrive. He was shaking, adrenaline coursing through his system.

The trajectory of the small vehicle was such that Newbury was never going to clear the bottom steps. The undercarriage of the tricycle collided brutally with the stone steps, cracking open with an enormous jolt. For a moment, Newbury honestly believed he was going to die. He opened his eyes to see one of the back wheels spinning away, and realised with horror that the furnace had cracked open, spilling burning coals in a hot trail behind him as the vehicle continued to skid down the stairs. Water, too, was gushing out of the tank, slopping across the steps and causing the hot coals to fizz noisily as they were doused. He clutched uselessly at the controls, finally realising that, to survive, he had to get out of the skidding vehicle quickly. The wreckage reached the bottom of the stairs, but continued to slide forward across the tiled floor of the station, leaving devastation in its wake.

The frame of the tricycle had buckled, and Newbury was practically hanging out of one side, his shoulder only a couple of feet from the ground, as the remnants of the machine continued their long slide across the floor. Wriggling his legs free, Newbury allowed gravity to take its course. He fell out of the ruined tricycle, his shoulder jarring painfully against the hard tiles. He slid to a stop, watching the wreckage of the machine slide away from him towards a nearby wall. His legs had come out of the machine twisted, but intact. He straightened himself out on the floor, surprised that he hadn't been seriously mangled in the crash. Around him, scattered coals still glowed with amber warmth and he suddenly became aware that people were screaming.

A young blonde woman rushed forward to help him to his feet, murmuring platitudes. He smiled at her, accepted her arm, scrambling to his feet and looking around for Ashford, who was getting away. The man moved fast, faster than Newbury could possibly conceive, but Newbury could see his black cloak fluttering along one of the tunnels as he barged his way through the crowd of passengers and he could hear the clanging footsteps of his heavy boots ringing out in the confined space.

Ignoring the burning pain in his shoulder, Newbury flexed his back and followed the sound. He hurtled along the white-tiled tunnel, pushing his way past rows of blank-faced civilians who stared at him, dumbfounded, as he forced a path through their ranks. Newbury had his prey in his sights once more. Things would end here.

Newbury charged along behind the rogue agent, skipping down a series of tiled steps towards the platform. His face was set with grim determination, but he nonetheless almost laughed out loud when he saw a faded, sepia-coloured bill pasted on the tunnel wall, advertising The Mysterious Alfonso's miraculous stage show. He swept past it, driving onwards.

Newbury burst out onto the platform a moment later, only to see the other man leap down onto the train tracks and dart towards the dark mouth of the tunnel at the end of the platform. Newbury ran to the edge of the platform and threw himself forward, jumping high into the air and coming down hard on Ashford's shoulders. Ashford twisted, stumbling on the steel tracks and toppling under the weight and momentum of the Crown detective. He banged his head, hard, against the curved tunnel wall, and it rang out with the sound of metal striking stone. There were shouts of alarm from the passengers waiting on the platform edge. Newbury heard a whistle blow. The police were on their way. Far from being concerned, Newbury was relieved. If he could only detain Ashford long enough, perhaps the bobbies would be able to help him restrain the man.

The metal runners of the track were hard against Newbury's back. He was growing weary now, but Ashford, seemingly indestructible, was already climbing to his feet. Newbury mustered his remaining strength. He jumped to his feet, punching at the rogue agent. His fist connected with the other man's chin, slamming his head backwards, but the blow was almost enough to incapacitate Newbury, whose hand felt as if he had driven it into a lump of solid iron. He glanced at his knuckles. They were shredded, bleeding, and sore.

Unperturbed, Ashford lurched forward, using the flat of his hand to slap Newbury hard in the chest. The blow was enough to immediately knock him off his feet. He called out as he scrabbled on the ground. "Ashford! What's the matter with you, man? Have you lost all sense? Give it up!"

Ashford's voice, when he spoke, was a grating, metallic whine. Every word was like a fragment of song. It sounded as if it were being squeezed from a clutch of miniature organ pipes in his throat, like a chorus of a hundred people all speaking the same words at once. But there was no emotion in it, no sense of the person Ashford had once been. The sound seemed to echo from a wheezing vent in his chest. It was cold and inhuman, just like the man himself. "Cease and desist, Sir Maurice. I don't want to hurt you." He stepped cautiously over the train tracks to loom over the prone Newbury. During the tussle, however, Ashford's long cloak had become tangled in the steel runners. As he stepped forward, the cloak tore open, momentarily exposing the horrifying figure underneath.

Newbury gasped in shock. "My God! What did they do to you?" The words caught in his throat. Newbury knew now the origin of that detestable stench. Ashford was less than half the man he had once been; less than half the *human being* he had once been. His body had been ravaged and then reassembled from a shocking assortment of flesh and brass, like a patchwork monster made real, a nightmare marriage of metal and blood. What flesh was still clinging to his brass exoskeleton was rotten, decaying, sloughing away in great hunks. In places, large patches of leather had been stitched indelicately to this remaining flesh in an attempt to give some semblance of skin, but that had only succeeded in exacerbating the man's monstrous appearance. Newbury had no idea whether this was a part of Dr. Fabian's original design or whether Ashford had tried to repair himself during his five-year exile in St. Petersburg. It mattered not. The result was grotesque.

The man's torso was perhaps the most disturbing aspect of all. The exposed skin of his chest was pustule filled and puckered around a large glass porthole that filled the space where his ribcage had once resided. In the murky depths it revealed, Newbury could see the grey muscle of the man's

heart beating in time with a flickering electrical charge that
shocked it at intervals, like the precise ticking of a clock.
Fluid burbled along four clear pipes that sprouted like giant
antennas from his shoulders, curling around the back of his
head and disappearing into the depths of his skull. The brown,
murky liquid appeared to be pumped around his brain cavity
by a further device buried deep inside his chest. His face
was just as alarming. The tiny lenses of his eyes flicked back
and forth over Newbury's prone body, their bright lights glowing in the darkness. When Ashford opened his mouth, Newbury saw that his teeth had decayed to black stumps. What
hair was left hung in long straggling clumps, and the flesh of
his scalp was torn, revealing the horrific juxtaposition of yellowed bone and metal plating underneath.

Newbury shuddered. So this was the disgusting genius of
Dr. Fabian, taken to its extreme. He could hardly believe
this had been sanctioned by the Crown. He pitied the man
despite himself. Newbury had no idea how Ashford could go
on living like this. It was a form of waking torture, that every
minute his intellect should be housed in this wreckage of a
frame, this parody of a human body. No wonder the man
had been driven insane. Newbury was amazed it had not
happened sooner. Indeed, he felt a kind of sickening sympathy for the man, an understanding of the desperation that
had led him to this point. Science had betrayed him and so
had the Crown. His life had been extended beyond the
point of death, certainly, but Newbury doubted it was a life
worth living. And now Ashford had turned to the occult,
hoping to find a means to restore himself, to reclaim the life
that once was his. It was tragic and Newbury was repulsed,

not only by what the man had become, but the means by which he had become it. Nevertheless, Ashford had committed two murders, and whatever happened there in the train tunnel, he needed to be brought to justice.

Ashford stooped low, as if to reach for Newbury's ankle. The detective rolled, using his momentum to spring up onto his hands and knees and then twist into a standing position. He fired out a blind kick in Ashford's general direction in an attempt to keep the other man at bay whilst he found his bearings. To his surprise, his foot hit home, although it appeared to have little effect other than giving Newbury some extra leverage to right himself. Again, Ashford tried to slap at Newbury with the palm of his hand, swatting at him as if he were a buzzing insect, but Newbury was able to skip away, watchful that his feet did not become entangled in the rails. He could not work out what Ashford was trying to achieve with such bizarre tactics. Surely a trained agent, a man who had lived rough in a foreign territory for over five years, would have developed more comprehensive combat manoeuvres? Especially a man with such power. If he were able to plant even one successful blow to Newbury's head or gut, Newbury knew it would be the end of him. He'd fought machines before, but this was an entirely different proposition. No, it was almost as if, with these flat-handed attacks, Ashford was genuinely trying not to wound him, instead choosing to parry Newbury's ineffective blows and disable him with the least amount of effort. Perhaps he was telling the truth? Perhaps he really didn't want to hurt him?

Confused, Newbury backed away. By now, people were shrieking loudly on the platform, but the combatants paid them no heed. Newbury wiped his sleeve across his brow. "Ashford . . . you have to come in with me. They'll hunt you down. *I'll* hunt you down, unless you stop me. Put an end to this now."

The half human, half machine rounded on him. Newbury found it difficult to get a measure of the man's facial expression; all subtlety was lost beneath the layers of peeling flesh. His voice chimed in its strange metallic tones. "I cannot."

Newbury sighed. "Then I fear I must detain you myself."

Launching himself from the tunnel wall with a kick, Newbury pounced on Ashford. It was then—too late—that he registered with horror the nature of the screams from the platform. People were shouting a warning. A train was coming. It was hurtling towards the station, heading directly for the mouth of the tunnel where Newbury and Ashford were now locked in combat.

Newbury landed on the other man, reaching for his neck. Ashford, however, was ready for this, and instead of fending off Newbury's attack, he grappled with him, grabbing him firmly around the waist. Newbury fought frantically against his captor, but Ashford was too strong and held him, pinned, as the train hurtled into the station. There was no way either of them could escape the roaring oncoming engine.

But then Ashford moved like lightning. He lurched to one side, heaving Newbury up and into the air and spinning him up onto the platform, where he landed with a painful thump. It happened just in time. The engine's brakes squealed loudly as the driver caught sight of the figure in its path, but it was too late for Ashford. The train slammed into him with a sickening thud, lifting him off the ground. His body was flung around the curved prow of the engine, trapped between the side of the tank and the tunnel wall. Newbury watched in shock as Ashford's elbows scraped against the dirty tiles, his metal bones on the hard ceramic setting a shower of sparks flying. The train screeched to a halt. Ashford, now partially obscured by the shadows of the tunnel, turned to regard Newbury, his red eyes flashing. Then, without saying another word, he eased himself out from between the engine and the tunnel wall, clambered around the front of the train, and dropped to the ground. Newbury could no longer see him but heard his footsteps disappearing into the depths of the Underground.

Newbury collapsed onto his back, breathing heavily. Ashford had saved his life. There was no doubt. The man had purposefully pushed Newbury out of the path of the oncoming train, at great risk to himself. It was only due to Dr. Fabian's enhancements that Ashford had managed to survive the encounter at all, if survive was the right word.

Sighing, exhausted, Newbury took in his situation. The civilians on the platform had formed a large circle around him, their expressions ranging from horror to admiration and everything in between. Newbury couldn't help but laugh out loud when, a moment later, a startled-looking Purefoy pushed his way through the press of people, rushing to Newbury's side. The boy looked dishevelled, tired, and anxious. "What happened to him? Where is he?"

"He got away."

"What . . . I . . ." Purefoy looked devastated. He glanced

down at his bloody hands, as if refusing to believe that everything he had been through that evening had been in vain, that all of their efforts had led to nothing but failure.

Newbury felt quite the opposite. "I should say, Purefoy, that I'm beginning to think I may have been wrong all along." Newbury glanced in the direction of the tunnel mouth, where Ashford had disappeared into the murky darkness. "That man saved my life." He looked up at the quizzical face of the young reporter. "Perhaps he isn't our killer after all."

CHAPTER

17

Veronica stirred into wakefulness.

Her eyelids were heavy and she had the bizarre notion that she was floundering underwater, her senses dimmed, her breathing thick and uncomfortable. She gasped for air, striking out with her hands, encountering only hard, rough panels in all directions. Her heart was racing. Probing her lips with her tongue, she found that they were dry and sore. She'd clearly been asleep for some time.

She wrinkled her nose. There was a cloying scent in the air, a heady aroma of flowers. The smell seemed somehow familiar, somehow comforting. It made her feel as if she wanted to curl up and go back to sleep, to lose herself in its floral embrace. She fought the urge, knowing

somewhere in the back of her mind that it would be dangerous to allow herself to slip away again. She had no idea how
long she had been unconscious or where she was. She tried to
get her bearings, but her mind proceeded at a glacial pace.
There was a light breeze brushing against her left cheek. She
turned towards it, allowing it to play over her face. The fresh
air was cool and sobering.

Slowly, unsure what to expect, Veronica peeled open her
eyes. *Darkness*. Nothing but impenetrable darkness. She
tried to remember where she was, what had happened to her
that she might find herself in this bizarre, uncomfortable
place. The memories came to her in stuttering bursts of images and colour. *Alfonso. The trapdoor. The box*. Suddenly it
all came back to her. She was still trapped in the wooden casket under the stage! Thankfully, she was still alive. But where
was the magician? Why had he left her here for so long?

Veronica felt around with her hands. The casket was resting at an angle so that she was no longer standing, but lying
on her back; the fibrous, untreated wood rasped against her
skin, even through the substantial fabric of her clothes. She
tried to sit up but there was not enough room and she caught
her head with a painful knock. Bracing herself, she lifted her
arms above her head, pushing at the roughly hewn panel
above her. There was no give. Shuffling a little, she tried instead with her feet, stamping down at the floor beneath the
bundled rags. To her surprise, the panel creaked slightly ajar
under the pressure. Frantically, she kicked down with her
heels, forcing the wooden floor to snap open on stiff metal
hinges. The rags spilled out beneath her and the dim impression of light seeped in. She shuffled out, using her legs and

hips to writhe free, her hands pressed against the sides of the casket to stop her from sliding downwards too quickly. The angle was awkward, but soon her feet struck hard stone tiles, and a moment later she spilled out of the box.

She sprawled on the cold floor and filled her lungs with clean air in an effort to clear the stench of chloroform from her nostrils. She sat up and the room swam. Her mind was still woozy, her reactions slow. At some point during the battle with Alfonso, she had lost her hat. Her long brown hair had come unpinned, cascading across her face. She brushed it to one side, tucking it behind her ear.

Veronica glanced around to get a measure of the room. She was deep underground, in a basement or cellar. Flickering gas jets danced in a series of glass bowls mounted at intervals around the walls. The walls themselves were bare, constructed from blocks of ancient grey stone, and the floor was comprised of red clay tiles laid in a neat herringbone pattern. They were cold and damp beneath her, and she shifted slightly, swaying as she almost lost her balance. The drug had affected her more than she had initially realized.

Near to where she was sitting, a long wooden workbench had been laid out, filling much of the room. It was covered in papers and unusual ephemera. Beyond that, against the far wall, was a strange-looking chair covered in a spidery assortment of brass arms and surgical instruments. She tried to focus on it, but her eyes betrayed her. She closed them for a moment, almost slipping back to unconsciousness, then snapped them back open with a start. Nervously, she glanced from side to side. She appeared to be alone.

Hauling herself into a more upright position, she turned

back to examine the wooden casket she had tumbled from. This was clearly the room in which the "disappeared" women were deposited during the show, after Alfonso had triggered the mechanism on the stage that caused them to fall into the box. It was ingenious. The young woman was carefully selected from the audience to ensure the correct size and shape, and when her weight was introduced to the casket it caused the device to begin rolling down an incline beneath the stage on rails or metal castors. The woman was trapped, of course, but her cries would be muffled by the shouts of the audience. Soon the rags soaked in chloroform would be enough to sedate her, putting her to sleep for—potentially— a number of hours. Until, Veronica supposed, either Alfonso or some secret aide could collect her from the casket and rouse her, or worse. The women who were set free would be so confused by the drug that they would never be able to ac- curately recall what had happened to them, and their the- atregoing companions would undoubtedly coax them into forgetting the matter with talk of their bravery and the mys- terious nature of their disappearance. The woman would briefly become the talk of her social circle, and for that alone she would make a point of dismissing any temporary discom- fort she may have suffered. After all, she had come to no dis- cernable harm.

That wasn't the case, of course, for all of the women. Veronica still had no notion of what fate Alfonso had in store for those young women he decided not to set free. Perhaps this room would reveal the truth.

Shakily, Veronica climbed to her feet and approached the workbench, resting her palms upon it whilst she waited for her dizziness to pass. Clearly, because there was no show that evening, there had been no one waiting to receive Veronica upon her impromptu arrival in the room. She wondered what had become of Alfonso. The man had had every opportunity to finish her off whilst she lay there drugged and incapacitated. Perhaps he had lost his nerve, or else he had assumed the chloroform would keep her sedated longer and was busy elsewhere in the building. Whatever the case, she was grateful to be alive.

She glanced down at the workbench. It was littered with bizarre paraphernalia. Large sheaves of paper covered in an elaborate language she did not recognise; vials full of a thin brown fluid and stoppered with bulbous corks; medical equipment, including scalpels; a pair of tan elbow-length leather gloves; pencils; and an assortment of small ancient Egyptian artefacts. She gasped in surprise. *Ancient Egyptian*. She picked up one of several little statuettes. It was an effigy of a mummified Pharaoh, made of clay and impressed with three neat rows of hieratic script which she could not read. It was certainly very old, of that much she was sure. She dropped it on the table. Nearby, a similar statuette had been broken in half. The two pieces lay side by side, revealing a hollow inside. She supposed that whoever had broken the ancient artefact had removed something from inside.

"My goodness," she whispered, realisation dawning on her. The presence of Egyptian artefacts could be no coincidence. This had to have something to do with Sir Maurice's investigation of the murder of Lord Winthrop. Did Alfonso have a hand in that, too?

She moved around the workbench, studying the other

artefacts. There were a number of similar ushabti, each of them broken, their hidden contents now removed. Someone— Alfonso, she presumed—had been conducting a detailed study of the objects. Many of the papers contained scrawls that deciphered the inscriptions, as well as strange mathematical drawings: stars within circles and other pictograms that reminded her of the contents of Sir Maurice's Chelsea library. She drew a deep breath and wiped her brow, then shook her head, trying to clear the drug-induced fogginess. It occurred to her, belatedly, to check the room for an escape route and get away. She needed to find Sir Maurice.

She glanced around. Her vision was still hazy. Across from her, on the other side of the room, was a door. She began edging around the table towards it, then stopped in horror. There, in the corner, a few feet to the left of the door, was one of the most ghastly sights she had ever encountered: a pile of female corpses, cast against the wall and left to rot.

The women had been piled haphazardly like discarded marionettes. Flies buzzed chaotically around their slack-jawed faces. Veronica felt bile rising in her gullet. There were five, perhaps six corpses. She'd had no idea the situation was this severe. Only two women had been reported missing in the area to date, but Alfonso had clearly been much busier than that down here in his secret slaughter-house. She was appalled by the sheer magnitude of his perversion. What had he done to the women? How could he continue to work down here with their dead, unseeing eyes fixed on his every movement? And the smell!

Veronica fished around in her jacket pocket for a handkerchief. Finding one, she held it over her mouth and nose and hesitantly stepped towards the sickening heap of bodies. She could not believe the lack of respect with which the women had been treated, even in death. They remained fully clothed, at least, although whatever *had* been done to them had clearly been appalling. What she could see of their faces showed frigid signs of terror. These women had stared death directly in the face.

Veronica crouched beside the nearest corpse. The woman was young—twenty, possibly—with long pretty curls of strawberry blonde and full pink lips. Her eyes had once been blue but were now a grotesque shade of milky grey. She was on her front, partially buried beneath the corpse of an older brunette woman. One of her arms was dangling free. Veronica grimaced as she turned the head slowly from side to side. A line of dark, dry blood ran from the woman's forehead down the side of her nose. Veronica followed this bloody trail, finding, with dismay, that the origin was a small hole in the woman's forehead. Flinching, she probed it with the end of her finger. It was about the size of a pen nib and was located at the very centre of the woman's forehead. Veronica frowned, checking another woman. The marking was exactly the same. A neat hole drilled for an unknown purpose directly through the bone and deep into the skull cavity. Clearly, Alfonso had been intent on extracting something from inside the women's heads.

Veronica moved around the pile of corpses. She was glad that the heady scent of the chloroform was still affecting her sense of smell. Some of the bodies were days old—weeks, possibly—and had begun to decompose. Their waxen flesh had become bloated and saggy, their eyes putrefying in their open, staring sockets. Their terrified, bloodied faces were an alarming juxtaposition to the gaudiness of their colourful evening clothes. Veronica felt an intense burst of sadness for these young women, for how their lives had been so drastically shortened, snuffed out in such a foul manner. She felt anger too—anger and a need for retribution. She had to stop this. She had to stop it before one more woman fell into the clutches of this terrible man. She knew now that the image of these dead women would be forever burned into her memory, their silent mouths crying out for justice. She knew also of her own predicament, and the fact that—still dazed from the chloroform—she remained in terrible danger. Nevertheless, she felt a need to understand the meaning behind the shocking slaughter of these women.

Veronica examined another of the bore holes, this time in the skull of a brunette. What was their purpose? There was clearly nothing sexual about the deaths; the manner in which the women had been discarded, carelessly, suggested that Alfonso was in no way objectifying the women. He didn't appear to *desire* their deaths, to treat them with any reverence or passion. No, it was as if he considered them animals, there to be experimented upon in his laboratory. The bodies were purely carcasses, immaterial; once he had extracted whatever it was he needed from their heads, he could leave them there to rot whilst he went about his business.

Veronica strode across the room to where the bizarre chairlike device stood against the wall. She needed to focus on something else, to blot out the horror of the dead women. She fought another wave of dizziness, holding on to the edge

of the workbench for support. *The chair*. She needed to con-
centrate.

Its frame was wooden and roughly hewn, with locking
iron bands where a person's wrists and ankles could be fixed.
Likewise, an adjustable band was attached to the backrest,
perfectly placed for clasping a person's head. At the centre
of this band was a small opening, and Veronica realised with
a shudder that this was the guide through which the holes
were bored into the women's skulls. Rust-coloured stains
around its edges confirmed that blood had been spilled on
the metal.

Rising from the back of the chair was a large multijointed
brass arm, which curved up and over the seat like a scor-
pion's tail, terminating in a fine drill bit. It gleamed in the
low light of the gas jets. The mechanism had two handles,
rods with rubber grips attached partway along its length so
that a person standing before the chair could easily manipulate the drill bit, moving it back and forth and adjusting the
height and alignment. The drill itself appeared to be powered pneumatically; cables stretched from the drill housing
and along the length of the brass arm, disappearing around
the back of the machine, where they snaked towards a large
grey cylinder of compressed air. Beside this, a glass bell sat
atop a chamber containing two brass pistons, which were
currently at rest. Tubing curled from two bungs at the top
of this glass dome, connecting with two smaller mechanical
arms, one holding a long-bladed scalpel and the other some
kind of bizarre suction device.

It was a terrifying machine. It looked to Veronica like an

engine designed for torture, but she knew it had to have an even more sinister purpose.

Beside the chair was a low wooden trolley which held a number of metal trays. One of these was covered with a scattered array of glass syringes, another with a series of small vials, each of them filled with what looked like the brown fluid she had seen in the vials on the workbench— some chemical or substance extracted from the skulls of the dead women. She realised that this liquid, whatever it was, must be the end product of whatever terrible process Alfonso was conducting down there beneath the theatre; the reason for the entire setup. Veronica felt sick to her stomach. She found it hard to reconcile the understanding she had developed of Alfonso's character with the concept of this monstrous laboratory. Yes, he was a thuggish brute, and egotistical, but this? Did he really have the gumption and the knowledge to pull off an operation such as this? And what of the links to Lord Winthrop and the ancient Egyptian artefacts? Surely Sir Maurice would have made the connection by now if it were obvious. She glanced around the room once more. No, this was the work of a scientist, not an illusionist. For the first time she considered the fact that Alfonso may only have been part of the story. Perhaps he was working with an accomplice. Perhaps—

There was a sharp pain at the back of her skull as she was coshed from behind. She crumpled to the floor instantly, the metallic taste of fear on her tongue, and once again slipped away into darkness.

CHAPTER

18

Newbury ached in every fibre of his being. He'd taken a number of serious knocks during his pursuit of Ashford, particularly when he'd driven the tricycle down the stairwell to the Underground station, and he knew he was lucky to be alive. His knuckles were bleeding and he had a painful red burn on his left forearm, where a hot coal from the tricycle wreckage had scorched his flesh during the crash. He suspected other minor injuries too, but he wouldn't have time to examine himself in the cheval glass for some hours.

And yet for all that, he had failed to capture Ashford once again. He lambasted himself because the chase had resulted in nothing substantial. He supposed he was able to take some solace from the fact that he now had a better understanding of the man, even if it had left him feeling more confused than ever. The certainty he had felt earlier, the sinister character of Ashford that he had constructed in his mind, all of that had now dispersed, become disassociated with reality. Now they were playing a different game altogether, and Ashford had shown his hand. Firstly, the rogue agent had never struck him during their battle on the tracks; aware, perhaps, of his own incredible strength, he had refused to risk Newbury's life with a direct blow. Secondly, at great risk to himself, he had thrown Newbury out of the path of the moving train. If it were not for that, Newbury would certainly be dead. It seemed to the Crown detective that Bainbridge had been right all along: Ashford was not the killer that Newbury had presumed him to be. Newbury had much to consider.

"Help me up, lad." Newbury smiled gratefully as Purefoy offered his arm, enabling him to heave himself to his feet. His back creaked. He straightened up, groaning at his protesting muscles. "What kept you?" he said, grinning.

Purefoy was still trying to catch his breath.

Newbury brushed his unruly hair back from his face. "I believe, Purefoy, that you could be a great deal of help in bringing this situation to a happy conclusion. Can I count on you?"

Purefoy's lips curled into a wry smile. "Absolutely."

Newbury glanced at the gathered crowd. Passengers were now disembarking from the stationary train, which sighed loudly at the platform. The driver had climbed down from the engine and was on the tracks, examining the scorch marks on the tunnel wall where Ashford's brass skeleton had been dragged across the tiles. He looked confused and not a little shaken by his experience. He seemed puzzled that there was no sign of a body on the rails.

Newbury knew that he needed to lose himself in the crowd before people began identifying him to the authorities, making it difficult for him to fade out of sight. He didn't have the time nor the inclination to answer the raft of irrelevant questions that would be put to him before he would be able to prove his identity or call in the aid of Sir Charles. He clasped the reporter on the shoulder. "Right, Purefoy. Let's get out of here."

They set off, forcing their way through the press of people. Newbury had a determined look on his face as he tried to ignore the flashes of pain from his sore limbs.

They soon found their way out of the Underground station, mounting the stairs, passing the wreckage of the tricycle, which was now swarming with police constables and transport officials in neat black suits. They were holding back the crowd of onlookers who had gathered around the wreckage and talking to witnesses in hushed tones. Newbury recognised the woman who had helped him to his feet after the crash and turned away, surreptitiously shielding his face from view.

Above the station, the street was dark and foreboding. Newbury drew his jacket closer, coughing a little at the syrupy vapour. He turned to the young reporter, who stood anxiously beside him, awaiting instruction. "Purefoy. I need you to fetch the police. Go directly to Scotland Yard and tell them that Sir Maurice Newbury has sent you to speak with Sir Charles Bainbridge. Charles is a good man. Fill him in.

Give him all the details of what has occurred here this
evening and then have him send his men round to Arbury
House. They need to secure Blake's apartment."

Purefoy smiled. "Of course." He hesitated for a moment.
"Surely you're not going after him again? The killer, I mean."

Newbury grinned. He took his pocket watch from his
jacket and held it for a moment in the palm of his hand,
studying the elaborate face. It was approaching seven o'clock.
"Me? No, I have an appointment with a beautiful young
woman."

Purefoy laughed. "Then may I suggest, Sir Maurice, that
you first of all find an opportunity to change your attire."

Newbury glanced down to see that his suit was now torn
and filthy, spattered with mud, grit, and oil. His green eyes
twinkled. "I think, my young friend, you make an excellent
point."

Purefoy's advice, whilst perceptive, proved not to be timely.
Newbury knew that if he were to take a cab to Chelsea he
would miss his appointment at Kensington with Miss Hobbes.
He was not prepared to leave her waiting for him once again.
So instead, bedraggled as he was, Newbury saw Purefoy into a
cab before hailing his own and instructing the driver to ferry
him directly to Miss Hobbes's apartments. She'd seen him in
worse states than this, after all.

The hansom clattered on through the effluvium-laden
streets towards Kensington. The fog had descended swiftly
and looked set to entrench. Newbury watched through the
window as figures flit past, ghostly shapes in the hazy yellow-

grey, like spirits attempting to escape the grasp of the afterlife. Every building, every corner, the mouth of every alleyway suddenly, in the sickly whitewash, became the haunt of
otherworldly things. Shapes hulked in the thick miasma,
taking on new roles: an avenue of trees became a row of forlorn soldiers standing to attention; a solitary flower seller became an ethereal ghost, haunting the abandoned streets in
search of fellow spirits. Newbury imagined shapes in the fog
just as he had since he was a boy, but these were no longer
the lucid imaginings of a child. Newbury now knew that there
were real monsters out there in the pale darkness, both human and otherwise. He had the scars to prove it.

Newbury sighed, and leaned back against the soft leather
of the seat. He hoped the fog would lift. If not, he was sure
that Mrs. Bradshaw's respiratory condition would return. It
had affected her badly throughout the winter months, and
he was concerned for her well-being. Besides, he knew he
couldn't live without the woman. She was a miracle. Unfazed,
undaunted, she catered to his every whim.

Newbury glanced again at his pocket watch. It was now
ten past the hour. He imagined Veronica in her Kensington
rooms, sitting before the fire, awaiting his arrival. He suspected
that she would be cursing him, in her own gentle way, for his
tardiness. But he would be there soon, and hopefully they
could take a moment to relax a little before continuing their
investigations. He needed a brandy. He needed *more* than a
brandy, but for now, a dose of alcohol would help to quell his
burning desire for the poppy.

Tonight he would give himself over to his assistant, enjoy
the pleasure of her company and attend to the details of her

own case. After a drink, they would repair to another carriage, take the short journey to his Chelsea lodgings—where he would wash and change into his evening wear—and together they would enjoy a fine meal at a restaurant on The Strand. He needed that.

Newbury's mind was still a whirlwind as he considered the Egyptian affair. He no longer fancied Purefoy for the crimes and was now more resolute than ever that he should take the young man under his wing. He'd arranged to call for the reporter in the morning, with Miss Hobbes in tow.

He must have dozed off in the back of the cab, for what seemed like only a moment later, he was awoken by a brisk knock from the driver on the roof of the cab. He rubbed blearily at his eyes and sat forward, glancing out of the window. The hansom had come to rest outside of Miss Hobbes's apartment. Newbury clambered out, paid the driver, and realised that he must have lost his hat at some point during the afternoon's excitement. Shrugging, he followed the path to the house and rapped loudly three times on Veronica's front door. Moments later, he heard footsteps creaking on the loose floorboards of the hall. The door opened enough for the slightest sliver of light and the eye of Mrs. Grant, Veronica's housekeeper, to appear in the opening. It took a moment for her to recognise Newbury in such a dishevelled state, but when she did, she flung the door open widely and ushered him in, offering him platitudes.

"Oh, my poor dear. Come on in. You look like you could use a pot of that Earl Grey you're always asking for. I keep some out the back for when you call."

Newbury smiled. Mrs. Grant was typically the most stoic

of housekeepers, rarely finding the occasion to even smile or raise her eyes to greet Miss Hobbes's visitors. Something about the state of his apparel that evening had moved her, though. He smiled warmly. "Now Mrs. Grant, fear not. I am quite well, really. But I *am* running rather late for an appointment with Miss Hobbes, who I gather had plans to meet me here this evening. Will I find her in the sitting room?"

Mrs. Grant frowned. She placed her hands on her hips, shaking her head in an exaggerated fashion. "Indeed not, Sir Maurice. Indeed not. Miss Hobbes has yet to return from the museum. I had hoped, upon seeing you, that you would be in a position to put my mind at rest regarding her good health." She looked him up and down once again. "I expected her over two hours ago, but I fear there has been no word."

Newbury nodded, thoughtful. "Hmmm. Well, I should not presume to fear too heartily, Mrs. Grant. It's not a long time to be missing. Perhaps she has simply been delayed in this dastardly weather."

Mrs. Grant nodded, but she did not appear to be pacified by this remark. "I take it you plan to wait for Miss Hobbes here then, Sir Maurice?" She looked hopeful. He nodded absently, then followed her into the sitting room, where she bid him to take a seat. "I'll just go and pop that kettle on the stove." She disappeared through a side door to the kitchen.

Newbury paced the room. What had become of Veronica? He recalled their conversation earlier that day, during which she had informed him of her intention to visit the family of the most recently missing woman. But that had been hours ago. Surely she must have returned to the office at the museum following her interview? He frowned. He feared he knew all too well what may have become of his assistant. He had appealed to her sense of duty and asked for her commitment that she would not venture to the Archibald Theatre to confront Alfonso alone, yet he had every suspicion that she had done exactly that. Whilst he was occupied chasing Ashford across the rooftops of Regent's Park, Veronica had most likely taken matters into her own hands. Why else would she not be here to meet with him? Newbury knew how badly she had wanted to speak with him regarding this matter, and she would not have been late for some trivial reason. Indeed, she certainly would have sent word ahead if she had found herself delayed.

Perhaps his night of relaxation would have to wait. He quit the sitting room, walked the length of the hallway until he reached a door that he presumed led to the kitchen, and then called for Mrs. Grant. After a minute, she appeared at the door, looking a little perplexed. "The tea will be with you presently, sir."

"Ah, no thank you, Mrs. Grant. I have a sudden notion of where I might find Miss Hobbes." The housekeeper's face lit up. "If I could dare put a stop to your tea making, I'll take my leave and see if I can't track her down and put your mind at rest."

Mrs. Grant smiled gratefully. "Thank you, sir."

Newbury bid her good evening, leaving instructions that should Miss Hobbes return home in his absence, he would see her the following morning at the office. Then, buttoning the front of his mud-streaked jacket, he left the house and went in search of transportation to Soho and the Archibald

Theatre, hoping that Miss Hobbes had not put herself in the path of danger.

The theatre was shrouded in darkness when Newbury hopped down from the cab a short while later. Upon seeing the bills pasted in the windows announcing that the show had been cancelled, Newbury almost stopped the cab driver as he trundled off down the road, thinking that perhaps his intuition had been wrong on this occasion. But knowing that he would be unable to rest without first establishing Miss Hobbes's safety, he decided to investigate further. A cancelled show would not have been enough to halt his headstrong assistant.

He tried a door and found it locked, but was surprised to find the second one he tried open. Evidently someone had been neglectful of their duties, or else the theatre was indeed inhabited that evening. Newbury crossed the large foyer in the dark, looking for signs that Veronica may have passed that way. There was nothing. The place was deserted.

Mounting a short flight of steps, Newbury pushed aside the curtain and entered the auditorium proper. Here, things were very different indeed. The only light was coming from a bright electric lamp on the stage, illuminating a grisly diorama of the type that, unfortunately, he was finding himself growing increasingly accustomed to. The body of a man—Alfonso, no less—lay spread-eagled on the stage, one of his own sabres protruding rudely from his chest. Beside him, a small round table had been overturned, and a top hat lay nearby. Surrounding the body was all the assorted paraphernalia of the show, most of it undisturbed. Newbury had no idea what had occurred here, but he sincerely doubted Veronica could be responsible for such a brutal act. As passionate as she was about discovering what had happened to the missing women, she would never lower herself to this. If she had come here, it would have been to apprehend the man, not to murder him in cold blood.

Hesitantly, taking care that there was no one watching from the shadows, Newbury passed down the long flight of wooden steps between two rows of seats and made his way slowly towards the stage. He hopped up and crossed to where the body lay. It was an appalling scene. The man's face was struck with terror, frozen in the throes of death. He looked battered and bruised, as if he'd put up some resistance. There was little blood, but Newbury assumed the blade had entered through the man's chest and pierced his back, so that the blood would have seeped out beneath him, probably dripping through the cracks between the floorboards. He tested the hilt of the weapon. It was stuck fast. Alfonso had been run through with such vehemence that the tip of the sword was buried deep in the wooden stage below. It was clearly a sadistic death, executed with great pomp. It was as if the theatrical nature of the setting had informed the manner of the death and the body had been left here on display.

Newbury glanced around, squinting in the harsh electric glare of the stage lamp. It was clear there had been a scuffle of some kind from the way the table had been overturned, but it didn't look as if Alfonso had been given much opportunity to defend himself. Newbury noted with interest that a small hatch lay open on the stage, right near where the table now rested. He moved closer to take a look.

Two hinged flaps had dropped aside, giving way to a fair drop. He looked around for any trigger that may have caused the hatch to spring open. Perhaps Alfonso's body was resting upon a pressure plate of some kind? He peered into the opening. He smiled grimly as it occurred to him that this was how the magician had affected the disappearing act. Alfonso was finally giving away his secrets in death. If Veronica had seen this mechanism, then perhaps she had gone through it to the underground. That would be as good a place to start as any.

Intrigued—and not a little disturbed—by the sight of yet another body, Newbury set out to search for his wayward assistant.

CHAPTER

19

When Veronica came round again, she felt sick with dizziness. The pain at the back of her head was like a hot lance inside her skull. She groaned and tried to move, realising with horror that her ankles and wrists had been bound. She opened her eyes and blinked blearily as they adjusted once again to the dim light. She was slumped with her back to the wall, facing the door and the pile of corpses at the other side of the room. A figure was standing by the central table, hurriedly collecting the scattered ephemera that covered it and throwing it untidily into a medicine bag. The man, who was tall and thin, perhaps a little under six feet, had his back to her. He was dressed in an immaculate grey suit with a crisp white collar. His hair was well kept and was beginning to turn a startling silver-grey, though it was still spotted with freckles of light brown.

The man turned to face her when he heard her shuffling. He had a handsome face with an aquiline nose. It was marred, however, by a deep, puckered scar that ran from just above his left eyebrow to his left cheek, blighting his eye. The eye was milky and blind, the colour of London fog, although a series of tiny red lights around the cornea suggested the work of a master craftsman, most likely Dr. Fabian or one of his pro-tégés. Otherwise, his skin was pale and unblemished, like a white mask. His fingers were long and bony. Veronica realised with shock that she recognised the man.

"Aubrey Knox." She croaked.

The man smiled almost imperceptibly. "That's *Doctor* Aubrey Knox to you, Miss Hobbes." His voice was like silk, smooth and warm and full of grace. He was impeccably well-spoken, and every word had the ring of perfection. She knew he was an Eton man and had once been the most charming of gentlemen. He clearly retained this affectation.

Veronica tried to sit up, but her bonds prevented her from gaining purchase on the tiles. She glowered at the villain who must have trussed her up in this manner. "So it was you. All along, it was you." Knox inclined his head in acknowledge-ment, a smile curling his lips. Veronica glanced at the pile of bodies in the corner. How cold must he be, how dead inside, that he could work in this room, even stand there smiling, while aware that he was responsible for those women's deaths? She could find no empathy for the man, no understanding of what might have driven him to this terrible series of acts.

She met his gaze. He appeared to be watching her with amusement. "What do you need them for?," she asked. "What is it you're trying to do?"

Knox's face changed, his mood darkening. He crossed the room to where she was bound and raised his arm, slapping her hard across the face with the back of his hand. Despite herself, Veronica cried out. She could feel tears welling in her eyes and her cheek smarted painfully. She forced herself to look him in the eye, her expression defiant.

"Miss Hobbes, I'd have thought you'd know better than that. This is not some ridiculous penny dreadful that we're playing out. I'm not about to reveal all of my carefully laid plans to you, now that you're finally here and close to death. Suffice it to say that you will exit this world as ignorant as you are now, and I shall take some measure of satisfaction in that." Grinning, he turned, crossed the room to the long table, and continued silently with his work. Watching him, Veronica realised that he was not indiscriminately taking everything from the workbench as she had at first assumed, but rather a selection of items, including the little vials of brown fluid and the ancient scrolls of papyrus.

Veronica bit her lower lip, searching for a reserve of strength. She twisted her wrists, trying to wriggle free, but the binds had been expertly tied, her ankles likewise. She was deeply afraid of what the renegade doctor was planning to do to her. It was unlikely, from what she knew of the man, that he would grant her a clean and simple death. That would not be enough of an amusement for him.

Veronica had been warned about Knox, of course, in her briefings about Newbury. Her Majesty and her closest aides had taken pains to describe the horrors that the man had committed in the name of progress and their need to ensure that Newbury did not follow a similar path. Knox had become obsessed with the occult and a desire to achieve extended life and pursued the cause with little concern for morality or human suffering. He saw himself as a progressive, the man who would finally learn to wed science with the arcane. That path had led him away from the Empire, and despite the best efforts of Her Majesty and her extended network of agents, he had not been seen for over two years. He was a danger, yes, but he was also an embarrassment: a worm that had turned, a betrayer deep in the bosom of the Empire. Victoria wished to make an example of him.

Veronica watched him warily. Knox had almost finished gathering up the scattered artefacts and papers into his bag. He glanced over his shoulder at Veronica, a wry smile on his lips. "So, tell me of Sir Maurice. I understand he's quite the dashing man about town." Veronica remained silent. Knox laughed. "I understand also that his taste for narcotics is dwarfed only by his taste for occult literature. I should dearly like to meet the fellow." This was a taste of the charming Knox again, the gentleman. Veronica understood that he lived by a code, but it was a code of his own devising, not one based on an innate sense of right and wrong. It was a code driven by insanity and a desire for self-perpetuation. Watching Knox now, Veronica could hardly believe the stunning outburst of violence he had demonstrated just a short while before. Her cheek, however, was a stinging reminder. She glared at him.

"Sir Maurice is twice the man you ever were, and twice the agent too."

Knox laughed. "What loyalty the man inspires! How interesting. One imagines he keeps you by his side like a pet dog, there to complement him with doe-eyed looks and pretty frocks. Personally, I imagine you to be far prettier on the inside." He paused. "I shall enjoy examining your brain." Knox moved around the table to place his medicine bag by the door. "I'm sure it would pain Sir Maurice terribly to know of your current predicament, my dear Miss Hobbes. Indeed, if I had more time, perhaps I could have made more of the circumstances. A shame." He gave a small, polite cough into his fist. "I must admit that in the end I'm disappointed, Miss Hobbes. I'd heard great tales of your derring-do, of your fiery passion. I'd been led to believe that you were perhaps even a worthy opponent. Regrettably, I find you full of righteous indignation. You are nothing but another insipid young woman, a prim and proper society girl who finds herself afraid and out of her depth. What has become of the young woman who aided in the retrieval of the Persian Teardrop from Milan? Who brought an end to the killing spree of the Liverpool Witch? Pushing papers behind a desk in a museum? What would your sister Amelia say of your decline?" He shook his head. "Victoria used to know better."

Veronica attempted to lurch forward, but succeeded only in toppling onto her side, prone on the floor. "Do not speak of my sister." The words were weighted with vehemence.

Knox was laughing now. "Idle threats, Miss Hobbes. Idle threats. It surprises me that Amelia did not find it appropri-

ate to warn you of this little encounter. Does she not speak
to you of the future?"

Veronica's eyes widened. How did this man, this terrible
man, know so much about her and her sister? She watched
him as he crossed the room, collecting the elbow-length
leather gloves from where they rested on the workbench. His
eyes flashed, and Veronica knew that her time was almost up.
With all her might she struggled against the bonds that held
her, but she knew it was useless. Knox had her now, and before long, she would be consigned to the sorry heap in the
corner with the other dead women. She wondered whether
she too would have a small hole burrowed through the centre
of her forehead. The thought made her shudder. She was
close to panic, her soundless lips frozen wide with fear.

Knox pulled one of the gloves over his wrist and wriggled
his fingers dramatically. Just as he was about to follow suit
with the other hand, there was a loud crash from somewhere
above them.

Knox looked up, as if he expected to somehow be able
to see through the ceiling to whatever had made the noise
above. Veronica assumed it must have been Alfonso—
presumably Knox's accomplice—treading on the creaking
boards of the stage. Knox, however, became suddenly flustered. He peeled the glove from his fingers and threw it on
the table, a frustrated look on his face. There was another
bang and a muffled shout. Veronica was unable to identify
the words or the voice. But something about the situation
had startled Knox. His plans had changed.

Knox snatched up a dirty rag from amongst his belongings

and approached Veronica, his expression fixed. He intended to gag her. Veronica forced her jaw shut and turned her head away from him. But it was a matter of mere moments before Knox, evidently an old hand, was able to force his fingers roughly inside her cheeks and prise her mouth open long enough to shove the rag inside. She did her best to push it out with her tongue, but it was no use, so she choked on its oily, dirty fibres.

Knox threw her one last, sneering look, his milky-grey eye flicking over her face, then turned and stepped through the door, disappearing into the passageway beyond.

CHAPTER

20

Newbury dropped to one knee, running his hands around the edges of the open hatch in the stage. It was dark below and there were no moveable lamps with which he could examine the trapdoor more closely. Nevertheless, he could see that the drop was around eight feet and terminated in two metal runners that appeared to slope away to the right, dipping under the stage and disappearing further underground. Clearly, during the disappearing act, Alfonso would position the woman over the hatch and then foot the paddle, dropping her swiftly into the hole beneath. Newbury guessed the victim would land in some kind of padded cart or box, which would then roll away on the tracks, depositing the woman somewhere else in the building.

It was ingenious, a masterpiece of engineering, and having seen the illusion performed, Newbury knew just how effective it appeared to the onlooker. He rubbed a hand thoughtfully over his chin. The strange thing was that the trap had been triggered at all. The weight of Alfonso's body had clearly opened the hatch, but what intrigued Newbury was the fact that the cart itself was missing from beneath the stage. The mechanism had been used but had not yet been reset. It could, of course, have been a simple case of tardiness, but in the back of his mind, Newbury feared that if Veronica had come to this dismal place, she may have discovered firsthand exactly how the women were being whisked away.

Newbury paused, suddenly alert. Somewhere in the shadows, off to the other side of the stage, he thought he had heard a footstep. He waited.

Nothing.

He got to his feet. There! Not a footstep, but something else. The rasping sound of a sword being drawn carefully from a scabbard. Newbury felt himself stiffen. There was someone there, watching him, in the shadows. Someone bearing a weapon. He looked around for something he could use to defend himself. The rack of Alfonso's swords was off to one side, near the source of the sound. There was the blade sticking out of the magician's rigid corpse, but Newbury knew that it would take him a moment to tug it free, and in so doing he would alert whoever was lurking in the shadows to the fact that he was aware of their presence. That could leave him dangerously exposed. He considered jumping into the hatch, but with the mechanism already triggered he did not know what to expect at the other end and did not want to find himself trapped in an underground shaft with no means of escape. His options were limited. Reluctantly, he decided to call his opponent out. Unarmed, he was choosing a dangerous course of action, but he wanted whoever was lurking offstage in plain view.

"If you're going to remain there in the shadows, I'll feel compelled to carry on with my investigation. I don't have the time to stand around waiting for you." His voice echoed around the empty auditorium. He heard a man chuckling in the darkness, then a figure emerged, drifting out of the shadows like a ghost adopting corporeal form. The man strolled boldly forward, his sword held, unusually, in his left hand. The blade glinted in the harsh electric light.

"Bravo! Bravo! I admire your panache." The man stopped as he entered the circle of light cast by the electric lamp. "So, you're Newbury! How I've wanted to meet my successor."

Newbury blanched. His successor? Then this was the much maligned Doctor Aubrey Knox. But how did he fit into the picture? Was he the one behind the missing women? And was it purely a coincidence that he and Ashford should surface in London at the same time? There had to be a connection. Perhaps Ashford really was looking for revenge. Perhaps that's why he was here, after all this time. But now was not the time to ponder that. Instead, Newbury met his opponent's gaze. "Doctor Aubrey Knox. I can't say it's a pleasure to make your acquaintance."

Knox laughed. "We're not so different, you and I. Not so

different at all. You shouldn't listen to everything that others tell you, Newbury. Perhaps it is only your misguided sense of duty that sets us apart."

Newbury shook his head. "No! I am nothing like you at all." He was curious to see how the situation would play out. He knew very little of his predecessor. He wondered if the man would live up to his fearsome reputation.

Knox came forward, further into the light. "You sound like Charles. How is the old boy?"

Newbury glanced across the stage at the rack of swords. His response was terse. "Well enough."

Knox grinned. "Yes, I always thought the job would wear him down. Still, I suspect he'll hold on until the bitter end. Wouldn't be like Charles to throw in the towel." He paused, smiling. "Oh, and Miss Hobbes sends her regards."

Newbury's curiosity about the man ignited into rage. Knox was taunting him. He clearly knew what had become of Veronica and more than likely had a hand in it. Newbury sprang into action. He rushed forward, catching Knox off guard so that he could batter the other man's sword arm easily to one side and bring his elbow up sharply into the pale man's face. Carrying forward with his momentum whilst Knox was dazed, Newbury darted towards the rack of swords, grasped one by the hilt, and swept it out from its wooden notch. He spun around, presenting the point of the weapon to Knox.

There was little more than three feet between them. Knox allowed his sword arm to idle casually by his side. He was laughing, spitting blood. "So, perhaps she *is* more than a pet, after all."

Newbury decided that enough was enough. He could not allow this man to slight Veronica in such a manner. He would wound him, force him to reveal what he had done with Veronica, and then take him in. Or, if it came to it, he would run him through. He lurched forward, the point of his sabre darting towards the other man's breast.

Knox moved like lightning. One minute, he was standing nonchalantly, eyeing Newbury and jesting with him, the next his arm had flashed up in a blindingly quick parry and he was facing the Crown detective, his wiry body poised for the interplay of the two weapons. He was still laughing as Newbury thrust again and once more was parried. Newbury had fenced in his youth, but Knox, it appeared, was an expert. He sent Newbury's thrusts wide each time with only the smallest flick of his wrist. He barely seemed to draw breath whilst doing so. Newbury recognised the tactic. Knox was trying to tire him out. He could not let that happen. Ceasing his series of ineffectual thrusts, he drew back, his sword at the ready.

"Oh, come, come, Sir Maurice. Haven't you the stomach for a good fight? I was quite enjoying our little tête-à-tête." He shifted again, reaching forward with his blade, his foot stamping on the floor as he threw his weight behind the movement. Newbury felt a flash of pain on his right cheek. As Knox recovered his poise, Newbury realised that blood was flowing freely from a cut on his face. He hadn't even had chance to react. He was clearly outclassed.

Knox smiled. He had a superior air about him, as if he were enjoying the encounter, knowing full well that he currently had the upper hand. When he spoke he was almost

genial, as if he and Newbury were nothing but two old ac-
quaintances sharing a conversation at a gentlemen's club.
"Fight me, Newbury! I can see the fire behind your eyes. You
want to know what I've done with her, don't you?"

Newbury, composing himself, rocked forward onto the balls
of his feet. He kept his blade low, ready, waiting. He would not
rise to the other man's taunts. "Tell me where she is, Knox, and
I shall let you live." His voice was a low growl.

"Hmmm. Quite a dilemma. I didn't have you down as the
sort of chap to make idle threats, Newbury. That's a crashing
disappointment." He was sneering now, his words dripping
with sarcasm. Newbury hoped he was coming to the end of
his game. If Knox had no time for idle threats, Newbury had
no time for cat and mouse. He may not have been able to
demonstrate finesse with a blade, but what he lacked in
theatrics, he gained in brute force and spirit.

"There is nothing idle about the threat, Knox."

Knox whipped out his blade, aiming high, but Newbury
caught it easily, their swords ringing out as the two men thrust
and parried frenetically. Searching for a means to gain the
upper hand, Newbury eyed the stage behind the doctor. The
hatch was still open. If he could manoeuvre the fight just a
few feet closer to that narrow opening, he might be able to
send Knox crashing backwards into it. The difficulty came in
circumnavigating the body of Alfonso, spread-eagled on the
boards between the two fighting men and the hole.

Newbury met Knox's gaze as their swords crossed, staring
deep into the other man's eyes. He repressed a shudder. The
man seemed to revel in the fight. Newbury recognised himself in that and it repulsed him. It was like looking into a

mirror and seeing his twisted reflection glare back at him, all sense of his humanity removed. He understood Charles's words now and they angered him. He would not allow himself to become a monster like the odious wretch he now faced. Newbury knew not to cross the line that made him human. Knox appeared to relish the opportunity to do so.

Knox's left eye twinkled, and Newbury watched the tiny red pinpricks of light describe a circle as whatever device had been buried inside the blinded organ turned, tightening Knox's focus. Newbury once again admired Dr. Lucien Fabian's work.

The two men broke apart, dancing carefully around the corpse of the dead magician. Newbury made a concerted effort to drive the other man back. Knox stepped backwards over Alfonso's legs, placing the body between them. Their swords hovered above the unseeing corpse. "So, what of your accomplice, Knox? Did he offend you in some way?" Newbury glanced briefly at the dead man.

Knox shrugged. "He'd outlived his usefulness. Besides, he was always a conniving toad."

"But he sourced the women for you through his stage act? And you cherry-picked the ones you wanted? For what purpose?"

Knox lips curled in amusement. "Newbury, if you want to discuss it we can down our blades and smoke a cigarette together like gentlemen. Otherwise, let us put an end to this encounter. It's becoming tedious." The man's flippancy was astonishing, but it provided Newbury with the opening he needed. He slashed out with his blade, causing Knox to lurch backwards to avoid having his chest opened in a streak from right to left. Still, the tip of the sword tore through his jacket and shirt, opening a wide smile in the fabric. As Newbury reached the end of the movement, he flicked the blade upwards, using the tip of his sword to catch the hilt of Knox's sword and whip it clean out of his hand. The weapon sailed across the stage, clattering loudly to the boards.

To Knox's credit, he barely allowed the situation to faze him. Whilst Newbury was recovering from his swing, Knox reached for the blade that he had left buried in Alfonso's chest and pulled it clear of the corpse. Blood sprayed in a shower as he brought the weapon to bear. Alfonso, then, had not been dead for long.

Blood was still trickling down Knox's chin where Newbury had caught him earlier with his elbow. Yet he still seemed to be enjoying the encounter, the rush of the battle, the opportunity to taunt the man who was so similar to him in so many ways. Newbury's face, in turn, was set with grim determination. With every second that passed, with every one of Knox's arrogant remarks, he grew more and more anxious for Veronica's safety.

Knox was now only a few feet from the open hatch in the stage. Newbury pressed on with a series of deft, forceful strikes. He thrust relentlessly at Knox, not attempting to strike the man, but to drive him backwards, forcing him to parry constantly, which distracted him from where his feet were taking him. Newbury knew he was leaving himself open to a counterattack, but at the same time, he was succeeding in forcing the other man back towards the hole. Stepping over Alfonso's body, trying desperately not to lose his footing, he pushed forward.

The two men fell into a smooth rhythm: thrust, parry, thrust, parry. The steel blades clanged noisily. Slowly, they inched towards the open hatch. Newbury was growing hot and tired. The rooftop dash and the fight in the Underground had taken it out of him and he knew his endurance would soon reach its limit. And the need for opium was a persistent itch, growing in intensity with every moment that passed.

As Knox neared the lip of the hole, Newbury took his chance. Using the flat of his blade to batter Knox's sword wide, he leapt into the air, kicking out, his foot connecting hard with Knox's breastbone. But the man had been expecting as much. Pivoting around on his left foot, he swung himself out of danger, narrowly missing the hole. He came to rest at a right angle to Newbury, his back to the empty auditorium. He was chuckling. "Really, Newbury, if you'd expected to—"

Knox's next words were lost as Newbury's fist thundered into his face. His head snapped to the side and Newbury stepped closer, dropping his weapon so that he could rain blow after blow on the other man with both fists. Knox sputtered and tried to raise his sword but Newbury beat him back, providing no opportunities for him to retaliate. Spittle and blood flew into the air as Newbury pounded Knox's face. He knew he did not have the finesse of a swordsman, but at Oxford he had taken to the ring and he was quick with his fists. Knox staggered backwards, heading towards the edge of the stage. Newbury saw his opportunity. He stepped in close again and aimed a powerful jab at Knox's kidney. As Knox bent forward with a rasping gasp, Newbury shoved him over the edge.

Knox tumbled backwards, crying out as he struck the ground. Newbury dashed forward to see. Knox was trying to gather himself. He shuffled backwards on his hands and feet, still clutching the sabre tightly in his fist like a talisman. He looked dazed and his face was raw and puffy from the battering. His good eye darted from left to right, as if he were trying to work out from which direction his assailant would come next.

Newbury could find no sympathy for the man. He wanted only to know what had become of Veronica and to bring the criminal to justice. At the back of his mind, however, he recognised that he also needed to prove, to himself and to Charles and the others, that he and Knox were not as alike as they had feared. He hopped down from the stage, standing over the rogue agent as he pulled himself into a sitting position, his back resting against the front row of seats. He rested there, panting for breath.

Newbury stepped closer. He needed to bind the man, to stop him from escaping. But he also needed some answers.

Knox had not given up, however. As Newbury leaned over to reach for Knox's collar, Knox flicked out his left hand, stabbing at Newbury with the point of his sword. Newbury was ready for him, though. He leaned back, grasping the hilt of the sword and following through with Knox's move so that the sword swept in a tight arc in front of him. He forced the blade down, hard, driving the point of the weapon through the outstretched palm of Knox's right hand, spearing him to the wooden back of the nearest seat. Knox howled in agony as Newbury pushed the sword deeper, pinning the doctor in place.

Twisting Knox's other hand free from the hilt of the sword, Newbury looked down at him in disgust and slapped him hard across the face. "Where is she?" Knox was laughing again, blood bubbling from the corner of his mouth. Newbury struck him again and repeated his question. "Where is she?"

Knox looked up at him, his strange, milky eye regarding the Crown investigator with something approaching admiration. "In the basement. She's still alive."

Newbury straightened. Grasping at his own collar, he pulled his necktie free then stooped, using it to bind Knox's free hand to a post between two seats. In this state, the man had no chance of escaping before Newbury came back for him.

Wiping his brow on the sleeve of his jacket, Newbury went back to the stage and staggered up the wooden stairs. He would find a route through the network of underground rooms beneath the theatre and from there, hopefully, find Veronica.

Glancing once more over his shoulder at the pitiful figure of Aubrey Knox—who lay with his arms outstretched, the sword blade pinning his hand to a seat, his body propped awkwardly against the front row—Newbury knew that he would soon have more answers. But one thing was certain: Knox was not the fearsome monster that Charles had claimed him to be. For that, he was more than grateful.

Sighing, Newbury slipped into the shadows behind the curtains.

CHAPTER

21

Veronica fought ineffectually against her bonds. The gag was dry and choking and tasted stale with oil and grime. She tried her best to spit it out, but to no avail; she could gain no purchase on it with her tongue. Knox had known what he was doing when he'd forced it so deep into her throat. She wondered where he had gone—perhaps to confront Alfonso?

Veronica tried to move into a more comfortable position, taking the weight off of her shoulder. Beneath her, the cellar floor was cold and damp with condensation. It was clear the laboratory was a makeshift operation, a temporary workshop, and that Knox did not spend a great deal of time inhabiting it. From what she'd observed—the cancelled show, the rush to gather his work into the medicine bag—she assumed he was now clearing out. Either he had what he needed or he had discovered that she and Newbury were on his trail.

Veronica glanced at the door, but her eyes kept flitting back to the disturbing heap of corpses just beside it. She couldn't take her eyes off the faces of the dead women. She thought it was perhaps the worst sight she had ever seen, worse even than all of those burnt, twisted cadavers she'd discovered on the wreck of *The Lady Armitage*, or the drained, desiccated corpses that she and Newbury had encountered at Huntington Manor. No, it was the heartlessness that disturbed her most, the careless manner in which the bodies had been used and tossed into the corner like commodities, like discarded meat. She hated the thought that a human being could be reduced to that. It was this, more than anything else, that offered her insight into Knox's cold, calculating mind. He was truly a monster. He would do anything for his own ends.

Veronica kicked at the ground in frustration. Knox knew what he was doing, that much was clear. The bonds with which she'd been tied were unbreakable. She could see no means of escape.

She heard footsteps in the passageway outside and flinched. Knox was returning, which meant that she likely did not have long left to live. The footsteps approached the door and it creaked open. It was hard to see the figure in the gloom of the passageway, but it was a man in a suit. He stepped forward into the room.

Her heart leapt. Sir Maurice! She tried to call out but was only able to offer up a muffled squeal. Newbury turned at the sound and saw her there, sprawled on the floor. He rushed to her side. Lifting her head, he reached inside her mouth and gently extracted the gag. Veronica gasped for breath. "Sir Maurice! How?"

Newbury smiled softly, the relief evident on his face. "Well, Miss Hobbes, it seems I have provided you with ample opportunity to save my life of late and you have done so on more occasions than I care to count. I felt this would be the appropriate opportunity to redress that balance."

"Oh, you foolish, brilliant man." Veronica smiled warmly, and Newbury swept her up in his arms, cradling her to him. He held her there for what seemed like an age. She could feel his heart hammering hard in his chest, his breath becoming shallow.

He brushed her hair tenderly away from her eyes where it spilled loose over her face. "I thought I'd lost you."

Veronica gave the briefest of nods. "I thought I'd lost me too." She expected him to chastise her, but he only held her close, trying to make her feel safe once again. She wanted to sink into that embrace, to be away from this horrible place with its stench of death and decay. Newbury knew her so well, knew where to find her in a crisis, knew everything about her . . . except . . .

She had to put it out of mind. There was still work to be done.

Newbury held her for a moment longer before placing her gently back on the ground so that he could attend to her bonds. She looked up at him, noticing the state of his suit. "Whatever happened to—"

"Later. First we have to free you from these damnable knots." He reached into his pocket, searching for a penknife.

"What of Knox?" Her voice was hesitant.

Newbury gestured upwards with his head. "Up there. He won't be going anywhere for a while. Except a cell and then perhaps a hangman's noose."

"And Alfonso?"

"Dead."

"What! Did you . . . ?"

Newbury shook his head. "No, Knox did."

Veronica looked thoughtful as Newbury held her ankles and cut the cord that bound her with a sharp flick of his wrist, slicing easily through the thin silken rope. He did the same to the tightly knotted cord around her wrists.

"He must be clearing out. He seemed close to finishing down here." Veronica felt suddenly tired.

Newbury slipped the penknife back into his pocket and got to his feet, dusting off his hands. He glanced around the room. He stopped, in startled horror, when he saw the pile of female corpses in the corner. "What the devil?"

"'The devil' is right. Knox is dangerous: cold, calculating, and murderous. He'll stop at nothing to get what he wants. He's always been the same."

Newbury nodded absently. He paused for a moment, moving over to the nearest corpse and stooping. "What's this? Holes in their heads?" His face wrinkled in disgust. Newbury grasped the woman's head and turned it slowly from side to side, examining the bizarre wound.

Veronica shrugged. "He's obviously used that device over

there to bore a hole in their skulls. I think he's been extracting a secretion or hormone from their brains."

Newbury straightened and turned to look at the chair that Veronica was indicating. He marched over to it, grasping one of the large mechanical arms and swinging it round so that he could see the deadly drill bit. He ran his fingers over the tiny pistons that controlled the movement of the arm itself, seeming to admire the craftsmanship. Then, with his fingertips, he followed the trailing cable that ran from the end of the arm in its wide loop around the back of the device. A moment later he emerged from the rear of the chair, a small glass vial clutched in his hand. It was filled with a brown, brackish fluid. He held it up for Veronica to see.

"Hmmm." Newbury's face was unreadable. "But what exactly was he extracting? And more importantly, why?" He looked at the bottle in disgust. "Let's see if we can have this analysed." He checked the stopper and then slipped the small glass bottle into his jacket pocket.

He crossed to the workbench, where a smattering of artefacts was still in situ: a few drawings, some scraps of paper covered in scrawled hieroglyphs, and the broken shells of three ushabti. Newbury's eyes widened as he recognised the items. He stared at the table for a while before picking up the remnants of one of the statues. "This is one of the pieces I saw at Lord Winthrop's house! Have you seen them? They've been broken in two. Knox must have been after the contents. My God." His voice was a low growl. "It was Knox all along." He cast the broken idol back on the tabletop. "The Osiris Ritual. That's why he's here, now, in London." He turned to her. "Miss Hobbes, that mummy—the screaming mummy that

Winthrop found in Thebes—was the remains of an ancient priest, a priest who was mummified alive and cursed by the pharaoh for attempting to extend his life in the physical world. I'll wager these idols contained documentation of his discoveries, that these poor girls gave their lives to provide some sort of ingredient for the ritual. Just like the women in ancient Egypt. He's been copying Khemosiri!" He slammed his fist on the workbench, realisation dawning on his face. "And here I was chasing Ashford all across London. Ashford would most likely have led me to Knox, given half a chance. It all makes sense now. Ashford saved my life earlier today. He may be rogue, but he's not a killer. He's out for revenge. He wants Knox."

Veronica sighed. "I should have realised. If I'd helped you sooner . . . if I'd been there. Knox was always your man, Sir Maurice. He was always obsessed with extending his life. It's the motivation that drives him, that gives him purpose, that makes him kill."

Newbury responded to this with a mystified expression, seemingly unable to take his eyes off of her. She realised, in a panic, that she may have said too much. She wanted so much to tell Newbury the truth about her secret affiliation. Had she told him the information about Knox as a means of revealing it? No. She had done so because the information was fundamental to the case: Newbury needed to know that Knox—not Ashford—was responsible for the deaths. She had done it for the good of the Empire, or so she wanted to believe. But somehow she still felt hollow inside.

Doubt was beginning to gnaw away at her. What was Her Majesty's intention in setting Sir Maurice on Ashford's trail?

Had she known about Knox in advance? She'd clearly only given Sir Maurice a perfunctory understanding of the situation, but to what end, Veronica was unsure. As an agent, she could hardly question the monarch's actions, but she resolved to develop a better understanding of the part she herself was playing in the Queen's machinations. She refused to be party to the undermining of another agent—especially Sir Maurice—whatever goal the Queen had in mind.

Unsure what else to do, Veronica joined Newbury at the table and began sifting through the remaining papers, looking for anything that might help explain her outburst. She felt her cheeks flush and silently cursed herself, though Newbury did not seem particularly fazed. He moved around the table, continuing to sort through the remaining pieces of ushabti.

Veronica was struck by a sudden flash of inspiration. "The bag!"

"What bag?"

"The bag by the door. The medicine bag. Knox was sorting through the items on the table here, stuffing them into his bag, grabbing vials full of liquid, papers, artefacts—clearly, the results of his experiments."

Newbury turned, looking for the bag. "What—where is it?"

"There, by the door. I thought I saw him set it down before he left." Veronica checked again but did not see it. She shrugged. "He must have taken it with him."

"Hmmm. We'll find it up there by the stage, no doubt. It'll be all the evidence we need to link Knox to the murders." He studied Veronica intently. "Can you walk?"

"Yes, yes, I'm quite well."

"Are you sure?"

"Sir Maurice . . ." Her voice was stern. Newbury met her gaze. He nodded once, then extended his arm, which she took.

"Come on. Let's find that bag and go and fetch the police. It's time to get Charles here." They left the dank room, stepping out into the passageway. Newbury guided Veronica along it carefully, allowing her to lean on him as he crept through the warren. It was long and narrow and must have wound under half the theatre. Veronica had no real notion of where they were in relation to the auditorium above.

After a short while, their feet scuffing on the rough stone floor, Newbury dipped his head under a stone archway and took a left turn, leading her to a wooden door. He had obviously come this way earlier. "Through here." He ushered her to the wooden stairwell. She mounted the bottom step.

Newbury cleared his throat, causing her to pause and look back. "Veronica"—she noted the use of her first name—"can you face him? After all of this, I mean?"

"Who, Knox?"

"Yes. He's quite incapacitated, of course. But if you'd rather leave by another exit, I wouldn't think anything less of you." He looked concerned. "I could see you to a carriage."

"Sir Maurice, I appreciate that very much. But it won't be necessary. I'm quite ready to face him again."

He nodded and they continued.

The stairs creaked as they made their way slowly towards the light. A moment later they emerged, squinting, from a small wooden trapdoor just off to one side of the stage. After hours spent in the gloomy depths of the basement, Veronica blinked blearily as her eyes adjusted to the sharp electric light. She righted herself on the stage, then turned to watch Newbury pulling himself out of the opening. She offered him a hand as he steadied himself. She could see where a large red carpet had been rolled away to reveal the secret trapdoor. The cellar in which Knox had set up his temporary workshop had, she supposed, once been a storage room for props or a space for the actors to rest or affect a quick change of costume as they traversed the tunnel beneath the stage, quitting the boards at stage right, only to reappear a short while later at stage left. She shuddered as she considered the way in which Aubrey Knox had repurposed it.

Newbury strode forward onto the stage, stopping to sweep up another sword from Alfonso's rack, clearly not underestimating the resourcefulness of the rogue doctor. Veronica turned her head, catching her first glimpse of Alfonso, his arms and legs outstretched, his chest covered in a dark crimson stain. His mouth was open and his eyes were staring at the rafters.

"Oh God," was all she could murmur. She had seen so much death that day already. Despite Alfonso's terrible role in Knox's plot, despite what he had done to her, she could not feel relief at the sight of his rigid corpse. She averted her eyes.

"Veronica! Here!" She turned to see Newbury throw the sword down upon the stage in frustration.

She ran to his side. "What is it?"

"Knox. He's gone." He indicated the row of seats just to the left of the stage. "I left him there, pinned to the chair, a blade driven through one hand. I trussed his other with my necktie. How the devil did he get away?"

Veronica glanced around, looking for any indication that the man may still be in the theatre.

"He's long gone. And no doubt his medicine bag has gone with him." He turned to Veronica, and she could see the anger burning behind his eyes. "You were right. He's clearing out. He has what he wanted and now he'll disappear, just like he did all those years ago. I underestimated him. I'm a ruddy fool."

Veronica sighed. She couldn't bear to see Newbury torturing himself in such a manner. "You saved my life. That has to count for something."

His face softened. "Miss Hobbes, it counts for everything. But it doesn't alter the fact that I allowed him to escape."

Veronica put her hand on his arm. "Let's check the rear exit."

Newbury nodded, but it was clear that he did not expect to find anything. He followed Veronica, alert, as she crossed the stage and took the steps down to the main auditorium two at a time. As they passed the seat where Knox had been bound, Veronica could see where the blade had pierced the wooden seat back, shredding the fabric and staining it with blood. Now both man and sword had gone. Newbury's black tie lay discarded on the floor, still knotted. He didn't pick it up.

Together they hurried around the side of the stage and pushed their way through the double doors that led to the actors' enclosure where they had first met Alfonso lounging idly in his dressing room. At the end of the long corridor, the door to the street was hanging open, banging noisily against the wall in the breeze. The hinges creaked and groaned with the strain. Outside, it was dark and the swirling fog gave everything a murky, hazy appearance. Veronica ran to the threshold, peering out into the night. There was no sign of Knox or the medicine bag.

Newbury was right. Somehow the doctor had escaped.

CHAPTER

22

Newbury awoke, momentarily disoriented. Slowly the room began to resolve around him. A bookcase. A writing desk. A fireplace with a low flame guttering in the grate. He felt dazed. He was in his drawing room.

After a moment, he realised there was someone standing beside him calling his name. He looked round. It was Mrs. Bradshaw, her hands on her hips. He had the sense that she had been there for some time. "Good morning, Sir Maurice. Will you be taking breakfast today?" she asked in her dulcet Scottish tones. She looked him up and down. "And whatever have you been up to for your suit to be in such a condition?" She said this with a weariness born of familiarity, of one accustomed to her employer's more

bizarre pursuits. She expected no answer. If she was concerned for his health, she showed no signs of it.

Newbury took stock of the situation. He was lounging in a
leather chair, still wearing yesterday's suit, which was torn at
the knees and covered in grime from rolling around in alleyways, rooftops, and an Underground station. His elbows
were scuffed and his jacket was sliced across the front from
the swipe of a sword blade. He had not attended to his
toilet, either, so his face was still crusty with blood and oil.
He must have looked a pretty sight to his housekeeper.

There was a heavy weight on his chest. He looked down
and saw a book resting there, Meyer's *Treatise on Futur-
ism*. On the occasional table beside his chair was a near-
empty glass of red wine, which of course had been laced with
laudanum. Sighing, Newbury looked up into the inscrutable
face of Mrs. Bradshaw. "What time do you figure it, Mrs.
Bradshaw?"

She glanced at the clock on the mantelpiece. "Time for
breakfast, I should say, sir."

Newbury grinned. "Very well. I shall make haste to my
rooms, where I shall endeavour to make myself presentable.
My thanks to you, Mrs. Bradshaw. I suspect I might have
slept all day if it had not been for your timely interruption."

The housekeeper smiled without saying another word and
quit the room. Newbury listened to the tread of her feet as
she descended the stairs to the kitchen below. Then, heaving
himself out of his chair, his bones creaking after hours spent
in a less-than-ideal posture, he repaired to his rooms to wash
and dress.

After washing and cleaning his wounds—which were more plentiful than Newbury had imagined—he partook of Mrs. Bradshaw's excellent breakfast and then headed out to meet Miss Hobbes at the museum, as they had arranged the previous evening.

As his hansom trundled along, Newbury considered the events at the theatre. After discovering that Knox had somehow managed to slip his bonds and escape the theatre, an exasperated Newbury had escorted Miss Hobbes to her Kensington home where, after he filled her in regarding the situation with Ashford, he insisted she take the opportunity for an evening's rest. There was very little else they could have achieved that night, and since they weren't aware of the full extent of Knox's plans, they were unable to predict his movements.

What was clear to Newbury was the fact that Knox had been hunting for the key to the Osiris Ritual. Winthrop's and Blake's deaths had been inconsequential to Knox; they were killed because they were in his way, regardless of the fact that they had been the ones to recover the artefacts he desired. That much was obvious. Knox had clearly gathered some notion of what the Osiris Ritual entailed—probably from the same material that Renwick had shown Newbury—and had been experimenting on the missing women for some time. The women had been disappearing for weeks, if not months, before Winthrop's death. Newbury assumed that they were somehow central to the execution of the ritual, that the secretion or hormone Knox had been extracting from their brains was an ingredient in the process. But now Knox had the documents from the ushabti, which were presumably the key, the final instructions for the ritual. It was all supposition, of course, but it seemed to fit the facts. Knox had learned of Khemosiri's work, and had tried to emulate it from the scant information available. Then Winthrop had returned from his expedition, full of pomp and ceremony, and Purefoy had made public the details of his finds. Knox only had to read the morning edition and connect the facts to realise that the final pieces of the puzzle were near at hand. They had practically been handed to him on a plate.

All of this led Newbury to two conclusions. Firstly, that Knox was planning to enact the ritual—and soon—in the hope of artificially extending his own life. Secondly, that Knox was entirely insane. Neither revelation filled him with comfort. Newbury would have to bring him in alive—of course he would. There were questions that needed answering. But he knew in his heart that the Empire would be a better place if the man were swiftly and decisively dispatched.

Newbury considered their encounter at the theatre. The experience of meeting his predecessor had shaken him, more than he cared to admit. The man was cold and calculating, yet there was a cool intelligence there too, an understanding of the world and the way that it worked. He was charming, resourceful, a master manipulator. He knew how to twist things to his own ends. Newbury knew that he had allowed the rogue doctor to get under his skin.

And where did that leave Ashford? He was still rogue too, still loose in the city and working to his own set of directives, ignoring the imperatives of the Crown. Newbury's mission had not changed, then. Ashford still needed to be brought in, even if he wasn't the vicious murderer that Newbury had originally mistaken him for.

That only left Miss Hobbes. What had she been trying to tell him down in that dank cellar? He thought he knew, of course, thought he understood the implication of her words. She knew Knox. At least, she knew *of* Knox. There could be very few ways in which she had come across that information, and she had divulged far more than she could have possibly learned from the man himself in such a short space of time. He felt torn. What had she been keeping from him? And for how long? The notion tied a knot in the pit of his stomach. If he couldn't trust Veronica . . .

Yet, how could he doubt her integrity? Everything he knew of her—from the manner in which she cared for her sister, to her recent concern over the missing women— spoke of a good heart. She had saved his life on numerous occasions. She knew everything about him. And besides, she was more to him than simply an assistant. She was . . . *important* to him. Yet he could not still the sharp sense of disquiet that had settled upon him. Throughout breakfast he had replayed the events of the previous evening over and over in his mind, trying to recall the exact look on her face, the precise tone of her voice. There was definitely more to it than a slip of the tongue. But what? He was not yet sure. If she had helped him *sooner*. . . . It was as if she'd realized that, all along, she'd held a piece of the puzzle that could have aided him in his mission. But how?

Whatever the case, he feared that he would cause an

imbalance in their relationship if he brought it up. He resolved to manage the situation carefully. He would not confront her outright. That, he thought, could only bring about disaster. He needed more time to ponder the consequences of what she had said.

First, though, he needed to act on the information she had given him. He needed to find Aubrey Knox. Knox was the key.

And Newbury had no idea where to start.

A half hour later, a smartly dressed Newbury, clean shaven and bright with energy, opened the door to his office at the British Museum and stepped inside. He filled his lungs with the familiar smell of the place. For all of his adventuring, Newbury enjoyed the calm respite he found here, the sense of stillness in a world so filled with chaos. He glanced around. Both Miss Hobbes and Miss Coulthard were sitting at their desks, studiously engrossed in their work.

"Good morning, ladies." Newbury removed his hat. "Do I smell a fresh pot of Earl Grey brewing?" He beamed at Miss Coulthard, who was quick to acknowledge his request, shuffling off towards the stove to fetch him a drink. Newbury crossed the room without removing his coat, then stepped through the partition to the smaller office where Veronica was working. "Miss Hobbes. Are you quite well?"

Veronica looked up at him, pushing her papers to one side. "I am quite well, Sir Maurice."

Newbury lowered his voice, glancing back at Miss Coulthard, who was still busying herself at the stove. "It's only . . . after yesterday's ordeal, I questioned—"

"There is no question." Veronica interjected. "Really, I am quite well."

"I am most pleased to hear it. Then we shall fortify ourselves with Miss Coulthard's excellent brew before setting out in search of our villain."

Veronica furrowed her brow. "Have you a notion, then, of where to begin our search for Knox?" She was toying absently with her left wrist, where a red mark showed how she had been viciously bound just a few hours earlier.

Newbury nodded slowly. "Perhaps. I still believe that Ashford could hold the answer. But first, there's someone I'd like you to meet." He looked round to see Miss Coulthard approaching, holding a large silver tray. "Thank you, Miss Coulthard. If you would be so kind as to set that down on my desk." He began unbuttoning his topcoat.

Miss Coulthard placed the tray on the rather cluttered desk as directed. Then, turning to Newbury, she reached into the pocket of her blouse and withdrew a small, neatly folded piece of paper, which she held out to him. "The information you requested, sir."

Newbury's emerald eyes widened in recognition. "Ah, marvellous! My thanks to you, Miss Coulthard." He took the note and slipped it into his trouser pocket without unfolding it.

"You're most welcome, sir. I also have a message from Sir Charles. He requests that you pay him a visit at Scotland Yard at your earliest convenience."

"I shall take it under advisement, Miss Coulthard. Thank you."

"Very good, sir." Miss Coulthard returned to her desk and

was back to work before Newbury had finished removing his winter layers.

Grinning, Newbury draped his coat across his desk and placed his hat beside it. Then, reaching for the steaming teapot, he turned to Veronica. "Tea?"

George Purefoy's apartment in Ladbroke Grove was above a tailor's shop that boasted two large bay windows, each filled with displays of exquisite dinner suits, hats, gloves, and canes. Through the window, Newbury could see the dark shapes of figures going about their daily business. To the left of the shop's frontage was a nondescript green door. This, Newbury fathomed, would likely be the door to Purefoy's apartment.

Despite Veronica's protests, Newbury had insisted upon taking a steam-powered carriage across town, keen that no further time be lost. She had taken the opportunity to make a sly comment suggesting that if he were so anxious for them to be on their way, they might have forgone their morning brew, but Newbury had only laughed and hailed the cab. Ritual was important to him. It gave him time to think.

After helping Veronica down from the carriage, which she glared at in disdain as she dismounted, wrinkling her nose at the smell of the throbbing engine, Newbury approached Purefoy's door. He removed his glove and rapped loudly with the brass knocker. Beside him, Veronica shivered in the cold.

A few moments passed in silence. There was no answer from the apartment above. Newbury knocked again then stepped back into the street, glancing up at the windows. Still nothing. No call from inside, no sign of movement at the windows. With a growing sense of unease, Newbury tried the handle and found that the door was unlocked. It swung open to reveal a steep, carpeted staircase up to the apartment.

Newbury crossed to the foot of the stairs. "Purefoy? Are you there, Purefoy?"

Then, with a look of horror, Newbury noticed something on the bottom step. He dropped into a squat, examining what he saw. "Oh no . . ."

Veronica stepped forward, trying to make it out. "What is it?"

"Blood. A footprint." Newbury's voice was barely a whisper. Feeling sick to the stomach and praying that what he had feared had not become a reality, Newbury bounded up the stairs two at a time. There were more footprints further up the stairwell; a man had passed this way only a handful of hours before. The imprints were still wet and sticky on the pale green carpet.

At the top of the stairs Newbury found himself presented with three white panelled doors. He chose the one to the right, judging that it would lead him to Purefoy's sitting room. He turned the handle, pushing his way inside. The sight that greeted him was enough to make him cry out in anguish and fall to his knees. He hung his head. He was too late.

Purefoy's corpse had been laid out on the sitting room floor to form the shape of a human star. Around him, his butcher had drawn a series of large concentric circles, each of them divided into precise intervals. Within these intervals he had carefully drawn an incredibly elaborate series of inscriptions, diagrams, and runes, each of them bearing its own dark, esoteric meaning.

Purefoy himself had been stripped naked. His belly had been rent open with a long, deep gash, and his bowels removed. His intestines had been stretched out around him and pinned within the circles to form a horrific spider's web of flesh, a web in which Purefoy himself had been caught, trapped at its centre like a fly awaiting its inevitable fate. Inside the abdominal cavity of the dead man, the killer had placed a series of small tributes: a holly leaf; the broken remnants of an ushabti; a small, rolled fragment of linen inscribed with some archaic scripture; and a single tarot card bearing the image of a goblet overflowing with water. The ace of cups.

The look on the boy's face was one of wonder, as if he had not yet come to terms with what had been about to happen to him, as if his reporter's instincts had remained engaged until the last, his curiosity somehow outweighing his fear.

It was immediately obvious to Newbury what had occurred. Aubrey Knox had tried to divine the future in the reporter's guts.

Newbury heard Veronica's footsteps on the landing behind him, and he turned to try to stop her from entering the room. But he was too late. She saw everything. He saw her gag reflexively and turn away from the scene.

There was blood everywhere, of course, thick and cloying. The smell of it filled Newbury's nostrils, seeming to penetrate everything. But under it all there was another smell, the familiar stench of rotting flesh. Ashford had been here, too.

Newbury felt a fury welling up inside of him, a burning rage deep in the pit of his belly. Knox would pay for this. He would pay dearly for it. There was one thing that Knox cared for above all else, one thing that drove him onwards: his own life. Newbury would have to take that from him. He realised this as he rested there on the threshold of Purefoy's sitting room, eyeing the devastation before him. The boy was dead, killed only for being in the wrong place at the wrong time, for being on the periphery of something that he didn't even understand. All of that potential, all of that enthusiasm, was gone, stolen for no end but Knox's wicked gratification.

Dark thoughts bubbled into Newbury's head. He would see justice done. Even if it meant that he had to become like Knox to do it. He would find Knox. And then Purefoy would be avenged.

Standing, Newbury looked back at Veronica on the landing. "He's toying with us."

Veronica coughed. "Knox, you mean?"

"Yes. What threat could Purefoy have *possibly* proved to the man?"

Veronica shook her head and swallowed. "I'm not sure that matters, Sir Maurice. The pattern is the same as before. He's tidying up loose ends. He must have been aware of Purefoy's involvement, his relationship with you, the article he had written about Winthrop's mummy. Knox clearly wanted him out of the picture."

Newbury nodded but didn't say a word. He stepped into the room, closer to the body. He looked down, his eyes filled with sadness.

"What does it all mean?" Veronica asked from behind him. She was hovering in the doorway, unwilling—or unable—to enter the room.

Newbury hesitated. "He . . . He was attempting to divine

the future. Many of the ancient rituals involve disembow-
elling cats, dogs, or flightless birds. He chose to use Purefoy."

"My God. . . ." Veronica's voice was full of pity.

"He must have been disturbed in the middle of it. By Ashford, I mean. Otherwise I can see no reason why he would
have left these items here."

"Why? Do they tell you something?"

"Perhaps." Newbury studied the objects that were resting
inside the carcass of his young friend.

Veronica shook her head. "We're running out of time. His
next move will be to disappear, to go to ground."

Newbury shook his head. Stooping, he gingerly removed
the tarot card from the bloody mess on the floor. "No, Miss
Hobbes. He's not going to ground. It seems old habits die
hard. He's going to water."

Veronica stared at him, wide-eyed. "What, the docks?"

Newbury nodded. "The ace of cups. Water. That's where
they found Ashford's body last time, isn't it? By interrupting
Knox, Ashford has done us more of a favour than he could
possibly imagine." His eyes flashed with steely resolve. "We
have Knox's trail."

Veronica straightened her back. "Shall I fetch the police?"

Newbury was studying Purefoy's face. His head snapped
up at Veronica's words. His voice was forceful. "No. No police. Not even Charles. We finish this alone." He saw Veronica shudder at the cold timbre of his voice. She looked at the
horrifying remnants of Knox's ritual.

"Will it work?"

"What, the divination? No."

Veronica shook her head. "No, not that. The Osiris Ritual. Will it work?"

Newbury sighed. "There are more things in this world of ours than I can possibly explain, Miss Hobbes. But it didn't help Khemosiri and I doubt it will help Knox."

"All the same . . ." Veronica let her sentence trail off.

Newbury gave her a weak smile. "All the same." He dropped the tarot card to the floor beside the corpse then turned and disappeared further into the apartment, returning a moment later with a large white sheet he had clearly stripped from Purefoy's bed. He knelt beside the body, laying the makeshift shroud neatly over the dead man to hide the ruination. Lastly, before covering Purefoy's face, he used the tips of his fingers to draw the reporter's eyelids closed.

Then, resolute, Newbury took Veronica by the arm and marched her out of the apartment, with only one goal in mind: revenge.

CHAPTER

23

Veronica bobbed up and down in her seat as the hansom cab bowled across the city. Newbury watched her from the other side of the cabin. Her head was turned away from him as she looked out of the window, and he admired her profile. There was no mistaking her beauty. What was more, she had flowered in the few months since he'd known her, growing in confidence. To Newbury, she was a near-perfect example of womanhood. He watched her strain to see through the fog, blinking, as if the action would have any effect on the cloying grey vapour through which they were travelling.

Yet, for all that, Newbury had never felt so far removed from her. Their relationship felt some-

how fractured, distant. Her actions towards him had not altered, of course. But he knew more now, knew that she was
holding something back from him, something fundamental.
His fury at Purefoy's death had not abated—if anything, it
was growing more and more forceful by the minute—and it
fed into the horrible sense of betrayal in the pit of his stomach. Unwelcome questions entered his mind. If she had acted
sooner, if she had warned him about Knox, would Purefoy still
be dead? Had she known about Ashford all along? Where had
she gotten the information about Knox? All of these questions
needed answers, but the very act of asking them was at odds
with how he felt about the woman. In questioning her, he
risked losing her altogether. For now, he decided that leaving
them unexamined was the lesser evil.

Veronica turned towards him, snapping him out of his
reverie. "Sir Maurice, I thought we were heading to the
London Docks."

Newbury nodded, slowly. "We are. But first, I must make
a brief stop." Veronica frowned. "I believe I know where to
find Ashford. I must talk with him."

Veronica nodded sagely. "Very well." The moment
stretched and they stared at each other in silence, neither
wishing to be the first to look away. After a while, Newbury
turned to glance out of the window. He had the terrible,
dawning sense that everything was unravelling around him.

Presently, the hansom trundled to a stop in the foggy
wilderness of Bethnal Green. Newbury stood. "You wait here,
Miss Hobbes. I shall return momentarily." He pushed open
the door and stepped down into the quiet street beyond. It
was still early, and this peaceful residential street had not yet

fully awoken to the morning. Newbury took a small cream-coloured card from inside his jacket pocket and unfolded it, revealing an address written in Miss Coulthard's neat cop-perplate that matched the house in front of him. It was sim-ilar, in many ways, to Newbury's own residence: a small end terrace house with two prominent bay windows, one on each floor; a small front yard filled with potted plants; and a pan-elled front door painted in a royal blue. A waist-high railing ran around the front and side of the yard. The mouth of a dimly lit alleyway separated the house from the next long terrace about six feet to the right.

It seemed to Newbury like a rather expensive dwelling for a widow on an agency pension. Nevertheless, this was the address that Miss Coulthard had found for him. Newbury slowly approached the building. For a moment he stood be-fore the door, considering whether to rap the brass knocker. Then, changing his mind, he edged round to stand before the window, peering into the living room beyond.

The room was lit brightly by a gas lamp and was well stocked with furnishings, including a sideboard, two arm-chairs, and a daybed. A large fireplace dominated the room, although its grate was cold and unlit. A pretty woman in her late twenties with strawberry blonde hair was sitting on the floor with two children: a boy, of around eight years, and a girl, slightly younger, who were clearly brother and sister. They were all playing a game with counters. Newbury smiled as he watched their faces light up whilst they laughed and carolled with their mother. He didn't turn his head as he be-gan to speak in a low voice. "You'll have to give yourself up soon, Ashford. All of this running around is doing neither of us any good. I'm supposed to take you in myself but I'm too busy with this blasted Knox business. I'm about to head to the London Docks to find him before he disappears again." He turned his head slightly to watch Ashford emerge from the shadows around the side of the building. The other man's eyes were piercing in the gloom. "I know you'll do the right thing."

Ashford lowered his hood and once again Newbury was appalled by the yellowed, rotting pallor of his skin and the disfigurements that Dr. Fabian's machinery had inflicted upon him. His black cloak was now shredded and hanging loose around his shoulders, exposing the mechanical pump in his chest, and Newbury could see where his encounter with the train in the Underground had scorched the flesh at his elbows, revealing the brass joints underneath. The tubing that curled between his head and chest flexed as he moved.

Newbury pitied Ashford then, not for what had become of him, but rather for the impact it had had on his life; left out in the cold, Ashford was separated from his wife and children by only a thin pane of glass. But that pane of glass represented a yawning chasm, a barrier that Ashford was forever unable to cross. It must have been torture to stand watching his wife and children and be prevented from reaching out for them, from holding them, from being a husband and a father to them. But Newbury knew that, to those children, their father was dead, and this *thing* would stand before them only as a monster, a creature drawn from their darkest nightmares. Ashford knew it too, and so had spared them that horror.

The former agent turned to regard the joyful scene inside the house. Newbury was unable to read any emotion on his grim visage, but he was sure that it still resided somewhere deep inside the man. "Thank you, Newbury." Ashford's voice chimed out in his grating, metallic tone. "I will do the right thing."

Newbury gave a curt nod then turned, making his way along the short path towards the waiting carriage, leaving Ashford alone to contemplate his nightmare. Just as he reached the railing, however, Newbury heard Ashford call out behind him: "Newbury." A brief pause. "Methuselah."

Newbury turned, a quizzical expression on his face, but Ashford had already gone, melted away into the foggy morning.

Newbury coughed absently as he helped Miss Hobbes to dismount from the hansom a short while later at the London Docks. The sun had done its work and burned away much of the morning fog, transforming it into thin wreaths of mist that still clung, determinedly, to the masts of the innumerable vessels that cluttered the harbour. The docks were teeming with boats of all shapes and sizes, from steamships to yachts to schooners. The quayside, in turn, was bustling with life.

Veronica wrinkled her nose. The docks had a distinctive aroma that was all their own. Laughing, Newbury paid the cabbie and sent him on his way. He held his arm out for Veronica. "I suggest, my dear Miss Hobbes, that we begin with the

major shipping lines and see if we can't discover the intended
destination of the doctor."

The offices of the shipping companies were, as one, small
and pokey, dimly lit, and without substantial furnishings. The
Crown investigators were forced to wait in line whilst mer-
chants, businessmen, and explorers all arranged passage to a
vast array of destinations—exotic locales from China to the
Continent, from India to Africa—booking berths on the large
steamers that were due to sail that week. Hours passed, and
innumerable interviews with office clerks—who were so alike
that Newbury considered they could have been stamped out
of the same mould—yielded nothing. There was no trail. No
person matching Knox's name or description had booked
passage on a vessel sailing that day, or indeed any day that
week. Newbury, frustrated, feared they had already lost
Knox, that perhaps his assumption back at Purefoy's apartment had been incorrect, or worse, that Knox had fooled
him, leaving a false trail. Had the ace of cups meant something else entirely? He was wracked with doubt.

Newbury and Veronica agreed to walk the quayside in
search of inspiration. Newbury was not hopeful that he
would find it. His sense of impending chaos was still bearing
down on him, still growing in force and magnitude. He had
the notion that he was at the centre of a vast maelstrom,
standing in the eye of the storm, looking out as everything
went to pieces around him. Purefoy was dead and Knox ran
free. Perhaps he could use Charles's help after all, but it was
too late for that.

They strolled along the water's edge, avoiding crates of

stinking fish, fine silks from the East, spices, tobacco, and any number of other goods being unloaded from the vessels that had moored along the quayside. Newbury scanned the faces in the crowds as they walked, until those faces became nothing but an indistinct human blur. *So many people*. If Knox really had come here, Newbury understood why he had chosen it. It would be easy to lose oneself amongst this vast cornucopia of nationalities and noise. Easy to adopt a false identity, or to slip down a side street, or even to stow away aboard one of the great ships that towered over the harbour like behemoths in the morning light.

His only clue now was that last, cryptic word that Ashford had muttered to him before slipping away into the darkness. *Methuselah*. Newbury turned it over and over in his mind. *Methuselah*. He knew the relevance of the word, the implication. He had studied the biblical texts as a schoolboy. It was clearly a reference to Knox, to Knox's plans. Methuselah was a watchword for longevity. He was the son of Enoch, who had lived for countless years in the early days of the Christian myth, his life supernaturally extended by the will of God. Newbury was not a religious man and did not consider the Bible as literal truth, yet he knew there were more things in this world than those he could see, hear or touch; he had even witnessed them himself on occasion. The supernatural realm was hidden only by a thin veil. The line between science and the occult was intangible. Or so experience suggested.

"Methuselah." He spoke the word aloud, trying to wring the meaning from it. He had come to a stop before a small

makeshift stall, behind which a burly man was selling cock-
les by the jar.

Veronica, who had been staring out across the water,
turned when she heard him speak. "Methuselah?"

Newbury nodded. "Yes, yes." He sighed. "The last word
that Ashford spoke to me before we parted company."

Veronica's eyes widened. "Methuselah . . . ? Ashford said
that to you?"

"Indeed. Clearly he was referring to Knox."

"Yes, Sir Maurice, I believe he was! But look!" He followed the line of her finger towards a small boat bobbing
gently as the river lapped against the harbour wall. It was a
bizarre craft: it had the look of a small ironclad about it, all
metal plates and reinforced glass portholes, with a tall funnel that would remain above water when the vessel dived,
providing a source of air for the inhabitants. There was a
wooden deck surrounded by a short rail, and a sealable
hatch for climbing down into the habitable space below. An
extendable periscope jutted from the deck. A submersible,
Newbury assumed, capable of spending extended periods
beneath the water. Submersibles such as this were rare, and
Newbury had only seen one or two of them in his lifetime.
This one sat afloat in the harbour, sandwiched between two
larger boats, and was tied to a mooring post on the quayside
nearby. On the side of the vessel, in small, black letters, was
the name: *METHUSELAH*.

Newbury turned to Veronica. "You don't think . . ."

Veronica nodded. "It makes sense. It must be Knox's ship."

Newbury couldn't prevent himself from grinning. "So

that's how he intends to get away. Underwater. Come on!"
He ran along the harbour edge, careful not to trip or lose his
footing. Veronica followed close on his heels.

The prow of the vessel was around three feet from the edge
of the harbour. Murky Thames water sloshed in the space
between. Glancing back over his shoulder to make sure Veronica was still following him, Newbury readied himself then
sprang from the edge of the harbour towards the small deck
of the *Methuselah*. He landed with a dull thud. Turning, he
held his arms out towards Veronica, willing her to jump.
"Come on! That bang may have alerted him. We need to
move quickly."

Veronica regarded the jump with trepidation. Then,
shrugging, she fixed her eyes on Newbury, bent her knees,
and leapt forward. Newbury caught her firmly, staggering
back a few paces before setting her down beside him. Their
faces were only inches apart. He could hear her ragged breath.
"Are you ready?"

"I'm ready."

There was a choking sound from deep beneath them, followed by a long, mechanical purr. The *Methuselah* began
to gently vibrate. Newbury's and Veronica's eyes met. "He's
started the engines. He must have heard us. We need to
move, fast. If he dives, we're done for. We need to get inside." Newbury moved quickly. He shot around the deck,
searching out the hatch that would allow them access to the
decks below. When he found it, it was nothing but a round
hole in the decking covered by a thick metal lip and a rubber
seal. Crouching, Newbury ran his fingers around the edge of
it until he located the catch. He pulled it open and the metal

plate eased upwards on a creaking hinge, revealing a steel ladder that disappeared into the shadowy depths below.

Swinging himself down, his feet caught on the metal rungs and he began his swift descent. Veronica followed suit, pulling the hatch closed behind her. Their feet echoed in the confined space as they climbed.

They found themselves in a small antechamber which branched off in three different directions. The decor was functional, at best; the walls and doorways consisted of grey, featureless steel. Everything was quiet, aside from the gentle slapping of water against the sides of the boat. There was a light, pleasant aroma of lavender and rosemary.

Newbury looked around for something he could use as a weapon but saw nothing. Giving up on that idea, he decided to follow his instincts. "This way," he whispered to Veronica, nodding towards the prow of the vessel. They crept through the small opening, treading carefully to ensure that their footsteps did not give away their position. Newbury kept his back to the wall. They inched further into the depths of the ship.

The small passageway terminated in an open doorway. Newbury peered through the opening. On the other side of the bulkhead was the main cabin. It was a relatively small space, with a single bunk, a square table fixed to one wall, and another open hatchway, which he supposed led to the control pit. The room was sparsely furnished but nevertheless cluttered with books, jars, and strange artefacts—in much the same manner as Newbury's Chelsea study—but filled also with the paraphernalia of normal life: clothes, a top hat, a pocket watch laid out on the table. The bedclothes were ruffled, slept in. This place, this boat—not only was it Knox's means of escape, it appeared to be his home.

The scene on the floor told an even more bizarre tale. A large pentagram had been marked out with string on the metal plating. Between each of the five points of the star within the large circle lay a curled, aged fragment of papyrus, each covered in an inky black scrawl. These, Newbury presumed, were the contents of the ushabti that Knox had fought so hard to obtain. The last words of Khemosiri. The instructions for how to perform the Osiris Ritual.

At the centre of the pentagram were arranged three tall glass phials, filled with the brackish brown fluid that Knox had extracted from the brains of the women he had killed. In addition there was a jar of thick, gelatinous blood; the clay effigy of a man, crudely formed; and a leather-bound book which lay open to reveal bright pages illuminated with decorations. There was no sign of Knox.

Gesturing silently to Veronica that she should follow, Newbury stepped carefully over the threshold, dipping his head to avoid banging it on the bulkhead. He heard Veronica steal in behind him. "What now?" she whispered.

"Now, my dear Miss Hobbes, you listen to me." The voice was a familiar, sensuous purr. As if on cue, Aubrey Knox appeared in the doorway of the submersible's control pit. He was dressed in an immaculate black dinner suit and was wearing a scabbarded sword on his left hip. In his left hand he bore a pistol, and his scarred left eye twinkled as he regarded the two investigators. His right hand was bandaged where Newbury had run it through at the theatre.

Knox was clearly about to launch into another oratory

when Newbury launched himself forward, carelessly tram-
pling the delicately arranged pentagram on the floor. He
charged towards Knox with wild abandon, driven by a fiery
passion for revenge. Grasping Knox's gun arm at the wrist,
he twisted the weapon away from him whilst bringing his
other fist down hard on the side of Knox's head. Knox had
not expected such a bold move and he floundered under the
impact of the blow, his finger twitching, firing off a shot over
his shoulder which pinged off of the toughened glass of the
Methuselah's viewing port and caused a spidery crack to open
in the glass.

"Fool!" Knox shouted as he kicked out at Newbury, catching him hard in the calf and causing his leg to buckle. Newbury stumbled backwards and Knox swung the gun round in
a fierce arc, cracking the butt of the weapon into Newbury's
temple. Pain ignited in Newbury's skull and lights danced
before his eyes. He tumbled to the ground, disoriented, unable to prevent his fall. Knox kicked him once more, this
time hard in the gut, and then turned the pistol on Veronica.
He pulled the trigger.

There was a loud report that echoed throughout the entire
boat. Newbury rolled to the side in horror just in time to see
blood spray in a wide arc from Veronica's shoulder, spattering
the wall as she screamed, the front of her jacket stained by a
spreading blot of crimson. She collapsed in a heap, whimper-
ing with pain.

Numb with shock, Newbury turned to find himself staring down the barrel of Knox's gun. The rogue doctor was
grinning. He didn't need to say anything; the look in his eyes
did the gloating for him. Newbury knew he couldn't move in

time. Knox's finger squeezed the trigger. The chamber clicked round in its housing . . .

. . . and stopped. It must have jammed.

Newbury tried to scramble to his feet, but Knox struck out again, whacking him hard across the back of the head with the gun before tossing it, frustrated, into the control pit. By this time the vessel was beginning its slow dive and water was lapping at the bottom of the portholes. The crack, caused by the errant shot, was beginning to groan. Soon the water pressure would cause it to give in altogether, flooding the vessel with river water. It would sink like a stone.

Newbury needed to get to Veronica. All he could think about was helping her. But stars were still dancing before his eyes. He shook his head.

He heard footsteps. Knox was standing over him. "What a terrible disappointment," the former agent spat at him in disgust. Then more footsteps, followed by the sound of Knox mounting the ladder in the antechamber. *Let the bastard get away*. There would be more opportunities in the future. For now, he needed to get Veronica to safety before she bled to death or drowned. He pushed himself up onto his hands and knees, his head spinning. He got to his feet, shakily, and crossed the cabin. Veronica lay unconscious, a dark pool of blood forming all around her. He hoped he wasn't already too late.

CHAPTER

24

Veronica stirred, semiconscious, as Newbury dropped to his knees, scooping her up and cradling her in his arms. "Oh, Veronica . . ." He held her like that for a moment, his heart breaking. Then, remembering that he needed to act, he stood, carrying her across to the daybed, where he propped her upright, trying to keep her wound higher than her heart. Cautiously, he examined her injury. The bullet had torn directly through her shoulder, leaving a ragged exit wound from which blood was gushing freely. "Hold on. Hold on, Veronica. You're going to be alright." He grabbed the lapels of her mauve jacket and wrenched it open, popping the buttons. He took up a fistful of her blouse and used both hands to tear off a long strip, exposing the alabaster skin of her midriff. He wrapped the strip of fabric around her shoulder and bound it tight, trying to compress the wound. She cried out in pain as he applied pressure and her eyes blinked open, frantically searching for him.

"I'm here, Veronica. I'm here."

The shock, the pain, and the loss of blood were evident in her eyes. She was unable to focus. "Newbury . . ." was all she could manage, her voice weak, tiny bubbles of blood forming on her lips as she mouthed the word.

Newbury tried to fight the rising sense of panic that was gripping him, making it harder to breathe. He had recovered a little from the blows to the head he'd received and adrenaline was coursing riotously through his veins, causing his hands to shake. He glanced over his shoulder, trying to get a measure of their situation. Knox had fled. Newbury had heard him scramble up the ladder and out onto the deck a few moments earlier, ditching the sinking vessel. The remnants of the Osiris Ritual were scattered across the floor, disturbed in the scuffle, but the vials of brown liquid were gone.

The boat's engines were still roaring, but Newbury heard a splintering crack sound above them. In the control pit, the fractured glass of the viewing port was splitting open under the pressure of the water. Newbury realised with shock that the *Methuselah* was nearly completely submerged. The glass would give way soon, allowing the river water to flood in. Not only that, but he guessed that Knox would have left the hatch open as he fled. If the upper deck of the vessel were to dip beneath the surface, there would be no stopping the onslaught of water, and their only route of escape would be blocked.

Newbury put his hand on Veronica's cheek. She was icy cold. "Stay with me, Veronica. Hold on."

Jumping to his feet, Newbury dashed towards the control pit. The vessel's control system made no sense to him whatsoever. Dials, levers, knobs; he had no idea where to start. He needed to reverse the direction of the boat. He grabbed the nearest control to hand, a lever that had been cranked forward and which he hoped controlled the speed of the dive. He pulled it back fully and felt the *Methuselah* judder as the engines whined, shifting into reverse. Triumphantly, he stepped back from the controls, only to see his relief dashed almost immediately. The crack in the glass had now extended across the whole of the viewing port, a vast spider's web with a small impact crater at its epicentre where the stray bullet had struck. Tiny beads of water were beginning to form along the fracture lines. He could see nothing but dirty, swirling river water beyond.

He had to get out of there, had to get Veronica out of there. He dashed back into the main cabin. "Veronica? Miss Hobbes!" He knelt, turning her head from side to side, but it lolled pathetically. "Veronica!" It was no use. She was fading fast. He was going to have to carry her. He bent low and placed his hands under her arms, heaving her up onto his shoulder, careful not to exacerbate her injury. She gave a low moan. The makeshift bandage was holding, but blood was still seeping through, pattering to the floor. He realised his hands were covered in it. He had to get her to a surgeon, quickly. He couldn't lose her. Not Veronica.

There was a loud bang from somewhere up above, the sound of metal striking metal, as something heavy landed on the upper deck of the vessel. The whole boat shook, rocking from side to side with the impact. He heard Knox cry out in dismay, although his words were lost, swallowed by the incessant roar of the engines. The reply was unmistakable, however: the dry, metallic croak of William Ashford, calling the name of his eternal opponent. "Knox!"

So Knox hadn't yet been able to get away. Newbury had lost all sense of time.

He steadied himself with a deep breath. His burden safely secured on his shoulder, Newbury rushed to the ladder in the antechamber. The space was small and he had to be sure not to knock Veronica's head against the wall as he mounted the first rung of the ladder. He began to climb, one hand hauling himself upwards, the other wrapped securely around the waist of his unconscious assistant. The going was tough, but he made steady progress, driven on by the sounds of the scuffle from above; a sword striking metal and the grunting of the two men locked in deadly combat.

Below, the glass pane finally gave way with a crash and water began to gush into the main cabin. Newbury didn't have long; he knew that. Soon the weight of the water would overwhelm the power of the engines and the *Methuselah* would resume its slow, ponderous course towards the bottom of the river. He was resolute, however. He would get Veronica to safety. This boat would not become their tomb. He pressed on.

Newbury emerged from the open hatch to find himself grasping at water. It was lapping at the lip of the hatch, about to start streaming over the side into the vessel itself. The *Methuselah* was almost completely submerged, its upper deck sloshing as it listed from side to side, its paddle engines straining against the sheer weight of the water that was flooding into the main cabin below. Gasping as the cold water slapped him in the face, Newbury struggled to pull himself and Veronica out of the hatch and onto the unstable deck. He knew he was exposed, but a quick glance reassured him that Knox was already occupied. The doctor had drawn his sabre and was facing off against the hulking figure of Ashford, who had now abandoned his tattered cloak and had his arms outstretched, taking sweeping blows at the other man. The remains of his discarded cloak drifted away lazily with the gentle current of the river, like a puddle of spilt ink.

Knox was grinning foolishly, his once-blind eye twinkling with glee. He was parrying deftly with his blade. Newbury, stumbling onto the deck and falling to his knees, Veronica still clutched tightly in his arms, winced at the sound of metal striking metal. Rotten flesh, flayed from Ashford's forearms by the constant thrashing of the sabre, spun away in great clods, exposing more of the bizarre brass skeleton beneath. Ashford barely seemed to register the blows. If he felt any pain, it was lost in the snarl of rage that Newbury could see writ on his face. This was why Ashford had come back. It had all been for this moment. He would have his revenge on Knox for separating him from his family, for turning him into a monster. Newbury thought he caught a glimpse of something else in that expression, too—sadness, perhaps? Ashford had reached the end. He didn't want to live any longer, not the abject half life he'd been forced to endure for the last five years. He was set on a path of self-destruction and he fully intended to take Knox down with him when he fell.

The huge re-created man staggered towards the prow, almost losing his footing as the *Methuselah* dipped into the water. He swung at Knox, his feet causing water to spray into the air as he stomped across the half-submerged deck. The fight between the two men was far less elegant than Newbury's earlier encounter with Knox, but was in many ways more effective. It was clear that Ashford had the upper hand, if for no other reason than that he seemed unconcerned by the shower of blows he was allowing Knox to rain down on him as he pushed forward, relentlessly, focused on his goal.

Newbury could hear the boat's engines choking now, and he knew it wouldn't be long until they were all pitched into the cold water. He looked down at Veronica. Her face was pale from loss of blood. Hastily, he tested the bandage he had placed around her shoulder. It was still holding, but she needed surgery, and soon. He needed to get her to the Fixer. But there was no way off the boat other than into the river. He dared not risk plunging into the cold river with Veronica already so weak. He feared she wouldn't survive the shock. He needed to get past Knox and Ashford. Perhaps then he'd be able to make a jump for the quayside.

As if reading his thoughts, Ashford took decisive action. Ploughing forward, he raised his arms and grabbed for Knox, ignoring the sharp downward swing of the other man's sword, which bit hard into the coil of tubing that stretched from Ashford's chest to the back of his skull. Blood and chemicals sprayed into the air, describing a wide arc, but Ashford paid them no heed. He chopped down hard at Knox's wrist, causing the doctor to lose his grip on the sabre. It spiralled away, clattering to the wooden boards, the weight of it causing it to slide across the uneven deck of the listing boat. Newbury watched it slip away into the water, disappearing into the murky depths of the Thames.

Standing, Newbury held Veronica tightly to his chest as Ashford grasped hold of Knox, wrapping his huge, sinewy arms around the other man's chest and lifting him bodily into the air. Mechanical servos squealed as Ashford applied crushing pressure, his feet planted firmly on the deck, water lapping at his knees.

Knox wailed and spluttered, wheezing as the air was forced out of his lungs by his slowly collapsing rib cage. His legs kicked uselessly as his body was constricted by his former victim. His head turned, his eyes fixing on Newbury. Newbury could see the panic there, the desperation behind those eyes. His mouth opened and closed. He was mouthing something. Newbury stepped closer.

"Help . . . me. . . ." Knox gasped. But all Newbury could see were the faces of the dead women in the cellar beneath the Archibald Theatre, Veronica's face as the bullet ripped through her shoulder, and Purefoy's disembowelled corpse, spread out on the floor like a butchered animal. He remained steadfast, unmoved by the doctor's pleas. There would be no redemption for this man. Hate burned within Newbury like a furnace. Charles was wrong. Knox was everything that Newbury was not. Perhaps they were two extremes on the same scale, but they were poles apart. He needed to believe that.

Knox spasmed, his neck jerking back, blood spouting

from his lips and his eyes rolling back in his sockets as, with one sudden movement, Ashford squeezed the last life out of him. The doctor's head lolled to one side.

After a moment, Ashford released the corpse, which flopped like a child's toy to the deck of the boat and then slid, ungraciously, into the river. A moment later there was nothing but a few escaping air bubbles to mark the departure of Doctor Aubrey Knox.

The *Methuselah* shook violently as its engines failed. Ashford stood watching the water for a moment, as if anxious to ensure that Knox would not suddenly resurface. Then he turned and staggered towards Newbury. The pump in his chest was still pushing fluid through the severed pipe, but it was now a pathetic trickle dribbling down the side of Ashford's head. The man himself had begun to tremble. With great difficulty, he raised his feet above the sloshing water and jerked himself over to where Newbury was still cradling the unconscious Veronica to his chest. River water was now pouring into the open hatch by Newbury's feet, and he knew he had only minutes to get Veronica to safety.

Before he could reach Newbury, Ashford collapsed to his knees. The red lights of his eyes were flickering, unsteady, and dim. Newbury realised that without the preserving chemicals his brain was drying out, starved of moisture and oxygen. He was near death. He looked up at Newbury, who met his gaze with a smile. "You did it, Ashford. You did it."

Ashford's ventilator was wheezing heavily, rasping as he dragged air into his artificial lungs. He seemed to be struggling to open his mouth. When he did, the tinny, metallic sound of his voice lacked its usual bass timbre. "Thank

Charles for me, Newbury." And then he convulsed, froze, and dropped to the sinking deck of the boat, the red lights of his eyes fading to a pinprick of light, then disappearing to a steady black. His head dipped below the water line.

Newbury lurched into action. Veronica's breathing was shallow. She'd lost a lot of blood, but the wound was clean, straight through. He only hoped he could get her to a surgeon in time.

Cautiously, he walked to the rear of the boat, his feet sloshing in the water. There was no way he could make the jump to the harbour, not with Veronica in his arms. He'd have to swim. He hoped Veronica could survive it. But there was no other option.

Cursing, he glanced up and down the quayside, looking for a means by which he could scale the harbour wall. His best option was to get to one of the other nearby boats, and from there to safety. Hesitantly, he lowered himself into a sitting position on the side of the boat and then pitched himself forward into the water, careful to buoy Veronica so that her head remained above the surface. It didn't seem that long since he was last in the Thames, since Veronica was dragging him from the belly of a sinking airship. He would have laughed aloud at the irony had it not been for the gravity of his current situation.

Long, powerful strokes soon propelled him towards the nearest moored vessel, a large white yacht bobbing on the water about a hundred yards from the sinking submersible. The owners were nowhere to be seen, but it wasn't difficult for Newbury to haul himself and his precious cargo up the small ladder to the safety of the deck.

Shivering with cold, his head pounding from the earlier blows, he didn't wait to catch his breath. Instead, he crossed the boat and took a running jump over the small gap to the dock, from where he could carry Veronica to a hansom, which would take them, swiftly, to safety.

CHAPTER

25

So, what did Her Majesty have to say about it all?" Sir Charles Bainbridge took a large gulp from his glass of claret and leaned heavily on the dinner table, regarding Newbury. The two men had only recently finished their meal, and Mrs. Bradshaw had yet to return to clear away the evening's debris.

Newbury shrugged. "Nothing, as yet. I'm seeing her tomorrow."

Bainbridge raised a knowing eyebrow. "Tomorrow? It's been, what, three days?"

"A day or two won't change anything, Charles. Her Majesty knows that." Newbury smiled.

Bainbridge sighed. "You'd do well to remember that it's not our place to take the law into our own hands, Newbury. I mean, why didn't you call me, man?" Bainbridge was adamant. "You put yourself, and Miss Hobbes, in great danger. I could have helped."

Newbury shook his head. "No, Charles. The Yard would have only gotten in the way. And besides, the police could never have mobilized quickly enough. Knox would have slipped through our fingers again."

"But Newbury, you're forgetting: I'm not just a policeman."

Newbury grinned, a twinkle in his eye. "You can take the man out of the Yard, Charles, but you can't take the Yard out of the man. You'd do well to remember *that*."

"Well, yes. Perhaps you're right." Bainbridge chuckled. "Dastardly affair, though. Do you believe that's the last we'll see of Aubrey Knox?"

Newbury's expression grew serious. He picked at the remnants of his pudding. "I believe so. I *hope* so. He looked quite dead when Ashford dropped him into the water."

"Quite . . . quite. But they're saying they haven't been able to find the body as yet."

"Charles, I'd be amazed if anyone could find anything by that dock, let alone a man's corpse. For all we know, it was caught up in the propeller of some passing steamship and dashed into a thousand pieces."

"Yes. I suppose you might have something there." Bainbridge placed his glass on the table before him and shifted position, leaning back in his chair. "But what about this . . . Isis Ritual? What would have become of Knox if he'd managed to complete his machinations?"

Newbury shrugged, dropping his serviette onto the table and leaning forward to regard his friend. "The Osiris Ritual, you mean? Charles, I don't believe for one moment that it would have had any effect at all. That's what makes the whole episode even more grotesque. What he did to all those young women, extracting some sort of hormone from within their brains. But that, coupled with some esoteric ritual from ancient Egypt? No. I believe it would have singularly failed to help him achieve his aim."

"Ah yes, his quest for extended life."

"I don't believe there's an answer, Charles. Knox was driven by an insane desire to live forever and in pursuing this folly, he surrendered what time he did have to it. What a waste. We should use our time on this Earth wisely, Charles. Ashford knew that."

"Indeed he did." Bainbridge looked momentarily forlorn. "So what of Miss Hobbes? I understand it was a grave injury she endured."

"Quite so. Have you been to see her?"

Bainbridge nodded. "Of course. She seems to be convalescing well. No doubt she'll be back on her feet within a week or so. She has a strong will, that one."

"That she does." Newbury felt tired. He studied the empty plate before him. "I feared for her, Charles. I feared for what might become of her, for the danger that my gallivanting has put her in. This whole affair . . ." He sighed. "I don't know. I just had the sense that I was losing control."

Bainbridge nodded sagely but didn't respond. After a moment, Newbury reached for his glass of wine and downed its contents in one long pull. He set it down again neatly before him. "Shall we retire to the drawing room, Charles? I'm feeling a need for my pipe."

Bainbridge grinned. "Excellent idea, old chap, excellent idea."

The two men abandoned the remains of their dinner and made their way through the large set of double doors into the drawing room. Newbury's clockwork owl sat on a perch in one corner, clicking its wings excitedly as they entered the room. A fire was burning low in the grate. Newbury felt immediately better. He strode over to the mantelpiece, collecting his battered old tobacco pouch and pipe. "Pour us a drink, Charles."

Bainbridge approached the worn, mahogany drinks cabinet, from which he produced two tumblers and a decanter of the finest brandy. Removing the glass stopper, he sloshed a generous measure into each glass and then turned and handed one to Newbury, who accepted it gratefully.

Standing by the fire, his sharp features cast in relief, Newbury looked almost statuesque, a picture of nobility. His proud, hawklike nose, his olive eyes, his finely chiselled jawline; they were as distinctive and unmistakable as any man in London. Yet there were dark lines beneath his eyes, dark lines that told of another life.

"You look tired, Newbury."

"I feel it, Charles."

"You need to go to her."

Newbury looked perplexed. "Who, the Queen?"

"No, Miss Hobbes."

Newbury placed his tumbler on the marble mantelpiece with a chink and began stuffing the bowl of his pipe with his usual fine, aromatic shag. He didn't raise his eyes to look at his friend. "Perhaps I do." He blinked, then buried the storm of emotions he could feel welling up inside of him. He needed to avoid that particular conversation. "So, Charles, it seems you were right about Ashford. Tell me, what connection is there between you and Mrs. William Ashford? Ashford intimated there was something, and in researching the background to the case . . . well, I found out about the house."

Bainbridge sighed and downed his brandy in one long draw. He reached into his pocket for his cigar case. "It's nothing untoward, Newbury. It's not what you might imagine."

Newbury shrugged. He looked up, meeting his friend's gaze. "I hadn't imagined anything, Charles. I'm in no place to judge. . . ."

Bainbridge smiled, a world weary smile. "Well, I don't believe that for a moment." He used his cutter to snip the end off his fat brown cigar. "You see, things were different in those days. The agents all knew one another, like you and I do. Now, I think myself lucky if I can spot another agent in the same room. Her Majesty keeps us all at arm's length. But in those days . . . Well, suffice it to say that I knew Ashford well, and I knew Catherine too. She used to get on well with Isobel." Newbury nodded. It was rare that his old friend spoke of his late wife. "I think I told you that I was the one sent to talk to her after Ashford died. Or rather, as it transpires, after Ashford died for the *first* time. I could hardly bear it, Newbury. It was the first time. The first time I'd lost a friend like that, a friend in the service. Yes, we'd lost policemen, and Catherine wasn't the first widow I'd had to break the bad news to. But this was different. Catherine was a friend. She cried on my shoulder the entire night. She wanted me to help her tell the children."

Newbury could see that even the simple act of recounting the story was a painful exercise for his friend.

"I spent much of the night comforting her and then managed a few hours of fitful sleep in the spare room. The next morning, I helped her to break the news to the boy. He was only three years old, Newbury. It broke my heart." Bainbridge paused, rasping a match across the rough strip on the back of the matchbook and bringing the flame up to the end of his cigar. He shook it out with a wave of his hand, then took a moment to puff in the cigar's acrid smoke. "It wasn't until afterwards that I became aware of their situation. She was destitute, and a Crown pension would be hardly enough to live on. She had two children, Newbury, two beautiful young children, and her husband had given his life in the service of the Empire. What was I to do? I couldn't see her cast out or sent to the workhouse."

Newbury sucked thoughtfully on his pipe, still standing by the fire, leaning on the mantelpiece with one arm. "So you took on the house in Bethnal Green. You paid the rent and moved her in there with her family."

"I did. I'm not ashamed of it, Newbury. She's a good woman, and I never asked for anything in return. You should see her with those children."

"I did see her. So did Ashford. He knew, Charles. He knew what you had done for him. On his death bed he told me to thank you."

Bainbridge smiled. His voice was filled with sadness. "I should have liked to have said good-bye."

"Better that you didn't, Charles. I'm not sure you would have liked what he'd become."

Bainbridge blew smoke through his nostrils. He regarded Newbury with a severe expression. "I'm not sure any of us like what we've become."

Newbury nodded. He recognised the truth in the other man's words. He turned and retrieved his glass from the mantelpiece, taking a long, slow drink.

Bainbridge stood, collecting his empty glass from the arm of his chair. He returned to the decanter. Beside it on the lacquered surface of the drinks cabinet was a tall, ornate object made of glass and bone with a small brazier on top and a curling pipe that terminated in a matching bone mouthpiece, carved like the head of a dragon. "What is this, Newbury?"

Newbury looked sheepish. "A pipe, Charles. A new pipe."

Bainbridge caught his meaning. "For God's sake, Newbury! I'll not allow a friend of mine to succumb to a slow death by narcotics, least of all you."

"It helps me think is all, Charles. There's nothing more to it."

"Like hell!" Bainbridge was red in the face. "You tell yourself that, Newbury, but in truth you're just like any of us, looking for a means of escape, something to hide behind. You've simply decided that this is your particular poison. And it is poison. You're killing yourself."

Newbury looked him in the eye. "Perhaps you're right. Perhaps I am looking for an escape. Then why is it you judge me so harshly?"

Bainbridge poured himself another large measure of brandy. "Because I don't want to be the one to put you six feet under. Because I know what it is you're doing and I have no time for it. Why the hell should *you* be allowed to hide behind a veil of narcotics whilst the rest of us have to suffer? We all have demons, Newbury." He placed the decanter back on the drinks cabinet. "For heaven's sake, Miss Hobbes deserves better than that."

Newbury sighed. "You're right. Of course you're right. She deserves far better." It pained Newbury that he was the one who always put Veronica in harm's way. But he feared that expressing his feelings to her would expose her to something far worse than physical danger. He knew that it could never lead to anything, regardless of whether she felt the same; knew that life with an agent was a life of fear and despair, a life dominated by concern for the other. For some, it was a life of mourning, too. He could not allow Veronica to become like Catherine: Ashford understood why Bainbridge felt the need to protect that woman, to save her and her children from the workhouse, to offer her a better life. He was giving her the life that Ashford could not, but he was also giving her the life that he *wanted*. That was what Bainbridge was hiding behind. He craved normality. He longed for ignorance. The life of an agent was lonely and it was lonely for a reason. He would do what he could for Miss Hobbes, but the kindest thing, he knew, was to do nothing. Charles was right. She deserved more than he could give her.

Newbury's pipe had gone out. He looked around, catching sight of a small carriage clock on a bookcase, surrounded by heaps of notebooks and journals. The night was still young. "I say, Charles. We're terribly maudlin this evening. What do you say to a trip to the White Friar's? A game of billiards and some banter."

Bainbridge smiled, his whiskers twitching amicably. "You know what, Newbury, that's the best idea I've heard in days."

"Come on then, old man." Newbury placed his pipe carefully on the mantelpiece. "Let's forget about the past for a while, and the future. Let's revel in the present."

Bainbridge nodded. "But first . . ." he raised his glass, "the brandy."

Newbury chuckled and did the same. "Yes, indeed. The brandy."

CHAPTER

26

Newbury stood by the window, holding back the netting and peering out onto the sprawling view of Kensington High Street below. It already felt like a lifetime had passed since the incident on Knox's submersible, but in truth it had only been a matter of days. The fog had lifted during the intervening days, leaving behind only a few thin fingers that clung obstinately to the street lamps or lurked in the quieter parts of the city.

Below, the street was a hive of activity. He watched a ground train rolling by, the passengers inside bobbing easily with the motion of the vehicle. Hansom cabs sent pedestrians scattering as they bowled along the cobbled road, and children ran circles around each other, frolicking in the morning sunshine.

This was the third time that Newbury had called on his assistant since she had been discharged from the hospital and on each occasion he had found her sleeping, unable to receive visitors. As she had on both previous occasions, Mrs. Grant had tried to send him away with assurances that her mistress was recovering well—no doubt concerned that his presence would in some way disturb that recovery—but today he had resolved not to take no for an answer. So instead, he found himself waiting in the drawing room as Veronica dozed peacefully nearby.

He turned to her, leaving the constant drone of the traffic behind him. She was resting on a chaise longue, her head and shoulders propped up, covered by a blanket that had been neatly embroidered with the design of a willow tree. Her shoulder was strapped to her body to protect her wound. She stirred and he crossed the room, stepping closer so that she might see him when she woke. Her eyes opened. She looked momentarily dazed, then her eyes fixed on Newbury, a pretty smile lighting her face. "How are you, Miss Hobbes?"

Veronica moistened her lips, then looked around for a drink. Newbury fetched the jug from the bedside table and poured her a glass of water. She drank from it thirstily. After a moment, she handed it back to Newbury and gave a small cough. She looked up at him. "I'm well enough, Sir Maurice. It takes more than a bullet to incapacitate me."

Newbury smiled. "I'm delighted to hear it. I've been . . . concerned."

Veronica's eyes were shining. "Really, I'm recovering well. The doctor was able to repair the wound, so now it's just a matter of time. Although I admit I find this convalescing business most tiresome. There is so much to be done."

Newbury laughed. "Yes, well. You'll recall how often you berated me for attending the office last December when I should have been at home, resting. I fear I set a rather bad example. I've never been the best at sitting still."

Veronica glanced at the door, as if to be sure that her housekeeper, Mrs. Grant, was nowhere in the vicinity of the room. "It's a good thing you were wrong about Ashford, isn't it?"

"How so?" asked Newbury.

Veronica shrugged, then winced as the gesture caused her shoulder to spasm in pain. "He said he would turn himself in after you'd seen him at the house, just before we set off for the docks."

Newbury gave a wry grin. "No, Miss Hobbes. I said that I was confident he would do the right thing."

Veronica frowned. "Oh . . . you mean . . ."

Newbury glanced away. His expression darkened. "I fear I used the poor man, Miss Hobbes. I used his anger, his desire for revenge. I used him as a weapon against Aubrey Knox. In truth, I suppose I engineered his death. I must take responsibility for that, just as I must take responsibility for poor Mr. Purefoy, and for your injury. I could hardly bear the fact that you were hurt."

Veronica shook her head emphatically. "No. Sir Maurice, the responsibility is wholly mine. I went after those women. I knew the danger I was opening myself up to. And as for

Ashford—he was dead long before you ever got to him. He was just a ghost in a machine, the remnants of a man, bound to steel and brass. If you offered him anything, you offered him a resolution, an end to his nightmare. You offered him a chance at peace."

Newbury took her hand and held it gently in his own. "You're too kind, Miss Hobbes. I don't deserve that. But I thank you for it all the same."

Veronica squeezed his hand. "You deserve more than you allow yourself room to imagine." They regarded each other in silence.

After a moment, Newbury brightened. "There is something I've been meaning to say." He looked her in the eye. "But I haven't been able to find the right time."

Veronica's response was almost breathless. "Yes?"

Newbury could see something in her eyes, in her expression. The weight of expectation. Hope. In turn, something inside him snapped. He could barely look at her. "It's about Amelia."

"Oh."

"No, it's good news!"

Veronica gave a weak smile. Clearly, she'd hoped for something different. But he couldn't give her that, couldn't put her through it. Couldn't put *himself* through it. He'd seen what had become of Charles and Isobel, of Ashford and Catherine. The risks were too great.

Veronica, of course, was brave enough to put it to one side, to hide her disappointment. She toyed absently with the edge of her blanket. "Go on."

"I've spoken with Her Majesty. She's in agreement. Amelia

is to be moved to a private establishment, the Grayling Institute, under the care of her personal team of physicians."

Veronica's eyes widened. "Oh, Maurice." She tried to sit up, but it was clearly too much. Newbury waved her still.

"I believe it is a sign of Her Majesty's gratitude towards you. For all your work on her behalf and for your help with the Chapman and Villiers case. Evidently, you're highly regarded."

Veronica sighed, as though a weight had been lifted from her shoulders. "That's quite wonderful news. Please extend my gratitude to Her Majesty."

"I will." He put his hand on her arm. "Just as soon as you're well, I'll take you to see her—Amelia, that is—in her new home. I'm convinced things will work out for the best."

Veronica smiled warmly. "More than that, Sir Maurice, I'm convinced this intervention will save her life. Or at least prolong it for some time." She glanced out of the window, as if seeing something that wasn't there. "I shall have to inform my parents."

"No need. Arrangements have already been taken in hand. Your parents have signed the relevant documents. Amelia is being transferred on Friday."

Veronica touched her damaged shoulder with an unconscious gesture. "I don't know how to thank you."

"By getting better. There's nothing more important now." Newbury paced back to the window.

"So what did Her Majesty have to say about the deaths of Knox and Ashford?"

Newbury shrugged. "I saw her this morning. She was sanguine. She gave little away. I suspect it puts a cap on a long and complicated story, a story that I'm only now beginning to understand."

Veronica nodded. "I suppose it does." Newbury studied her expression. What was it that she wasn't telling him? For now, he knew, he had to forgo all such thoughts. What was important was that she recovered, as quickly as possible. "So, what next?" she enquired.

"Next? Next we do what we always do. We return to our sedentary lives, to fine wine and cigars, to meals with Sir Charles, and to our office at the British Museum. To filing papers and writing dry academic treatises as we await further instruction. It doesn't sound so bad when you put it like that, does it?"

Veronica looked longingly out of the window and sighed. "I'm not so terribly good at waiting."

Newbury's face cracked in a wide grin. "Nor am I, my dear Miss Hobbes." He crossed to where his coat was draped on the back of a chair, preparing to leave her to rest. "Nor am I." He studied her from across the room. His eyes twinkled. "I'm sure it won't be long before something comes our way. Besides, it's nearly spring. It wouldn't do to miss the fine weather, stuck indoors behind a musty old desk." He located his hat and placed it on his head with a flourish.

"You're leaving, then?"

"For now. I've had word that an old friend of mine is in town. It's high time I paid him a visit. In the meantime, you need to rest. I'll return on Friday with news of your sister."

Veronica allowed herself to sink back into the cushions of

the chaise longue. "Be sure to do just that. Friday seems like an eternity away."

Newbury gave a dramatic bow. "Until then, Miss Hobbes."

"Until then, Sir Maurice."

And without further ado, he was gone.

CHAPTER

27

Amelia Hobbes rocked back in the carriage seat, brushing the window drape aside with her hand. She stared out at the city beyond. The streets rushed by like a series of still, blinking images, grey and unfamiliar. It had been so long since she had left the grounds of the sanatorium, she'd lost all sense of time. Was it months? Years, even?

Sighing, she allowed the drape to fall back into place, casting her once more in darkness. She felt tired and weak, yet filled with a new sense of optimism. She had yet to see that optimism reflected in the eyes of others, however. Doctor Mason had been kind, as always, seeing her off at the sanatorium gates, even suggesting that—time permitting—he would consider making the long trip to the Grayling Institute to pay her a visit. But Amelia could see what was really reflected in his eyes: he did not think that she was long for this world. Perhaps he was right . . . but perhaps not.

Amelia knew little of the mysterious Dr. Fabian but she was well aware of his status as the personal physician to the Queen, and Veronica spoke highly of his reputation. She could hardly be bestowed with a greater honour. She had much reason to thank the enigmatic Sir Maurice Newbury, although she didn't doubt that his motives had been less than altruistic, more to do with winning the affections of her sister than with truly aiding Amelia in her plight. But that didn't matter. Whatever his motives, Sir Maurice had given her hope: hope that Dr. Fabian might see her visions as more than just a facet of her supposed insanity; hope that in doing so, he might help her to find a way to control those visions and prevent her body from descending further into wrack and ruin. Not that there was much of her body left, she thought bitterly, glancing down at her bony knees, clearly protruding through the thin fabric of her dress.

Amelia had once been pretty; as pretty, at least, as her sister. But now, emaciated, subjected to a harsh life in the sanatorium, and covered with scars from wounds she had earned during her numerous "episodes," she looked older, worn out. There were lines on her face, dark rings beneath her eyes. And she was disgusted by her own fatigue. Above all else, she hoped that Dr. Fabian could help her to restore her energy, her enthusiasm for life, her desire to get out of bed in the morning. Dare she consider that Dr. Fabian might even find a cure for her? No, that was too much of a fantasy. But nevertheless, she felt the little germ of hope seed itself in the back of her mind. If she chose not to acknowledge it, perhaps it could grow unimpeded.

Tired, Amelia rested her head against the cool leather of the seat back and closed her eyes. She would sleep now. Soon, she would have much to remain awake for.

Amelia came to as the carriage juddered to a brisk stop. She sat forward, urgently scrabbling for the window drapes. The carriage had come to rest at the far end of a long gravelled driveway, and through the window she could see the corner of a grey stone mansion. They were here. She felt her heartbeat quicken. This was it. Her new home. The Grayling Institute.

Amelia clasped her hands on her lap, letting the curtains fall back into place. It wouldn't do to display her impatience. She waited. Unbearable minutes ticked by, although in truth she had no way of judging how much time had actually passed. After what seemed like an eternity, she heard footsteps crunching on the gravel outside. Someone called up to the driver, but the words were lost in the breeze. The footsteps approached the cab. She realised she was holding her breath as the handle turned slowly and the door of the cab was pulled open. Light flooded in through the open doorway, stinging her eyes. She blinked away tears, momentarily bringing her hand up to her face to shield her eyes from the glare. She had spent too long in darkened rooms at the sanatorium.

Framed in the doorway was a diminutive man, no taller

than five feet four, balding, with trailing wisps of dark hair still clinging resolutely to his temples. He blinked up at her through the small, wire-rimmed spectacles that were perched on the end of his nose. He was dressed in a smart brown suit and a white collar and black tie. His face split in a wide grin. "Good morning, Miss Hobbes. It's a pleasure to make your acquaintance. My name is Dr. Lucius Fabian."

Amelia smiled, edging forward in her seat. "Good morning, Dr. Fabian. It truly is an honour. I—"

He cut her off with a wave of his hand. "No need, Miss Hobbes." He looked her up and down. "I'm sure you are tired after your long journey. I think it would be best if we saw you to your new rooms inside the Institute, where you can take some time to rest and recuperate. Then later we can talk of how we intend to manage your . . . affliction." He grinned. "Come now. Are you able to walk?"

Amelia sighed. "A little, perhaps. I fear that these days I am rather weak."

Dr. Fabian searched her face with beady eyes. "Yes. We'll have to see what we can do about that. Now, if you can manage to climb down from the carriage, we have a wheelchair on hand to assist you to your rooms."

Amelia nodded. With a huge effort, she lifted herself up from her seat, clutching at the sides of the cab for support. Dr. Fabian stepped up onto the footplate and offered her his hand. She took it gratefully, noting that his fingers were fat and soft and well kept. Hesitantly, leaning on the doctor, Amelia stepped down from the cab onto the driveway below. She glanced up at the building as she dusted herself off. The Grayling Institute was an enormous country house, probably two or three hundred years old, once the domain of princes and kings but now given over to science and more practical pursuits. This was Dr. Fabian's private establishment, managed on behalf of Her Majesty the Queen. This is where he did his great work, where members of the Royal Family themselves were brought for treatment, whether it be a dose of syphilis or a case of the "family sickness." She'd learned all this from Veronica and consequently found herself in awe of the place, of the doctor, and of her wondrous surroundings. To live in a palace! Already she felt her spirits lifting. How could she not recover here? Just the look of the place was enough to imbue her with energy.

Dr. Fabian adjusted his glasses. Amelia wondered if it was a nervous tic—it was the third time she'd noticed him do it in as many minutes. He glanced at the open doorway of the Institute, which sat behind four Corinthian pillars at the top of a long slope. Amelia suspected that there had once been a set of stone steps, but these had now been replaced by a ramp to improve access for the infirm. Dr. Fabian's reedy voice echoed out in the empty courtyard. "We're ready now, Mr. Calverton."

Amelia sensed movement in the shadow of the doorway. She watched intently. Sure enough, a moment later a figure appeared pushing a small wicker wheelchair, which she assumed would be used to help her into the premises. But as the figure emerged from the shadows of the doorway, Amelia felt her breath catch in her throat. *The man with no face!* The figure she had seen in her visions. She felt suddenly gripped with panic. The man pushing the wheelchair barely had the look of a man about him at all. His face was entirely hidden behind a featureless, porcelain mask designed to give the impression of a blank human face. Two slits allowed his startling blue eyes to peer out from behind the mask, and his head was closely shaved, covered in a fuzz of auburn stubble. His upper torso was still human, and he was wearing a smart black jacket and a cravat. Below the waist, however, Mr. Calverton was more machine than man. His legs had been replaced by gleaming brass contraptions that parodied their biological counterparts, pistons spitting furiously in his thighs, servos grinding in his knees.

Mr. Calverton cocked his head as if to acknowledge Amelia, but otherwise remained mute. There was a long pause before he edged forward with the wheelchair, his pointed metal feet scraping on the flagstones. The servos squealed and whined as he slowly descended the ramp. When he reached the gravel path he rolled the wheelchair forward, gesturing for Amelia to take a seat. She noticed he was wearing white gloves.

Amelia felt a shiver run along her spine. There was something about the man, something she'd seen in her visions, but was not yet able to place. He had a story. A story that had not yet come to an end. She wasn't sure if she wanted to know what that end might be.

Dr. Fabian seemed to notice Amelia's alarm and put a steadying arm around her shoulders. "Come now, Miss Hobbes. There is no need to be afraid. Mr. Calverton will see to your every need."

Trying not to grimace, Amelia allowed herself to be led towards the entrance. Mr. Calverton came forward to greet her. She studied his blank expression, realising that it was this, more than anything, which had inspired her unease.

She was unable to read his face. She had no idea if behind that plain, porcelain visage, the man was smiling or frowning at her. His eyes looked vacant. Dead. Suddenly, she felt a longing for her old room, back at the sanatorium. She closed her eyes and tried to suppress her fears.

Dr. Fabian gently placed his hands on her arms and lowered her into the wheelchair. Amelia gave him a brisk nod of acknowledgement, then the small party wound its way slowly towards the stark edifice of the Grayling Institute.

Inside, the reception hall retained many of its original features: the bold, galleried staircase, the glassy marble floor, and the high, decorative ceiling. Rooms and passageways branched off from the hallway in all manner of illogical directions, like arteries winding away from a heart. It was quite different from the sanatorium; Amelia allowed herself a brief smile. Perhaps she had been hasty. Perhaps her earlier hopes had been right. This was a place to heal.

Dr. Fabian led them down a small passageway to the left of the staircase. The space had obviously been converted from old servants' quarters and now, Amelia realised, the rooms that stemmed off from the main corridor had been remodelled as apartments for the patients. The wheelchair creaked as they rolled along the corridor, the sound of Mr. Calverton's clicking feet a constant distraction.

Presently Dr. Fabian came to a stop. He gestured through an open doorway on the right-hand side of the corridor. Mr. Calverton brought the wheelchair to a stop. Dr. Fabian coughed into his fist. "These shall be your rooms, Miss Hobbes, for the duration of your stay. I hope you find them to your liking." He stepped to one side, allowing her a clearer view. Amelia gasped. The apartment consisted of two rooms linked by an internal door, with tall sash windows that looked out upon the perfectly manicured gardens at the rear of the old mansion, where topiary sculptures described creatures from ancient mythology and birds wheeled in the sky above a glittering lake. The rooms themselves were panelled in dark oak and well furnished. A four-poster bed filled the antechamber, and in the large drawing room, an ornate marble fireplace dominated one wall, a low fire crackling in the grate. Two armchairs, a chaise longue, and a sideboard completed the arrangements, and an ancient portrait hung on the far wall, showing a regal-looking fellow in plate armour standing beside an immense globe.

Amelia began to climb out of her wheelchair, but Dr. Fabian waved her to remain seated, instead ushering Mr. Calverton to wheel her forward into the room. "Really? This is really where I shall stay?"

Dr. Fabian's lips curled. "Indeed it is, Miss Hobbes. I am sure you will be comfortable. Now," he stepped back as if suddenly galvanised into action, "we shall take our leave. No doubt you're tired after your long journey. Perhaps this evening we could dine together and I could tell you a little more about our work here at the Institute?"

Amelia nodded. "I'd like that very much."

"Excellent! I shall return to escort you to dinner at seven o'clock. In the meantime, your belongings will be delivered shortly. Good day to you, Miss Hobbes."

"Good day to you, Dr. Fabian." She glanced warily at the other man, who stood to one side, regarding her, unblinking. "And to you, Mr. Calverton." The masked man remained silent, turning to stomp unceremoniously from the room. Dr. Fabian gave a curt bow and then also took his leave, pulling the door shut behind him.

Amelia gazed longingly out of the window. Then, surprised, she turned back to regard the door as she heard a key pushed into the lock and bolts slide shut in the doorframe. The doctor had locked the door behind him. Why should he do that? She wheeled herself over to the door and tested the handle. It was locked firm. She was trapped.

Frustrated, Amelia considered her situation. The lavishly furnished room, then, was nothing but a lavishly furnished cell. What was this place? It certainly didn't seem like a hospital. And what of Mr. Calverton? What affliction had he endured to wind up like that? Amelia gave an involuntary shudder. Perhaps, with him wandering the premises, it was better that the door to her room was locked after all.

Easing herself out of the chair, Amelia crossed to the chaise longue and took up a position at the window. She watched the birds dancing in the sky above the lake and hoped it would not be long before her sister was able to pay her a visit.

EPILOGUE

The morning was crisp and chill, and the sun had yet to poke its way through the hazy layer of yellow fog that clung to the treetops and surrounding buildings, cloaking everything in a fine, gossamer web.

Newbury watched his breath form plumes in the frigid air. The cold was penetrating, bone deep. He longed for the comfort of his Chelsea drawing room and the roar of an open fire. It was early—too early—and he had not slept. In truth, he'd been unable to sleep properly for a week, not since the events in the Archibald Theatre and his conversation with Veronica in Knox's makeshift laboratory. He'd managed to lose himself in laudanum-inspired dreams, draped on the daybed in his study, but sleep—real sleep—had continued to elude him. Instead, he'd been reduced to lying on his bed, staring not at the ceiling but at an elaborate reconstruction of events, as conjured by his mind's eye. He kept replaying their conversation, over and over, attempting to tease meaning out of half-remembered looks and hastily spoken words. What had Veronica been trying to tell him? He thought he knew, now. The evidence was incontrovertible: her knowledge of Knox had helped to bring a swift conclusion to the case. But if he was right, why on Earth would she reveal the truth to him in such an opaque fashion? What else was there that he still did not know? There had to be another dimension to it, something that was staring him in the face.

Newbury hated the thought that he was working in the dark and that he was forced to resort to such clandestine activities as loitering outside of her apartments and following her across town. The emotional conflict was enough to make his stomach churn. But he needed to know if he could trust her.

Still, he had little time to consider the implications now. He'd been following Veronica for over an hour, first by hansom cab and then, for the last mile, on foot, since she'd abandoned her transport and taken instead to the footpath. He watched her slight figure sway from side to side with every footstep as he kept pace, careful to remain out of sight. It was clear she was still suffering from her damaged shoulder; her gait was a little awkward and she held her upper body stiffly, like a soldier, erect and alert. He knew if he asked her later, she would tell him she had remained at home, convalescing under doctor's orders.

Ahead of them loomed the splendour of Buckingham

Palace, towering out of the mist like a grey monolith. There could be no mistaking her destination.

Hanging back, Newbury watched Veronica approach the gates. To his surprise, she was acknowledged immediately by the guard, who pulled the iron portal open and admitted her to the palace grounds without a word. Newbury crossed the road and followed her progress through the tall railings, catching glimpse after stuttering glimpse as she strode purposefully across the courtyard. Newbury could see she was heading around the side of the building. He stopped in the shadow of an ash tree, watching, waiting, his heart in his mouth.

Moments later, he watched as she stopped before a familiar door and rapped loudly, three times. He heard the wooden panel slide open and imagined Sandford, the agents' butler, peering out. A second later the panel slid shut and the door swung open. Veronica disappeared inside.

And there he had it.

Veronica Hobbes: Agent to the Queen.

Newbury felt a growing tightness in his chest, like a dead weight had been laid upon him, forcing the air out of his lungs. So he'd been right. Veronica worked for the Queen. The duplicity made his head spin. To what end had it been kept from him? Did Charles know? He'd suspected her of keeping a secret since their conversation in the cellar, but to have it confirmed . . .

Newbury was surprised by the bizarre sense of vertigo he felt, standing there in the cold morning in the shadow of a tree. He didn't want to acknowledge what he knew in his heart to be true. Veronica had been employed by the Queen to spy on him, to monitor his actions and report back to the palace. Even now, he could hear Charles's words echoing inside his head: "The Queen is worried . . . even the best of men is fallible."

Victoria was concerned he would turn out like Knox. He cursed under his breath. He didn't know where this left him with the Queen, with Veronica. The feelings she'd intimated . . . had they even been real? A ruse to draw him closer? The implication was too awful to bear.

Sighing, Newbury turned and walked away into the hazy morning. He could be at Johnny Chang's place within the hour, chasing the dragon, losing himself in the sickly sweet vapours. The pull of it was like lightning in his veins.

Gathering speed, he allowed himself to be swept up in his cravings. He was tired and, after all, he had a great deal to consider.